MISSION CREEK

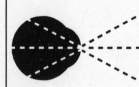

This Large Print Book carries the
Seal of Approval of N.A.V.H.

Mission Creek

A WESTERN DUO

Frank Bonham
edited by Bill Pronzini

THORNDIKE PRESS
A part of Gale, Cengage Learning

GALE
CENGAGE Learning®

Detroit • New York • San Francisco • New Haven, Conn • Waterville, Maine • London

GALE
CENGAGE Learning®

LIBRARY OF CONGRESS CATALOGING-IN-PUBLICATION DATA

Bonham, Frank.
  [Novels. Selections]
  Mission Creek : a western duo / by Frank Bonham.
    pages ; cm. — (Thorndike Press large print western)
  ISBN-13: 978-1-4104-5680-9 (hardcover)
  ISBN-10: 1-4104-5680-3 (hardcover)
    1. Large type books. I. Pronzini, Bill. II. Bonham, Frank. Rodeo killer. III.
  Bonham, Frank. Mission Creek. IV. Title.
  PS3503.O4315M57 2013
  813'.54—dc23   2012047555

Published in 2013 by arrangement with Golden West Literary Agency

Printed in the United States of America
1 2 3 4 5 6 7 17 16 15 14 13

ADDITIONAL COPYRIGHT INFORMATION

TABLE OF CONTENTS

■ ■ ■ ■

Rodeo Killer

■ ■ ■ ■

"Rodeo Killer" is one of Frank Bonham's early Western stories, first published in the March, 1942 issue of *All Western Magazine.* It is the tale of smoldering and violent conflicts among New Mexico cattle ranchers, cattle buyers, and breeders of horses for the rodeo circuit. It is also the story of young Hugh Talbot, son of the ramrod of Snake Track Ranch, willful Lass Towne, daughter of Snake Track's rawhide-tough owner, and a blood sorrel racehorse named Little Sister that everyone except Lass believes to be a wind-broke man-killer.

Greed, deceit, trickery, and murder mix with romance and human and animal courage in this action-packed novelette. The climactic scenes at the Alamo Rodeo, in which "racing silks and hot lead" figure prominently, are among the most evocative to come from Bonham's pen in the formative stages of his career.

B.P.

I

Lass was always the first one up around Snake Track headquarters, rolling out of her blankets before sunup to be down in the pasture with Little Sister by the time the first golden flakes of dawn came sifting into Poverty Valley. So it was Lass whose cry emptied the bunkhouse of half-clad cowpunchers that morning. Hugh Talbot was still buttoning his shirt when he came out the door, stockingless feet tromped into spurred boots, blond hair rumpled.

The empty corrals were bleak in the chill predawn. All was peaceful, save where Lass, down by the water pen, was trying to saddle her pony. Hugh's eyes hunted the trouble. Then it hit him solidly in the stomach. "Crawled out, the breechy sons!"

Mike Talbot, long-time ramrod of the Snake Track, came out behind him, tucking in his shirt tail and swearing. Mike always knew, at the first alarm, what needed looking after when trouble hit the ranch.

He turned to confront the hands who had grouped behind him, still logy with too little sleep on top of too much work. "Will somebody quit batting his eyes and get the horses," he snapped. "Yonder's the hold-up, belly-deep in grama. I'm telling you for sure, if them critters ain't back under the pole before Dennis gets here, they'll be some old faces gone out of the bunkhouse tonight."

Mike stomped down to the open gate, Hugh beside him. Two of the Snake Track boys grabbed their bridles from the harness shed and went after the wrangling horses. Mike's jaw was set like cement. The beef buyer was due at 7:00, a man who insisted on his twelve-hour shrinkage, and the hold-up was spilled all down the creek.

Lass was mounting her pony when Mike reached the gate through which nearly three hundred prime beef animals had broken out during the night. She watched him examine the latch, a simple arrangement consisting of a horseshoe on a chain bolted to the gatepost. The open end of the shoe, dropped over a gate bar, made an absolute lock against range-seeking cattle.

"That's how I found it," she said. "Hanging just like that. The shoe isn't bent or the pole cut. The steers couldn't have pushed it open."

"Reckon they got to jostling the gate," growled Mike.

"You mean you think they could have opened it?"

Hugh watched her, not missing the pinch of worry between her eyes. His wide mouth began to smile.

"Let's see. . . ." He closed one eye and pondered. "Maybe we ought to think back and remember who was the last one in last night."

Lass Towne's tawny-gold eyes blazed. Her lips pressed tight, but it was Mike who grunted: "Yonder comes your dad. Why don't you skedaddle and get the critters drifting up thisaway?"

"All right." Lass's reply had a reluctance. She was still staring at Hugh, whose grin was broadening.

She had hardly left the corral when Mike grabbed the horseshoe latch again.

"By golly, look here."

Hugh examined the shoe. The inside edge, through years of wear, had been honed like a knife. Now that edge was splattered with brown, dried blood.

"That ain't steer blood." He frowned. "Somebody unlocked that gate in a hurry or else somebody didn't savvy to yank the shoe off by the chain. But who in this outfit don't know about it?"

The yard gate banged, and they looked back to see Barney Towne standing by the harness shed. He stood there, short legs outspread, baldhead swinging like that of an angry bull, bloodshot eyes sweeping the empty corral. It took him several scowling seconds to analyze the trouble. Then he let out a roar.

"Talbot! Where in tarnation are the cattle?"

Mike took a deep breath and went back to him. "Down by the creek. They busted out during the night."

Towne breathed heavily through distended nostrils. The flush of his red features, vein-shot by twenty years of tippling, deepened while he sought strong-backed words to carry the weight of his fury. "Busted out, hell! Why don't you admit you forgot to close the gate?"

"Because I didn't," Mike replied doggedly. "Now, there's no use getting your blood hot. Mark Dennis ain't due for an hour. We'll have them back before then."

Towne's lips had a sour, sadistic twist. "Here's one to raise your own temperature on. If Dennis gets wise and clocks me five

14

percent for his damn' twelve-hour shrink-age, you're done! I ain't hoorawing. Talbot, maybe you figure you're the brains of this layout. But maybe you're going to find out who does the hiring and firing hereabouts, in case you've forgot."

One of the wranglers brought up Barney Towne's horse. He swung up heavily and, not looking back, rode off. His fists knotted, Mike stared after him. Then he turned on his heel and went to saddle his pony.

Hugh held his temper until they were riding out of the yard. He rode with an easy slouch, but under the old jumper his body was stiff as a whipstock. Then he said, his eyes bright with a hard shine: "He's asked for it once too often, Mike. We're getting out. To hell with this lousy iron. We can make a heap more money glory-holing like we used to, and not have to take his guff."

Mike's quick glance was testy. "That's foolishness. Man's liable to say 'most anything when he's tapering off a six-day drunk."

"But when he's drunk five days out of seven, you finally get your belly full. We've had ten years of it, and that's enough. You pulled the Snake Track right out of bankruptcy court when you first signed on, but Towne's kept it in the red ever since. Not that I haven't asked it a hundred times before, but what have we got to gain by staying?"

"Give him an inch, boy," Mike muttered. "If I was to quit him, the iron'd go under in six months."

"We've given him miles already. If he drinks the Snake Track onto the rocks, it isn't our fault. I've heard Towne get the credit for being a top-hand cowman too long. They say he can bring a weanling to prime on a handful of corn and a bucket of water. That he savvies rodeo stock better than any man in New Mexico. The whiskey-logged cull. When they say those things, they're talking about Mike Talbot! All Towne savvies is to pop a cork."

Mike made no answer. Hugh knew that, as usual, he was getting nowhere. "At least," he grumbled, "you could have told him the truth about the gate . . . that Lass left it open."

"We don't know that. You can forget about her being the last one in." Mike's words crackled. Where Lass was concerned, he was as fiercely protective as an old mother grizzly.

Hugh shrugged. His glance went off across the billowing, tree-dotted range land, the blue of far distances shining in his eyes.

"Remember Calico town, Mike?" he said, after a moment. "Deadwood, Leadville . . . Tombstone? We had fun, those days, glory-holing around wherever the sign was right. Scratching in played-out claims for bacon and beans. A little silver here, a little gold there. . . ."

Mike's scowl did not mask the longing in his face for those unforgotten, carefree times. But he shook his head doggedly. "As far as I'm concerned, glory-holing is all a played-out claim. We had seven years of it, and we ended up as broke as we started."

Just as broke, Hugh thought, *but not half as happy.* Tragedy had brought them together, and he considered it tragic, for Mike, that they had ever settled on the Snake Track. The last ten years had tucked many a wrinkle into the tough skin of his face. Hugh had watched him grow heavier and solid in his joints, and his short, stiff hair turn iron-gray, had seen his vitally blue eyes fade and become tired.

He remembered the first day he saw Mike seventeen years ago, when they dragged him out of a cave-in in a Deadwood gold mine, more dead than alive. His memory was one part of him that never did come alive after a stull timber had smashed against his skull. Nobody could identify him. He was new in

17

town, one of a hundred muckers in the mine, most of whom were pulled out dead.

Hugh's father had been one of these, leaving the eight-year-old boy orphaned. After Mike was on his feet again, he took pity on the half-starved kid who was making his grub watching miners' horses and wagons while they cavorted in the saloons.

"So you've got no daddy," Mike had said to him one day, when he was back at work. "Well, I'm just as bad off. I've got no name. The boys call me Mike, but I've got to have a longer handle than that to sign the pay sheet. Suppose we make a swap? I'll take your old man's place, if you'll loan me your name till I can think of my own."

It was a deal, but in seven years of glory-holing around the mining camps Mike Talbot never did remember his own name. Until one day the clouds began to break. To Hugh he had said: "We've got to go to Denver, kid. It seems like . . . like I sort of remember living there once. Maybe I'll see somebody I know."

He never told Hugh about it if he did. But from that visit to Denver, and a subsequent hurried trip to Alamo, the new life and the new Mike Talbot dated. A worried, gloomy Mike, who hunted up Barney Towne and signed on. Maybe there was ranch experience in Mike's past; at any rate he showed himself to be a top hand, and Towne made him ramrod. It was the end of their easy-going life. Mike lived within himself most of the time from then on.

Towne needed him, as badly as Mike needed a job. Since the death of his wife he had hardly been sober in five years. Mike had stayed on, taking more from him than Hugh had thought he would take from any man. How much did Lass have to do with their remaining? Hugh wondered. And he knew the answer was — plenty.

"Poor kid needs somebody to side her, living under the same roof with Towne," Mike would argue sometimes, when Hugh got the traveling itch. "If we pulled out, the place would go bankrupt, and where would she be?"

Toward Hugh, Lass was as coldly impersonal as a gambler's handshake. They had scrapped every day in the ten years he'd been here. He didn't try to varnish his feelings about her with friendliness. He felt too strongly that Mike was sacrificing everything for her — needlessly and thanklessly.

II

Full daylight was over Poverty Valley by the time the last steer was choused into the pen. Barney Towne himself locked the gate. Mike loped to the back.

"Throw them dinked ponies back in the trap," he ordered.

Over the bawling of cattle, someone answered him: "What's the matter, Mike? Afraid I'll see they've been working overtime?"

Mike's stocky body twisted in the lowdown roping saddle. But he failed to find the speaker until two men walked from the harness shed. It was Mark Dennis and a man in a plaid shirt and lemon-colored chaps, and both were laughing.

When they had all gone over to the shed, Barney Towne demanded: "Where'd you two come from?"

"Over the hill from Beaverhead Creek," said Dennis. "Stayed at Charlie Davis's last night. So this is how you shrink your beef cattle, is it?" He was still grinning, but it was a hard smile without humor.

"I reckon it wouldn't make any difference if I swore they only busted out an hour ago?" Barney Towne appealed. "I tell you they've been penned up all night."

"Contracts are made to be kept," Dennis told him. "If you can't keep your stock penned up for twelve hours, I'm not going to take the loss for you. I've got to write off five percent for shrinkage, Barney."

Dennis was black Irish, his square-set eyes dark, skin swarthy, black hair showing thin in back. He was forty-five but he carried his trim, wide-shouldered five-ten like a man fifteen years his junior.

"Shrinkage," snorted Towne. "What will you buyers think of next to make it tough on the cowman?"

"I don't set the styles," Dennis said crisply. "You could have kept those animals penned up away from feed and water for twelve hours, as the contract specified. Well, let's go to it. How many are you offering?"

They went down to the scales, a high-walled, rectangular pen with a wooden floor onto which each steer to be weighed would be prodded.

"Two hundred yearlings and seventy-five steers and heifers," Mike Talbot told him.

"I can use them," Dennis said. Then he laid a hand on the shoulder of the young fellow with him. "You all know my boy, Larry. He'll tally the weights for us."

"Him and me both," corrected Towne slyly. "I'm only aiming to take one cut on this deal."

"If your cows are in the kind of shape they were last fall," Larry Dennis replied, "you'll take more than that. But read them off yourself."

Larry had been cast in the same mold as his father, but he slept a longer night and worked a shorter day, with the result that he packed more weight than he needed. The fat around his eyes gave them a piggish look. He wore a thick brown mustache. The shirt and fancy yellow chaps he wore needed the seasoned look only hard work could give them. He wore pigskin gloves. A tailor-made cigarette dangled from the fingers of one gloved hand.

The job got under way, with Hugh cutting out the steers, Mike doing the chousing, and the others on the weight tally. Barney Towne, squatting by the indicator, called off the tally.

The weighing went on for two hours. From time to time the buyer would reject a steer. Rednecks were undesirable in the yards; long horns and overlarge brands counted against an animal. Dennis was a sharp trader. He bought top-rate beef, and that only after haggling the seller into a price that nearly brought the blood.

Finally Dennis made out a check for

$8,600 — far less than the Snake Track would need to get through the coming year. Barney Towne blew up.

But all Dennis said was: "Tell you the trouble with you, Towne. You've turned a first-class iron into a dude's idea of a ranch. Bucking stock. Brahma bulls. Goats. My Lord, this ain't a cattle ranch any more, it's a game preserve."

"There's money in rodeo stock," Towne snapped. "I cleared five thousand last year with my string. Besides, mister, I notice you've built up a sizable bucking string yourself. Figger to give me some competition?"

"I pick up a bucker now and again." Dennis's drawl was a little too casual. "Figger to resell when I find a man with the *ganas* and the cash. I notice you're fooling around with racehorses, now."

"Fooling? I got a mare down yonder will beat anything you ever saw."

"Not that Little Sister sorrel."

"She's the baby."

Dennis laughed. "I make no claims to being a racing man, but I'd give daylight money on my stallion, Heelfly, to beat Little Sister under the wire at the brush meet next week."

Barney Towne cornered him. "How much?"

"Horse against horse."

Towne's grin was wolfish. "You've just lost a horse."

Dennis only smiled. He pocketed his tally book. "I'll arrange for a string of cars the night before the brush meet. You can bring your plug in with the beef herd. She'll be right at home with a bunch of cows."

Hugh had been watching Larry Dennis for some time, and now, as the pair rode off, he drawled: "I'll bet a purty there's a cut on that Larry's thumb, under those gloves."

"I don't get it," Towne said after a moment.

Mike's jaw dropped. "I do. The dirty sheepherders have reamed us. We found blood on the gate and reckoned one of the boys got cut on it. But what really happened was that that lard-gutted cub of Dennis's sprung the gate last night and cut hisself on the latch doing it."

Towne's features were blank, then they reddened. "Why the dirty, slimy . . . ! They done it to nick us for that five-percent penalty."

Suddenly Hugh, staring at the scales, started. Then he began to laugh. "And you

24

came out ahead at that. Look."

Dusty, bedraggled, Lass Towne was dragging herself from the balance pit. There was a small trap door through which a man might crawl beneath the big platform to adjust and grease the working parts of the scales. The girl had been down there all during the weighing. Corral dust had sifted down upon her and perspiration had traced streaks of mud down her face.

Towne gasped as she came up. "How long have you been down there?"

In Lass's grimy features her eyes had bright glints of anger. "Ever since the weighing started. I knew I locked the gate when I came in, so somebody else must have opened it. That would be a man who stood to profit by it. So I crawled down there, and every time a steer was weighed, I sat on the balance arm."

Towne chuckled. "Good girl."

Lass's blonde hair tossed, and her chin tilted. "I hope you'll still say that after I tell you we aren't going through with that bet you made. Little Sister's not going to race that Heelfly."

Towne put a cigar between his teeth and began to chew on it. "Ain't we? I had a notion Little Sister was my horse."

There was a panicky catch in Lass's voice.

"She is, but you know what it would mean to me to lose her, after the way I've brought her to the chutes myself. You can't do it, Dad!"

Barney's face was bulldoggish. "She's going to run. That's the end of it."

Lass turned to Mike. "She isn't ready to run, Mike . . . tell him that. She hasn't found her stride yet."

Mike Talbot patted her arm. "Don't you worry, little lady. She's got a stride that'll take her under that wire a length ahead of Heelfly. Anyway, it's only daylight money we're bucking. Sister can't lose."

"Unless," Hugh pointed out, "she gets one of them pitching spells of hers. That mare never will be one you can count on. If I was you, Barney, I'd put her in my bucking string."

The pupils of Lass's eyes were black with anger. "You probably would," she said, acid putting a thin, sharp edge on her words. "But if you hadn't botched the job of breaking her, she'd be as track-wise as any of them now. I suppose if the bet's made, it's made. Only, if I were you, I'd be pulling for her pretty strong. Because if she loses, I'll be looking for someone who knows how to break horses so they win."

■ ■ ■ ■

That was how things stood when they trailed the beef herd into Alamo the next week. The threat didn't worry Hugh. Almost, he hoped, Little Sister would lose, so that Mike would be more or less duty-bound to string with him after he was fired, if Lass stuck to her threat.

The meet was into the last day before Little Sister and Heelfly were matched for a half. Both had turned in stopwatch performances the first two days.

That last night, Mike got Hugh to stay with the mare while he went for a bait of grub at the café. Hugh spent his time currying the horse, feeling the rippling muscles under the brush, the nervous tremors that went through her when he laid his hand on the warm, sleek neck. It had not been so long ago when he had gone up on Little Sister for the first time. He had come down in under ten seconds. She had a mind to pitch, had Little Sister. She was still a demon to get into the chutes. Let a jockey mount her who betrayed any nervousness, and he would finish the race on all fours.

Hugh bent to inspect a slight cut she had acquired on the pastern, when she had

27

tripped over a hidden fence wire. He was squatting like that in the dark stall, the mare standing with head high, nostrils dilated, when the sound of men's voices suddenly came to him. They were not entirely clear. Seeming to come from Heelfly's quarters, in the opposite run of stalls, the voices were those of Mark and Larry Dennis and some third party Hugh could not identify.

"You can put your money on Heelfly, Sam," Dennis was saying. "He'll double it for you. That's a guarantee."

The man called Sam laughed. "It's as sure as that?"

Hugh stood up, a straight shadow in the corner of the stall. Sauntering on, the men passed a point where he could see them clearly among the litter of wagons, bales of hay, and harness.

"By the way" — Mark Dennis's voice was not entirely casual — "who's promoting the rodeo at the state fair next summer?"

"You ought to know that. That's what I'm down here for. Hunting a man to supply the stock I'll need."

"Then you can stop looking right here," Dennis told him. "Did you see Johnny Mullins's bunch of wild animals at Magdalena?"

"He's got a string of plenty mean critters."

"Not any more, he hasn't. I bought him

28

out last month. That's why I'm saying you can leave that contract right here with me."

The other tucked a cud of tobacco into his cheek. "There's no rush," he said. "I'll be running down to El Paso in the morning to see what Champ Grayson's got to offer."

Dennis spoke hurriedly. "Look, Mister Cotton, I want to save you some trouble, as well as do myself some good. It ain't for publication, but I'll have double the stock I've got now by next spring. You'll have your pick of the best in New Mexico."

"How's that?"

"An old booze-fighter I know of is going to be washed up and willing to sell *muy pronto.* When the time's right, I'll take over. So why not let me have the contract tomorrow before you leave?"

Sam Cotton laughed. "Don't crowd me, Mark. I ain't committing myself ten months ahead. I'll be around again for your spring rodeo. Then we can see how things stack up."

What else was said Hugh could not make out. But the conversation left him with plenty of meat to chew on.

Sam Cotton was the biggest rodeo promoter in the Southwest. A man with a first-class rough string could make enough out of stocking him for the Albuquerque show to pay all his expenses for a year. And Mark Dennis intended to be that man. Heretofore, Hugh had looked on him simply as a shrewd trader who hewed, on occasion, too close to the line. He loomed as a more sinister figure now. This was October, and the Snake Track was in no such immediate danger of collapse as Dennis had intimated. Unless — did the buyer have traps set to snare old Barney Towne?

III

Hugh was out in the crisp, bright dawn, walking the stiffness out of Little Sister's legs. The blood sorrel was bulky under three blankets that he whipped off, one by one, as she warmed up. As always on the morning of a race, the feeling of excitement went into Hugh like an electric current.

When he had been walking the horse for nearly two hours, Hugh saw Lass Towne signaling from the paddock.

"Cesario's going to work her out," the girl told him, when he had gone over. She was in a fawn-colored skirt and a white blouse, a bright ribbon in her hair. Her smiles, if she had any on a tense day like this, apparently were not for Hugh.

Cesario had ridden for Barney Towne

before. He was a Mexican of forty years, with sharp eyes that kept as busy as a weaver's fingers. Hugh leaned on the rail while the Mexican took the horse around. Cesario was having trouble. Little Sister danced sideways every time she passed the wheeled chutes at the side of the track. She threw her head whenever another horse got close.

Part of Hugh's attention was caught by the comments of the track crowd standing near him.

"If it was a quarter, I'd give you the mare by a half length. But them pipe-stem legs of hers won't never carry her to the half pole."

"They're saying Dennis has spotted her a length. That's liable to make a race out of it. But I'll still put my four-bits on Heelfly. He's tough and he's fast."

"You talk like a passel of old women. Heelfly ain't got a show with that horse."

The voice, an unpleasant sort of snarling whine, made Hugh look at the speaker. He was perched on the railing, a disreputable figure in patched Levi's and a striped jersey, an old Union cap on the back of his buzzard-like head.

One of the other men said: "Ain't he? You're crazy as a one-eyed road lizard, Johnny. Look at the reach in them legs of

31

his. Lightning."

Johnny launched a stream of tobacco juice onto the track. "While you're in a noticing mood, look at his ankles. Limber as a whalebone. It's him that's the Quarter horse, not the mare."

There was a pause, the men watching Heelfly as the jockey, Santos Luna, paced by. Little Sister was pulling in beside him.

"Maybe so," the other said. "But I'm betting on the stud."

The man called Johnny said: "So'm I."

"But you just said. . . ."

"I said the mare would win . . . in a fair race. This ain't going to be one. Her jockey's going to throw it. She's going to come out of the chutes fighting him. Look at her right now, nervous as a cat."

Little Sister chose that moment to buck-jump sideways into Heelfly. There was an instant of quirting and cursing, of high-strung horses squealing. Suddenly Cesario was across the horse's head in a flat dive. He landed in front of her. Head high, Little Sister bolted. One hoof hit the Mexican's knee and he doubled up, groaning.

Hugh was over the barrier and running across the field, hoping to head off the mare. But it was the old-timer, Johnny, running like a deer, who crossed the field first and captured the runaway's reins, throwing himself at the horse with no apparent regard for broken bones.

Hugh hurried back to Cesario. Barney Towne was there, now, and Lass. Mark Dennis was coming up with his jockey. Cesario, with a broken leg, was white as chalk.

"Tried to quirt me," he groaned.

Santos Luna, a spindly, fox-faced youth with gopher teeth, did not deny it. "*¡Seguro que sí!* Any man that try to pace my horse . . . *por Dios,* I quirt him, too."

Hugh's natural sympathy for Cesario was tempered by suspicion. He had violated track ethics by pulling in beside the other horse, trying to size him up.

Barney Towne tried to bluster it through. "This'll cost you your jockey," he threatened Dennis. "I ain't racing my horse against no quirt-handy Mex. I'll have Luna barred off every track in New Mexico."

"You'll run against him or forfeit your horse," Dennis retorted. "I reckon these boys will back Santos."

There were those who nodded and others who seemed dubious. The old-timer who had captured Little Sister settled it, walking the horse up to the group just then.

"Santos done right," he said. "Cesario was trying to pace him. It looks, pardner, as if

33

you're the man that needs a jockey. How'll I do?"

Towne's bloodshot eyes lifted. "Who in Tophet are you?"

"Cap'n Johnny."

That was all he said, but Barney Towne said — "Oh." — and blinked.

Hugh Talbot remembered him, too. You couldn't have a meeting without Captain Johnny any more than you could run a race without horses. His whiny voice, raised in profane advice to a losing rider or cackling praise to a winner, was as unavoidable as the thunder of hoofs. He had a legion of enemies and a few friends, the latter mostly horses. Going on seventy, Johnny had announced his retirement in ten more years, to run out his days breaking horses.

Towne rubbed his nose. "Come on over to the paddock," he grunted.

So Captain Johnny was signed on to ride Little Sister. Hugh watched him rub her down an hour before the race. The old jockey slipped the wire basket onto the mare's muzzle, to keep her from eating anything this close to starting time.

"I'll be getting into my colors," he said.

Hugh opened the door of the stall. "They're down in the tack room. You've got a savvying way about you, Johnny. A man

34

like you could calm Little Sister down right nice."

Johnny gave him a toothless grin. "Folks nowadays have forgot how to reason with 'em. I just talk things over with a horse and we usually make some kind of a compromise."

Mike and Barney Towne were in the tack room. Towne was carrying several drinks already. He was raw-tempered and on the butt about trading a good jockey for a dubious one.

It was Hugh who saw it first — the wire basket lying in a corner. Little Sister had her nose buried in a sack of bran and was eating as fast as she could bolt it. Then Captain Johnny saw and let out a yell.

"She's a-foundering herself! Somebody slipped her muzzle!"

With something like a chunk of ice in his stomach, Hugh flung the sack of bran from the stall. Captain Johnny stood back, almost sobbing as he looked at the horse.

"She's swelling already."

"Thank God she couldn't get at any water," Mike Talbot said. He glanced at the sack, trying to estimate how much she had eaten. "Lord, she's downed a couple of gallons, if that thing was full."

The jockey pulled off his cap. "Well, there

goes your race, gents."

But Towne, head jutted forward, fists clenched, and short arms drawn up, said slowly: "Get a bridle on her."

The tough skin about Johnny's eyes crinkled. "What for?"

Towne roared his answer: "I'm going to run her!"

Mike gripped his arm. "You'll ruin her, Barney. You can't run a horse in that condition."

"Can't I? Maybe I ought to forfeit the race and trot her over to Dennis. That's what he figgered I'd do, I reckon. But, by heaven, if I'm going to lose her, it'll be a string-halted, wind-broke critter Dennis will take home."

He clung to his purpose like a leech. Presently they heard the race being announced. Barney Towne himself put the racing bit in the horse's mouth and led her out. Captain Johnny could do nothing but follow.

Hugh saw Lass coming from the judge's stand. He headed her off, making talk while the two horses were paraded before the stands. But as they were saddled and mounted, she realized there was something wrong.

"What's the matter with Little Sister? She acts sluggish. . . ."

Hugh said quickly: "She's doing fine. The

Cap'n's just holding her in."

"Hugh! She . . . she looks as if she's foundered."

Striking off the hand he put out to hold her, she ran down the track toward the chutes. But she was too late. Little Sister was too sick to put up her usual fuss at the chutes. The horses broke clean from the barrier, and the stands' roar swept the field like an explosion.

Hugh pulled her off the track. Her body was rigid, not seeming to breathe, turning slowly to follow the horses as they rounded the track. Already Heelfly's deep-chested dun body was straining ahead of the little blood sorrel. Santos Luna, humped over like a monkey, was quirting viciously.

Old Captain Johnny was all but invisible. Plastered along the mare's neck, he was like a part of the horse. He wasn't using his quirt, but somehow Hugh knew he was getting all the horse had to offer.

They hit the home turn, Heelfly pushing Little Sister farther behind with every slamming impact of his hoofs on the track. Uncertainty came into the sorrel's stride. The smooth rhythm of her flashing hoofs was broken. It was a daylight race, for sure. You could line three horses up between them.

Then, as they whirled past Hugh and Lass, they could see that Captain Johnny was easing in on the reins. Probably he had been doing that for a quarter mile. It was Hugh's guess that, if he hadn't, the mare wound have run herself to death.

When it was all over, Lass leaned against Hugh, her face against his shoulder. "Oh, Hugh. Hugh. They've ruined her."

IV

The crowd wasn't making much noise about it. They knew, if only by Little Sister's staggering progress back to the paddock, that the race had been run under a cloud.

Then, in one of those breathtaking changes of which she was capable, Lass pulled away. "You could have stopped them," she said. "You knew she wasn't right."

"We all knew it. But did you ever stop your old man from doing what he wanted?" Lass's look, full of scorn, stung him with quick anger. "I'm not trying to pass the buck," he said on the defensive. "We tried. . . ."

She was going toward the paddock before he could finish. Hugh followed slowly, his lips pale with anger. Down at the end of the stables, among the wagons, he found Barney Towne, Mike, and Captain Johnny. Towne was laying it on with the big trowel.

"I've got my belly full of you and your lunkheaded tricks. Last week you cost me five hundred dollars' worth of beef. Today it's a six-hundred-dollar mare."

Anger pumped the blood darkly through Mike's square-cut features. "You know whose fault it was that Little Sister ran," he snapped. "The job ain't on my head."

"No?" Towne closed one eye and squinted through the other. "Who left her alone to be tampered with?"

"You as much as me," said Mike.

Towne began to curse him, taking a sadistic enjoyment in it. When he could listen no longer, Hugh stepped in. Grabbing a handful of shirt front, he jammed the Snake Track boss against a wagon. Towne began to struggle, but against his liquor-rotted bulk Hugh was all tough muscle and hone.

"Take a dally on your jaw, you whiskey-guzzling old boar hog," he told him. "I can't speak for Mike, but me . . . I'm accepting your invite to get out. You've been itching to show who's the brains of the outfit. Well, I hope you find out. When they talk about Barney Towne savvying to raise beef, they're talking about Mike Talbot. When they say

39

you're the best man with rodeo stock in New Mexico, they're still talking about him. Mike kept you in drinking liquor for ten years. He's kept the ranch from going under while you lay sleeping off your drunks. And I hope to hell he's got enough of it now."

Barney Towne, wriggling from his grasp, made sputtering sounds. He swung a haymaker that Hugh caught on the shoulder. Hugh struck him just once, on the ear, and Towne reeled away, ran into a wagon tongue, and crashed face first in the dirt.

Mike's face was wrinkled, as if with pain. "Hugh. You . . . you shouldn't have done it."

"I should have done it five years ago." Breathing hard, his face ridged with sinew under the brown skin, Hugh demanded: "For the last time . . . are you staying, or coming with me?"

Mike gripped his arm. "Don't you see the spot I'm in? I can't leave Lass now, with him like this. . . ."

The girl, as always. A flush, perhaps of jealousy, darkened Hugh's cheeks.

"Always the girl, eh, Mike? It isn't what you owe yourself . . . it's how she'll make out. Luck to you, anyway. I'll be around to pick up my war sack. Have the boys cut out my calves, will you?"

Mike's eyes were full of searching. "What do you aim to do?"

"Take a government lease on a few sections of forest. Raise beef, maybe some horses. I've got the calves I've taken for wages, and those colts Harley Dalker gave me for busting horses last summer. I'll make out."

All Mike could say as he turned to leave was: "If you ever need a few bucks, son. . . ." But he did not try to stop him, and Hugh knew, then, that the bond that held him to the Snake Track was a strong one.

Captain Johnny, still in his colors, came up as Hugh was saddling his horse. He stood watching him, chewing his perennial cud of fine-cut.

"Couldn't help hearing the fireworks, pardner. Maybe you won't mind a suggestion from a gent that's been around horses so long he's commencing to whinny. Get hold of that Little Sister horse."

Hugh frowned into the eyes that were like blue brilliants set in seasoned cowhide. "What do I want with a wind-broke mare?"

"Matter of sentiment, you might say. Never seen a horse get a rawer deal. I'd like to try my hand at bringing that horse back."

"Little Sister's not worth a gamble. I can't afford a trainer, anyway."

41

Captain Johnny fetched to his lips the grin that a man could not help answering. "That's the point. I go with the horse. All I'll cost you is a little grub. You buy her and I'll put her back on her feet."

The idea awoke a warm pulse within Hugh. If Captain Johnny thought the horse could be salvaged, maybe it was possible. He liked the notion of Little Sister stretching the tape in front of a field of the best horses in New Mexico. In the end, he dropped the reins of his horse over the rack. "You could talk a gopher into climbing a tree," he told Johnny. "Let's find Dennis."

So Hugh made a trade with Mark Dennis. Five yearlings for one broken-down race horse. Dennis didn't want her enough to bicker. But, for Hugh, making a deal with Dennis was the hardest part; he couldn't doubt that Dennis was the one who had foundered the mare, not knowing Barney Towne was the stripe to kill a horse rather than forfeit her.

At the Land Office next day, Hugh took an all-year lease on thirty sections of forest range in the Magdalenas. Driving seventy head of cattle and two dozen horses, he and Johnny crossed the Snake Track and began the climb into the mountains.

Staked about by lofty peaks, his range lay

42

in a rugged timberland broken into deep cañons as if by a giant plow. At the foot of a frowning cliff of blue granite lay a small park, a green patch of grass, and pines watered by a cold, deep creek. It was between the stream and the cliff, in a scope of incense cedar, that Hugh and Captain Johnny built the Padlock headquarters.

One day in late November Lass Towne rode up.

Hugh hadn't known, until he saw her, how her absence had left a little empty pocket in him. Maybe, he told himself, he needed somebody to scrap with.

"How's Mike?" he asked her.

"He's fine." Her gaze went appraisingly about the yard and outbuildings as they began to walk toward the barn. "You're building a real ranch here, Hugh. I'm proud of you."

"Surprised, I reckon, that I didn't decide to run sheep."

Lass stopped and looked up at him. "Please, Hugh . . . let's bury the hatchet for a while."

"If it suits you."

Reaching the barn, Lass glanced inside. Hugh watched her, grinning. "Where's Little Sister?" she asked.

"Over in Big Cañon somewhere."

"How is she?"

"Good enough."

"Captain Johnny's still working with her?"

Hugh began to play with a rope. "He gave up a couple of weeks ago. Says she's too wind-broke for anything but a bucking horse. Even if she could run, she ain't to be trusted. She's still a pitching fool."

Gone was the color from Lass's cheeks, and her voice was unsteady. "You're just saying that to . . . to make me angry, aren't you?"

"No, why should I? If she wants to pitch, I'll let her . . . for a profit. She hasn't got the *tripas* to last long, but even for one season it would be worth it. Afterward I'll still have a good stock horse."

"But they'd kill her!" Lass exclaimed. "She isn't strong enough for a tough game like that."

"You'd think she was tough enough if you'd been the one that broke her. I figured I'd let that Mexican, Pete Chavez, have her this winter. If she isn't a bad horse when he gets through with her, then Pete's forgot how to use those Chihuahua spurs of his."

Lass's face was white. Words came through a lump in her throat. "If you do that to Little Sister, I'll. . . ."

"You'll do what?"

Tears blurred the girl's eyes. In lieu of speaking, she slapped him. Then she ran back to her horse.

Regret piled upon Hugh, suddenly, and he started after her. For the first time, he knew he didn't really want to hurt Lass. Yet he was forever doing it, deriving a vicarious revenge on Barney Towne. He didn't dislike Lass, as he'd made himself think. He could like her a lot, if. . . . But there was that *if* between them, and always would be, while she was the anchor that held Mike down.

Hugh saddled and rode up the pasture, but the strange new loneliness he was trying to escape stayed with him all that day, and for many more.

V

In December, Hugh made a trip to Fort Selden and got a contract for fifty trained horses. Buying very shrewdly all the way home, he hit the Poverty with a score of good broncos. He and Captain Johnny worked them over until March. It was hard work — men's work. Hugh would have been lost without Captain Johnny. In Johnny's equestrian lexicon, there was no such word as *outlaw*.

"Me and them bronc's," he told Hugh,

"just naturally talk the same language. We savvy each other. It's no use to fight a horse. I learned that long ago."

He would let Hugh take the rough edge off the broncos. Then he'd take them in hand, work with them, break them to rope, to stand, to handle on their hind legs. They were ready far ahead of schedule.

"By hokey, did I ever see a horse reach," Johnny marveled one morning about Little Sister. They were standing in the middle of the small, circular track, the horse loping easily at the end of the long rope Captain Johnny held.

"Think she'll ever run a half again?" Hugh wanted to know. "She's still dragging her hind legs."

"When I'm done with her, she'll be a miler."

"That's strong talk," said Hugh. "How long is this miracle going to take?"

The trainer's gray, stubbly jaws worked a handful of tobacco down to eating size. "Confidentially," he said, "Little Sister could run the plates off Heelfly right now, in a half. I aim to run her at Alamo in June."

"But she hasn't shown anything, yet." Hugh instantly regretted the statement, because Captain Johnny turned the scorching heat of his contempt upon him.

46

"P'raps you'd like to change trainers? Maybe I don't know my business, after fifty-five years. Mister, when I say a hoss is ready . . . she's ready."

"You're the boss," Hugh assured him. "If you say we take her to Churchill Downs, we'll do it. I'm only saying she hasn't raised much dust while I've been watching."

Captain Johnny grunted. "That's because I've held her down. Them legs will loosen up, once I let her step out."

The idea took hold of Hugh. "Race her in June, eh? That gives us two and a half months. I'd give a lot to see her take the whole field."

"You will." Coming from Captain Johnny, that was a promise.

When spring came to the valley, one day Hugh left Captain Johnny to tend the stock and took the wagon down to Alamo to buy roundup necessities — vaccine, dehorners, and a load of chuck.

He ran into Mike for the first time in months. While they drank beers, Hugh noted the weariness of his face.

"So the iron's still sliding downhill," he remarked.

"Danged near to the bottom," Mike admitted. "We've lost a heap of stock somewhere. I'm starting roundup next week, but the count's going to be twenty percent off. The worst of it is, I can't blame Towne."

With almost a physical start, Hugh remembered the conversation he had overheard between Dennis and Sam Cotton at the brush meet eight months ago. He asked quickly: "Any idea where they're going?"

Mike pushed the beer glass around in the spilled foam. "Some kind of fever's knocking them over. Carcasses around all the tanks. I had the water tested, and it's all right. It looks like sleeping sickness . . . but twenty percent?"

Hugh looked into Mike's eyes, his voice held low. "I wish I'd had sense enough to tell you this before. I heard Mark Dennis promise Sam Cotton, the rodeo promoter, that he'd have taken over the Snake Track by June. That was last October. When did you start losing cattle?"

Mike's eyes were as hard as chilled steel, and his fingers made a vise on the handle of the mug. "Three months ago. Just after Dennis tried to buy the iron."

"If I'd only told you," Hugh said. "You could have had men riding the rims all year. Somehow, Dennis has got to your cattle."

Mike shook his head. "The way it looks, I reckon we'll go under before the beef

48

roundup. I wouldn't give a damn, except. . . ."

"For Lass." Hugh's wide mouth smiled.

Mike linked his stubby fingers and scowled at them, hunting for the words he wanted. "You hurt her when she was up there, Hugh," he said finally.

"Just threw a scare into her," Hugh told him. "I let her think I'm making Little Sister into a bucker."

"That wasn't all. She came to me the day after she was up and she'd been crying. She said . . . 'Why does Hugh hate me, Mike?' . . . and I said I didn't guess you did. But she said she was sure you did from how you always acted. I said I guessed she wasn't wasting any love on you anyway, and she told me . . . 'That's just it. I like Hugh . . . a lot, Mike. I wish I didn't. I wish I could hate him like he does me.' "

Hugh's grin was to hide his real emotion. "You aren't going to pull a John Alden on me, are you?"

"Not exactly. But I'm going to tell you something I've dodged for a long time. You remember the trip we made to Denver that time?"

"When you thought your memory was coming back?"

Mike nodded. "Well . . . it did come

back . . . and I wished to hell, then, that it never had."

"Mike, you never told me that."

"I had my reasons. You see, I wasn't exactly prideful of who I was, or what I'd done, after it came back to me. I'd had a wife, Hugh, as fine and lovely a woman as ever married a worthless glory-holer. We had a little place in Denver, but I wasn't there more'n a month or two out of the year. But the last time I wandered off, I swore would be my last. We had a six-months-old baby girl by then. All I wanted was a decent stake to support them right. What I got that time, instead of a pot of gold, was a crack over the noggin with a twelve-inch stull timber. When we went back to Denver, I got the shock that made me wish I'd never remembered. They'd reported me as dead in that cave-in. My wife had waited three years and then married a cattleman from Alamo . . . Barney Towne. I guess you can figure the rest. She'd been dead a couple of years when I found Barney Towne. But there was still my daughter. I thought of taking her away from Towne. But I knew that wouldn't have been fair to him. He loved her like his own kid, and he had troubles enough without my making things worse. Besides, I wasn't sure she'd go with . . . with a stranger. After I'd been with them a couple of years, I knew she wouldn't. She's got too much loyalty, that kid. Naturally I never told either of 'em about who I was. It would just have messed things up. But I guess," he finished, smiling wryly, "it couldn't have messed 'em up much worse than they are anyhow."

Mike stood up, blowing his nose. "Well, that's why I've hung with it. I just thought I'd tell you, so, if you do feel that way toward Lass, you can do something about it before it's too late, Hugh."

They walked up the street toward Hugh's buckboard. Hugh's thoughts were so confused that he could not separate and pigeon-hole them.

He was still searching for the right phrases when across the street he saw Lass coming toward them. As cool and haughty as ever, she gave Hugh a look that made him wonder how a man would ever get close enough to this girl to talk about love.

"Dad would like to see you over in the Land Office, Hugh," she said.

"Me? What's up?"

"I don't know. Something about the old Baylor place, I think. You might want to go along, Mike." With that she walked on down the street and passed into a store.

Crossing the street, Mike growled: "What's that yahoo up to now? He's made four visits here in the last month."

The land agent, a vulture-eyed little man, was tracing with his forefinger across a big map spread on the counter as they entered. Barney Towne looked up from it.

Hugh went over and asked: "What's on your mind?"

"I've been asked by Mister Towne to have you vacate certain of his lands which you are now occupying," Spreckles began. "Namely a parcel of government forest reserve bounded by a line commencing at a brass-capped cement stake. . . ."

Hugh straightened as though a ramrod had been threaded down his spine. He glanced into Towne's vein-webbed, grinning face, then spun the map to examine it.

"Show me. If I'm using one acre of his land, I'll stock it with black-polled Anguses free of charge."

Spreckles's face showed no eagerness for the job ahead. "You are using," he said, "exactly fifteen sections of land now owned by Mister Towne."

"*Now* owned?" Hugh's eyes snapped to Towne. "All right, Towne, what's the game? Fifteen sections is half of my range."

"Remember the old Baylor place?" Towne asked.

Hugh nodded. "Baylor ran cattle up in the Magdalenas, near my place. The ruins of his shack aren't far from me. But he's been dead five years. Any lease he had must have reverted years ago."

"He didn't have a lease."

"You mean he was trespassing all that time?"

Spreckles came in again: "Mister Baylor owned the land. He was an old Civil War man and took out his soldier's bonus in a plot of government land. I don't know how I missed it when I granted you your lease. Mister Towne's lawyer ran across it and . . . er . . . Mister Towne bought the plot for back taxes."

Hugh stretched the map out in his two hands, his eyes hard. "What's the extent of it?"

Barney Towne showed him. "It takes all of that Granite Springs section, and about half of the rest of your lease. Including Cold Springs, Granite Creek . . . all your water rights, you might say."

Hugh put the map down. He faced Towne, his features pale and hard. "All right, you buzzard, you've asked for it." Suddenly he took Towne by the neck and rammed him

53

against the wall. Towne squalled as his fist drew back.

Spreckles was yelling excitedly: "See here! You can't pull anything. . . ."

But it was Mike, pulling Hugh back by the shoulder and snapping — "Take it easy. One good lick would kill the old sot." — who brought him to his senses.

Inside, Hugh was shaking. This was wipe-out. The dry Magdalena Mountains didn't offer another all-year spring within fifty miles. Eight months' work and most of his cash were forfeit to Barney Towne's revenge.

"I start roundup tomorrow to cut out my strays and throw your animals over on your own lease. Headquarters will be at Long-Time Corral, if you're going to send a rep," Towne said, then stalked out.

Hugh and Mike left a moment later. Hugh remarked: "Dumb like a lobo wolf, isn't he? I've still got the Padlock, but he's got the key."

Mike laid a hand on his shoulder. "I've got an idea." he said, his words slow and full of thought. "You go on back. Be at Long-Time Corral around ten tomorrow. Larry Dennis will be there, repping for his father. I'm putting all our chips on one card . . . and I hope it's the right one."

VI

Dawn was a grayness against the dusty windowpanes when Barney Towne awoke the next morning to the knowledge that someone was standing beside his bed.

"Towne," he heard a man's voice say. "Git outta there."

Towne tried to focus his bleary gaze but made out only wide shoulders against the pale square of the window. "Who in hell says it?"

"Mike Talbot. Horses are saddled, mules packed, and we're waiting on you."

"Waiting for what?" Towne sat up in bed.

Mike Talbot leaned over and hooked a big hand around the back of his neck. "For you to get in your work clothes. A top-hand rancher always rides roundup with his crew. Shake a leg."

"Mike, you damned jughead!" The ramrod's jerk pulled him out of bed. Towne tried to push him away. "I say I ain't riding. Get out of here now or I'll beat the living tar out of you. Well, what are you waiting for?"

"For you to get dressed or beat the tar out of me. You're riding, mister. Maybe you thought I'd swaller your breaking Hugh, like I have a thousand other insults. But we've crossed the bridge. I don't reckon you know why I've held this broken-down spread together so long. Not for you or the salary . . . for Lass. Take a deep breath, Towne, prepare yourself for a shock. Lass is my daughter."

Towne grunted. "Hell, I've knowed that for years."

"You . . . you knew?"

"Ever look in a mirror? Chips off the same block. And if I hadn't been able to see it, I'd've savvied it because you've hung around so long, hating my guts as much as you do."

Mike rallied from his shock. "Which makes me hate your guts more than ever. If you knew, why didn't you say so?"

"Reasons of my own," growled Towne. He turned to go back to bed. "Now get out of here."

"Not so fast." Mike reached out and held him. "My plans ain't changed none. I aim to show you some things you've forgot. That a ranch don't run itself. That somebody works his head off to keep it in the black. And maybe you think Hugh didn't put out a little work to build the Padlock up. That's rough, tough country, Towne. I think you'll agree along about next week when you've put in eighteen hours a day on one meal a day and no likker. Now, mister, get into your duds."

In the poor light, Mike Talbot did not see Towne's fist until it landed on his ear. There was power in the blow. Mike went to his knees, heavily. But in a moment he was coming to his feet. Towne swung again; Mike parried the fist and sank a blow into the rancher's belly.

Mike slammed a fist into the side of Towne's head. Reeling, the rancher grabbed at the dresser. The thing went over with a din of broken bottles and mirror. Snorting like a galloping bull, Towne lunged into the foreman.

That was his last mistake. A dozen men seemed to be throwing fists at him. They spatted all over his body, bruising, crippling, drawing blood — but never finishing him. Pawing out with his hands, the Snake Track owner backed down the wall and into the corner. He took more punishment than Mike Talbot thought he could stand. His face was a welter of blood and puffy swellings; his chest must have ached from the booming blows that thundered against it repeatedly. But in the end Barney Towne gasped: "I'm . . . done . . . Mike."

Mike stepped back, rubbing his skinned knuckles. "All right. I told the boys last night that you'd be riding with us. So don't try to back out now or they'll think you've gone yellow. Pack up your war sack and be out in twenty minutes."

Camp was pitched at Long-Time Corral, the remains of an old Mexican goat camp at the head of Green Rock Cañon. Old Dirty, the cook, was stewing because everything breakable in his moonshine packs had been broken. The country, too rough for a chuck wagon, had necessitated packing in all his equipment.

Hugh had only half expected to see Barney Towne. When he rode in and got a look at him, he experienced a shock. Towne looked as though he had been dragged at the end of a rope all the way from the Snake Track. His face was skinned, his eyes black, one leg was lame. He was whipping loose the ropes that held his war sack on the pack animal when Hugh rode in.

Mike Talbot shouldered him aside and took over the job. "Go grab yourself some chuck," he said. "I'll finish for you."

Mike winked at Hugh when he had thrown off the square hitch. He lifted the heavy pack, weighing all of one hundred and fifty pounds, carried it to the trees, and dropped it heavily. Barney Towne sat watching.

Theoretically the pack consisted of blankets rolled around a miscellany of odds and ends a cowboy found necessary in his rambling life. But what Hugh heard when the pack dropped was the muffled jangle of broken glass.

Affecting astonishment, Mike prodded the roll with his toe. "Sounds like something broke, boss. Bottle of liniment, mebbe."

Barney Towne said nothing. But there was black desperation in his eyes as he turned away and poured coffee with a hand that shook.

Mike paired Hugh with Larry Dennis for the afternoon circle. Dennis was seeing that his father's interests were protected. Should any Frying Pan strays be found, Dennis would cut them out and drive them back when roundup was finished.

Barney Towne took a sad beating that day. For the first time in years, he had gone all day without a drink. The effect was evident in the putty-like pallor of his face and the jerking of his muscles when he tried to handle knife and fork. He sat hunched with his back against a tree, slopping his food down and drinking coffee by the quart. Nerves twitched his eyes and mouth grotesquely.

For the two days the roundup crew

59

combed the rugged cañon country for Hugh's cattle. They had about seventy head bunched up in the corral, among them a few Frying Pan and Snake Track animals. By now Barney Towne looked like a dissipated ghost. He hadn't found sleep in three nights. There were brown patches under his eyes. He couldn't smoke because his fingers threw the makings all over the landscape. Hugh, hating him as he did, knew a growing fear that he would throw a fit on them.

When they came in that last night, Hugh saw Larry Dennis motion Towne over to his blankets. A little later, while they were eating, Mike Talbot suddenly leaned close to Towne and smelled his breath. Then he sat up straight and announced: "Some dirty son has brought likker into this camp!"

No one spoke. Mike got up and went back to Larry Dennis's blankets. With a choked sound, the Snake Track owner leaped up, spilling his food. He reached Mike in five seconds, but by this time the ramrod had the bottle out. Towne grabbed at it and Mike shoved him away. He gave the pint flask a sling into the creek. Towne went rigid as the crash of broken glass hit his ears. Then, without warning, he went after Mike Talbot.

He swung once and stopped. Stiffening, his body toppled forward like a plank. A moment later he began to thresh in wild convulsions. Mike was on him with a yell. He pinned him flat while cowboys ran to help. Somebody jammed a wadded handkerchief between the rancher's teeth to keep him from biting his tongue.

For fifteen minutes Barney Towne continued to kick and jerk in delirium tremens. One of the cowpunchers said finally: "It jest looks like we'll have to bat the old boy over the head to calm him down. Somebody fetch a rock."

"To hell with that." Dirty, the cook, yanked a blanket from a bed and laid it out flat on the ground. "I've heard some place you can roll them up so tight in a blanket that they can't move an eyelash. Lug him over here."

Rolled up like a cocoon, Towne was quiet. Presently he passed out. When he regained consciousness, he was lying on his own blankets. Dirty carried him a cup of ink-black coffee. Towne drank it. Before long he was asleep.

He was still sleeping when Hugh rode out with Dennis the next morning. Their circle took them down into the foothills bordering the Snake Track range. By a small tank

Hugh found a dead cow so bloated her legs stuck up like the legs of a sawhorse. Dismounting, he scooped up a handful of water and tested it. It tasted sweet enough.

Suddenly Hugh threw the water aside. Dennis watched him walk to a salt block almost hidden in the brush. The cowpuncher squatted by it. Then, turning his head, he called to Dennis: "This is a damned peculiar-looking saltlick. It's been bored full of little holes and then filled up with something that ain't salt."

Dennis's piggish eyes were unsteady as he regarded the block and glanced at Hugh. "What . . . what do you reckon it is?"

Hugh growled: "I'll know better after I have a chunk of it analyzed. But my guess is . . . poison."

With his pocket knife, he hacked off a piece and stuck it into his jumper pocket. He saw little of Dennis the rest of the day, and that night, when he came in, driving a few cattle, he saw that the cowboy hadn't shown up yet. He had the quick suspicion that Dennis had pulled out fast.

But in a short time Dennis came in. Chuck time was a utensil-rattling interval of intense eating. Dirty stood by his fire, watching with satisfaction as the ravenous roundup hands put away third portions of

62

son-of-a-gun stew.

"How's she go, gents?" he asked presently. There were grunts of satisfaction. Dirty began to grin. "I allus did say a cowhand didn't rate no better grub than a cow. And now I've proved it."

Startled eyes lifted to his mustached face. "Meaning what?" Mike asked.

"I ran low on salt. Knowed you'd holler if I fed you unsalted stew, so I throwed in a chunk of saltlick. But I reckon what's good enough for a cow ought to be good enough for rannihans anyway."

Larry Dennis tossed his plate at the dishpan, then frowned. "Where'd you find any lick around camp?" he demanded.

"Oh, some jigger left a hunk in the knife drawer. I don't know what for. But I just throwed it in the stew and. . . ."

"God Almighty!" Dennis came straight up. His features were pea-green. He began to retch. "Water!" he gasped. "Some-body . . . get . . . water!"

Hugh was suddenly before him. "What's wrong, Dennis? Just because a cow licked off it before you did. . . ."

Dennis looked like a rat in a corner. He started to speak, his slack lips shaking. "I . . . I. . . ." His mouth clamped shut and he bolted for the water keg. He stuck his

63

head in and began to drink in great, noisy gulps.

Hugh's voice went through the silent camp. "All right, Dennis. You can relax now. I just wanted to make sure you and your old man left that poisoned block there. Thanks for the help, Dirty. You see, I've still got the salt right in my pocket, Dennis. . . ."

Dennis came up with his face dripping. A look of amazement spread through his features, then rage came to make his eyes sooty and distort his mouth. Fist drawn back, he went after Hugh Talbot.

Hugh let him come close. Then his long body pivoted, right hand driving straight to the cowpuncher's face. Dennis's neck snapped. His forward rush carried him on for several feet before he stumbled and fell. He lay there like a shot beef.

To Mike, Hugh said: "So that's how Mark Dennis plays the game. Now that you know the rules, maybe you can even up the score one of these days."

Dennis left that same night. But if finding the poisoned lick had been a surprise, Barney Towne pulled a bigger one the next day.

After his fit of drunken horrors, he had begun to look better. There was a clearer look to his eyes. His skin had lost that fishbelly color. He startled the whole camp at breakfast by telling a joke — something no man had heard him do in years.

Afterward, when the cowpunchers were preparing to leave, Towne said: "Come back here and set down. I've got some *habla* to make. And I want it down on record that I'm not drunk or crazy. It's the first time I've been able to say that in fifteen years. Mike," he said, putting out his hand to the foreman. "I've thought and said some mean things about you this week."

Mike's eyes studied him as if fearing a trick. "Can't blame you," he grunted. "Tapering off ain't exactly salve for the temper."

"I'm not tapering off. I've quit." Towne looked about the ring of faces, as if calling them to witness. "You've done a job for me, Mike, that I hadn't the guts to do for myself. I wish you'd've done it years ago."

Mike was smiling. "So do I."

"But in a way," Towne added, "you were responsible for me getting into this blind alley. I was jealous. I knew what Lass meant to you . . . and I knew she cared for you a sight more than she did for me."

"Not that she ever showed it," Hugh put in.

"She knew better'n to. Knew I'd get crazy

65

jealous and be worse than ever. You've got a kick coming, too, son. But maybe you'll feel better when I tell you I'm signing over that Sam Baylor claim to you. You can throw your cows back on the range anytime you like. Far as I'm concerned, the roundup is over."

Hugh glanced at Mike, his mouth softening. "Mike, you'd better smell his breath again. He talks *muy borrachado* to me."

"No, by hell, I'm sober. But I'm going to ask a favor of you in return."

"Name it."

"I want you to ride with my outfit at the rodeo next week," Towne said. "I had a talk with Sam Cotton and Dennis in town. Seems like Cotton's looked over all the bucking stock in the state and likes Alamo's best. He's on the fence as to whether he wants me or Dennis to supply him for the state fair. It means five thousand dollars to the man he picks. So here's how he's going to decide. Me and Dennis have both got a nice bunch of riders. We're going to match them at the rodeo, my boys to ride his buckers and 'dog his bulls, his boys to tackle mine. The outfit with the most points wins. Will you side me?"

"You've just got a bronc' stomper," Hugh told him.

VII

Rodeo time found Alamo primed to the exploding point on the news of the Snake Track–Frying Pan wager. Alamo knew defeat would mean Barney Towne was finished. But the town knew Mark Dennis, too, and understood he was playing to win.

Hugh and Captain Johnny kept Little Sister hidden in a rear stall at the livery stable. Fearful of tampering, they brought her in at night and bribed the liveryman to secrecy.

Captain Johnny vowed he had never seen a fitter horse in his life. She was a different mare from the one Mark Dennis had supposedly ruined in October. As far as Dennis knew, Little Sister was growing fat in some Magdalena park, her racing days done.

Johnny's plan was to save the horse for the sweepstakes the last day, when every top race horse in the county would run. For the little shriveled-up racetrack man, those two days were a torment of waiting. Watching Heelfly win every race he entered was the bitterest pill he had to swallow.

But for Hugh, they were two tough days of getting his insides shaken up on those Frying Pan buckers and risking his neck bedding down mean-tempered bulls. Lap-

and-tap rules were in force, and the toll of injuries was already high.

By morning of the third day, the Snake Track was running behind. Towne showed his boys the tally sheet while they waited behind the chutes for the calf roping to finish.

"We need a pair of firsts and half the second and third money to win," he told them dispiritedly. "It kind of looks like we need a miracle. That Larry Dennis tramp, for all his fancy yaller chaps and silk shirt, has got the lot of you licked in the saddle-bronco riding. But if Hugh don't draw another Chihuahua outlaw, I hope for a first in the bulldogging. You, Taggart, I'm counting on to take first money in the bareback-bronco riding."

Taggart, a stringy redhead, looked at the palm of his hand, from which the surcingle had peeled most of the skin the day before. "If my danged hand gives out," he said, "I'll be lucky to finish third."

And Taggart's hand did give out. Consternation hit the Snake Track camp when he was thrown in less than the short limit, and the Dennis boys took first and second money.

An hour later the pendulum swung back, when Hugh grabbed a surprise first in the bronco riding right out of Larry Dennis's hands. Mark Dennis had jobbed him with the meanest outlaw in his string, but Hugh had hung in the hooks and circle-saw-spurred the bronco all over the arena. He hadn't been breaking horses all winter for nothing.

Up on the judge's stand, Sam Cotton was announcing the final event. "The bulldoggin' contest, folks! Free-for-all rules . . . and the devil take the hindmost! Watch Chute Four . . . Larry Dennis coming out after Yellow Fever!"

The barrier banged open, and Dennis rocketed after the big Chihuahua bull. Bulldogging bat slapping his pony's flank, he pulled in beside the brute and dived for the slick horns. The bull went down in churning brown dust. Dennis wrenched the big head over and, sitting on the neck, held his hands aloft. A yell went across the field like a tornado. Hugh groaned. It had been a beautiful job — too beautiful. Cotton was waving his arms.

"The time . . . eight and one-half seconds!"

Up on the chute bars, the Snake Track outfit was silent. Dennis had set a new arena record. Then Hugh heard his name being called. He jumped down and hurried over, conscious of one thing — that what happened in the next half hour would decide whether the Snake Track was to be shuffled into the limbo of old outfits that had outgrown their time.

Waiting behind the foul line, he was nervous, jumpy. As the barrier slammed open, he saw, from the corner of his eye, a flash of movement behind the chute, and he guessed what had happened. Someone had given the brute a jolt of high-life, the stinging concoction that turns a horse or a bull crazy. He knew he couldn't beat Dennis's time before he ever swung the bat. The steer was going like a cannonball. Hugh's cutting pony gave him his try. He came down heavily on the broad neck, popping the sinews with the wrenching power he put into his arms. His heels dragged the animal to a stop. Hugh bedded him down and the field judge's red flag flashed.

"Nine seconds!"

On a wrenched ankle, Hugh limped off the field. He was surprised at the time, the best he had ever made. Still it was one-half second too slow. He had only one more chance, one more ride in which to set an average better than Dennis's.

None of the other riders came close to Dennis's mark. The second round came up with the Frying Pan bunch already cocky with victory. Larry Dennis went out after his second bull. It was a ride that brought every spectator in the stands to his feet. Dennis was out there like a bolt of lightning, knocking over his bull before it had time to pick up its full speed.

Hugh knew before they announced it that it was even better time than Dennis's former ride. He knew, too, that it had been dishonest. One of the gatemen had held the barrier long enough to throw the bull off balance.

Mike protested. But the judges hadn't seen it, and Sam Cotton let the time be announced — eight seconds!

Hugh was about to swing into the saddle when someone touched his arm. It was Lass who stood behind him. All the hardness was gone out of her manner.

"I thought you might need this . . . for luck," she said,

Her hands went up to Hugh's face. She pulled him down to her and for a moment her lips were warmly soft against his. But when she released him, Hugh's arm went around her waist and he caught her to him. They were calling him to the chutes, but he held her there a moment, gripping her hands.

"Some people would call that a promise."

"If you want me, Hugh, that's what I'll call it." Lass's eyes were serious, with little shadows of fear darkening them. "But we've got to win, or I can't keep it. I'll never leave Barney while he's down. So you see . . . you'll have to win . . . for us."

From his position beside the bullpen, Hugh could see the bull he had drawn. It was a powerful-shouldered, short-legged animal with pink-rimmed eyes set in a massive head. Its long, down-curving horns were sharpened to needle points on the brush tangles of Chihuahua, where Dennis had bought him. He would be fast and tough, and Hugh, his arm raised with the bulldogging hat, knew only luck would let him spill the brute in less than ten seconds.

Now the gate was open, the bull thundering into the clear. Hugh's pony shot after him. Coming alongside, Hugh leaned out across the shaggy red back. The certainty was lead in his heart that he could never bulldog this brute down in time to do the Snake Track any good. Then he remembered what he had almost forgotten, that the rules were free-for-all. Anything went, and the plan that came into his mind was sheer suicide.

The stands went silent as they saw what

he was going to do. He dived on the bull's neck and took an over-under grip on those blade-like horns. Then his legs gave a kick, hurling his body in the path of the animal's hoofs.

That was all the spectators could see of it. Up on the chute bars Captain Johnny let out a high-pitched yell as the bull stumbled and went down on the bulldogger's body. The brute's hindquarters semaphored over his head. Dust obscured the rest. When the field judges rode in, they found the bull lying with a broken neck, ten feet from Hugh Talbot. Hugh lay as he had fallen, one arm crumpled under his head.

It was Captain Johnny that Hugh saw when he came back to consciousness. He was lying in the shade behind the judge's stand. Lass was wringing out a wet cloth to put on his forehead. Mike and all the Snake Track boys except Barney Towne were standing around him.

The rodeo doctor was closing his bag. "Keep him quiet a while," he said. "He's shook up considerable. But the crazy jughead hasn't got a thing wrong with him that I can find."

Hugh's eyes flicked over the faces about him, trying to read in them what he wanted to know. His hand stayed Lass's as she started to place the compress.

"Did they announce . . . ?"

"Seven seconds." Captain Johnny cackled. "A new record on anybody's track."

"And we won?" He knew as soon as he said it that they hadn't. Mike shook his head.

"A tie! Twenty-seven points apiece. They're up there, now, trying to decide whether to flip a coin, or what."

Hugh sat up. "Gimme a hand. I'm going up there. I've got an idea of my own."

They tried to stop him, but Hugh staggered over to the stand, and Mike had to hurry to keep him from falling. When they reached the little knot of officials, in which Mark Dennis and Barney Towne were standing at opposite sides with glares for each other, Sam Cotton was saying: "Well, a coin has always settled every argument I ever got into. I've no preference in the matter. You've both got a good string of stock."

"I've got an idea, Mister Cotton."

Sam Cotton looked at Hugh as he shouldered into the circle. He smiled, noting the mud and blood on the bronco rider's face. "I suppose you want to run the 'dogging match over again."

"Not today." Hugh grinned. "Dennis, do

74

you still think that Heelfly of yours is a race horse?"

"You won't catch him pulling no wagons. What have you got that's faster?"

"A blood-sorrel mare called Little Sister."

Dennis's jaw loosened. "Little Sister! That plug I sold you last fall? She'll never run in anything but the Stringhalt Handicap."

"If that's what you think of her," Hugh remarked, "you ought to fall right in with my notion of how to settle this. Little Sister belongs to Lass Towne. I'm giving her back as of right now. Lass will match her horse against yours tomorrow for a mile. Winner takes the contract."

Sam Cotton made the decision for him. "That's one I could go for. How about it, mister?"

Mark Dennis's face was marked with the lines of distrust and surprise. But all he could say was: "Heelfly will be ready. Eleven o'clock?"

"On the nose." Hugh nodded. "Better feed that hoss on dynamite, Dennis. We're keeping an eye on Little Sister this time."

Captain Johnny almost swallowed his fine-cut when he heard it. "Did I ask for a race?" he chortled. "By pokey, we'll run the plates off that stud. Little Sister's a-coming back, and New Mexico's going to know about it.

I'm sleeping in the paddock with her to-night."

Later, when the mare was installed in her new quarters, they ate supper in front of the stall. At 9:00 P.M. Hugh got up to go to the wagon where he had spread his blankets.

"You'd better let me bring you a tick of hay and sleep in front of the stall," he counseled Johnny. "A horse that's been mean once is never safe to take chances with."

"Don't you fret yourself 'bout Little Sister," said Captain Johnny. "She's so soft-hearted now she won't switch her tail at flies."

Those were the last words Hugh ever heard from the old man's lips. At midnight the sounds of kicking and squealing dragged him from his bed, but when he reached the paddock Captain Johnny was lying in a corner of the stall, dead, while Little Sister continued to kick at his limp body.

VIII

It was a scene of horror Hugh would never forget. They had dragged the jockey out on the ground and covered him with a canvas. But in the yellow light of a lantern, while track followers clustered around, Hugh

76

could see the brown-red stains coming through the tarpaulin, and he remembered the ghastly horseshoe mark on the Captain's face.

Barney Towne came from the hotel with Lass. Hugh and Mike leaned on the gate, looking in at the mare. She stood against the back wall, getting as far away from the odor of death as she could.

"I . . . I can't understand it," Hugh muttered.

He was trying to keep from his mind the recollections that came bitterly to crowd it — days in the meadow with Johnny, working out Little Sister; times when they yarned of race horses before the fireplace on wintry nights; these and a thousand other memories of a gallant little old man who loved horses and won their love with understanding.

Barney Towne said huskily, beside him: "She never brought us nothing but grief, that filly. And she's done it for sure, this time. Won't a jockey in the county ride her now. Even if she could be mounted."

Hugh felt a tremor in Lass's body, as she pressed against him to look in at the mare. "I've ridden her . . . I'll ride her again. They aren't going to whip us this easily."

Ice seemed to form along Hugh's spine.

"Good Lord, no. She'll never wear a saddle again. She's a killer horse if one ever lived."

"I'm not afraid of her. She's never tried to hurt me."

"But if you'd seen Captain Johnny as I did. . . ."

Lass's eyes were narrow. "I don't think she did it. She's never kicked in her life."

This mad idea of hers had Hugh breathless. "I tell you I saw her kicking him," he retorted.

"Any horse would do it with a dead man in the stall with her. They can smell death. Captain Johnny might have been . . . stabbed, or something. Dennis thought we could never get a jockey to ride her if she'd killed a man. But he was wrong."

Mike's big hand fastened on the girl's shoulder. "I'm saying you aren't going to ride her."

Lass pulled away and faced them angrily. "No, this is the end of it . . . Little Sister belongs to me, now. There's no rule against an owner riding her own horse. So if you don't want to see it, you'd better not be here eleven hours from now."

That was far from the end of it, however. They started arguing again when she showed up for breakfast in the hotel dining room. But at 10:30 she was in the Snake

Track's old purple-and-white silks, snap-brimmed cap on her golden curls.

Hugh was the first one to approach the mare after the tragedy. She had gentled down completely, taking the snaffle bit without a fuss. He led her out. Lass stood by the gate, blanket and pad over her arm, quirt in her hand. Hugh watched her reach up and stroke the sorrel's neck. Little Sister bent her head and nuzzled in the girl's pocket for sugar, as she had done with Captain Johnny.

Lass's eyes went to him in relieved triumph. "A killer horse, is she?"

Hugh only wagged his head. There was a frowning wrinkle between his eyes. There were pieces in this puzzle that didn't fit.

A whistle blast rode the breeze to them. The track was cleared. Heelfly was being walked out by Santos Luna, his jockey, and a trainer. The stands, a jam of color, surged with excitement.

Lass looked up at Hugh, standing there, frowning, hesitant. "Post time," she reminded him.

Suddenly Hugh gave Mike the reins. "Take her around, will you? I'll see you all later."

He watched them parade before the grandstand. Then the horses were saddled and Mike gave the girl a boost. This was the moment the crowd had been waiting for, and a dead silence blanketed the field. Little Sister walked down toward the turn. Hugh saw Lass wave at him.

Still he stood there before the empty stall. Presently the track was cleared again and they began maneuvering the horses for the start. Abruptly the starter's whistle shrilled, and the horses broke away. That was when Hugh turned from the track, went to the back of the stall, and climbed the rear partition. In his ears was the swelling roar of hundreds of voices. But his attention was for Heelfly's empty stall.

He began crawling gingerly down the two-by-four partition. Twice he stopped and examined spots on the new wood. Reaching the stallion's stall, he dropped into the deep straw. Now he began to grub around in the stuff. He had covered almost the whole space and was burrowing into a far corner when his hands struck it — a smooth length of hickory.

It had been an ordinary single-jack sledge-hammer, until someone welded a racing plate across the head of it. On that steel horseshoe there was brown blood, caked deep. This was the killer horse. This was the deadly tool that someone had carried from

Heelfly's stall, down the partition to where Captain Johnny slept almost beneath the mare's hoofs. That someone had struck the old man in the head, and the mare, terrified, had begun to kick at the limp thing that smelled of blood. Returning, the murderer had left splotches of blood along the partition. And he had buried his bloody weapon where now it had been found.

Hugh turned to leave. It was then he saw Mark Dennis standing in the portal, a gun in his hand. Behind the Irishman loomed his son.

Hugh's move was reflex action. He sent the sledge-hammer spinning into Dennis's face. Dennis ducked, firing as he did so. The slug splintered wood behind Hugh, giving him time to pull his own .44.

The murderer was thumbing his Colt again when Hugh's weapon came up. Lead burned deep through the muscles of his shoulder. Pain shook him, but his aim held steady. He saw Mark Dennis jerk as a bullet caved his ribs to find the heart.

Larry Dennis was running away before his father's body hit the straw. Hugh stepped into the sunlight, gun held low. "All right, Dennis."

Without slowing, his face showing over his shoulder, Larry Dennis thrust a gun barrel under his left armpit and fired. The slug threw grit over Hugh's boots. Hugh's finger squeezed the trigger. Dennis came up on his toes, hands pressing against his thighs. Hugh Talbot turned away.

When he went back to Little Sister's stall, he could see them leading the mare across the field. Lass was running ahead of the horse, her cap off, blonde hair tossing. When she reached him, she threw her arms around his neck and hugged him.

"Oh, Hugh! Little Sister did it . . . by two lengths!"

"That . . . that's great." Hugh tried to sound enthusiastic, but the girl pulled back and looked at him.

"Darling, what's wrong?"

Hugh lifted the sledge that leaned against the wall. "This. I found it in Heelfly's stall. Mark and Larry Dennis jumped me, and . . . I shot straighter. I guess somebody'd better get the law."

That night they sat long over their dinner. Alamo was returning to normal, with a long string of ranch wagons rattling back into the hills.

"If there's got to be a coroner's investigation," Mike Talbot told Hugh, "there'll be

82

time to take that advice I gave you last week."

Lass shook her head. "If you're referring to what I think you are, I'm not going through with it. It's too risky. How would I look if you two began wrangling over who was going to give me away? One of you my legal father and the other my father-once-removed?"

"There'll be no wrangling," Barney Towne assured her. "That's a promise. Ain't either of us so anxious to lose you that we'll fight about it. In fact, I'd like to borrow the pair of you down to my place till after the Albuquerque show. I need a good bronc' stomper to help shape up the bucking string I've promised Sam Cotton."

There was a little silence, all of them expecting Hugh to say something.

"I'll help all I can, Barney," he said at last, "but I've got another duty that comes first. There's an ornery, tobacco-chewing little *hombre* who'll be watching to see whether I let him down. I'm going to put his horse in shape for that Albuquerque show before I do anything else. And when she runs, I'll see him up there in the saddle, whispering things in her ear that only the two of them savvy. That's why Little Sister can't lose. Captain Johnny told me so himself."

▪ ▪ ▪ ▪

MISSION CREEK

▪ ▪ ▪ ▪

"Mission Creek" first appeared as a six-part serial in *The Saturday Evening Post* in May and June of 1954 under the title "The Feud at Spanish Bit," Frank Bonham's second Western novel to be serialized in that well-regarded slick-paper weekly magazine. The first, "Outcast of Crooked River," appeared in five installments three years earlier. The Red River region of Texas is the background for this fiery tale of Ruel Starrett, an uncompromising, land-hungry rancher and breeder of humpbacked Brahma cattle, and his level-headed and idealistic son, Rex, and the misunderstanding between them that flares into hatred — until volatile circumstances bring them together again in a bitter fight against a common enemy.

As in all of Bonham's well-crafted Western novels, a realistically portrayed background, unflagging action, and strong character development are the featured attractions of "Mission Creek." The Starretts are both memorable creations, as are beautiful and unpredictable Susanna Dalhart and the old Mexican sinner, Lisandro Garza.

B.P.

I

Ruel Starrett caught sight of the horsemen as they slid down a bluff to the river two miles north, their dust mounting above the gray uplands that crumpled into the wide bosque of the Red River. Although he had awaited the return of the trail crew for days, Starrett patiently finished shaving at the mirror that hung against a cottonwood in the ranch yard. He was a large, deep-chested man of early middle age, massive in the shoulders, dark as old copper, horn-hard, with the look of a tough and capable man. He wore a buckskin shirt and gray trousers with faded red slashes down the seams. A Colt revolver hung on his right thigh. He wore his hat on the back of his head.

He glanced again in the mirror and hummed as he whetted saber points onto his long sideburns. They were the only touch of vanity about him, his leather shirt having been traded from a Comanche, his trousers being one of a bale purchased from a Confederate quartermaster after the war. With a flourish, he flicked peppery lather at the tree trunk. Behind him stood the main ranch building — two stories of plastered adobe with reeling wooden balconies. Somewhere he heard Mexican girls chattering as they pounded corn. Starrett glanced across the hills once more. The dust was clearing. Now a wagon topped the bluff and hung groping for the cliff-side trail. Starrett's excitement began to mount, but he kept it locked in his eyes.

Suddenly from the upper gallery of the ranch house a girl called: "Mister Starrett! I believe I see them."

"Yes, ma'am." Starrett glanced at the girl on the balcony. She stood at the railing, slim as a candle, her hair hanging dark and free, a silver brush in her hand. "Me and Rex will ride out directly and meet them," he told Susanna Dalhart.

The girl hesitated. "Mister Starrett, I don't know how Zack Markley will take it, that I've got a partner, with my father dead only a month. Will you let me ride ahead and tell him myself?"

Starrett's thumb slicked lather from the razor. "No, ma'am. I'm sorry. I'd planned on breaking it to that young rooster myself. To tell the truth, one of the reasons I bought in with you was to square things with your ramrod."

He could see the girl's lips firm. "Perhaps you don't realize how much this means to me."

"Probably I don't." Starrett squinted and with the razor picked off two hairs he had missed at the point of his sideburn.

The girl struck the railing with the hairbrush. "You'll please wait for me!" she cried. She vanished from the gallery.

Starrett chuckled and rinsed the razor. He saw his son Rex come from the bunkhouse. Gazing at him, he was touched with pride. *Every day,* he thought, *he looks more like I did at twenty. But he's got the chance now that I never had. He'll set this cow country rocking one day. Clean, tough, and smart, like I was at his age. But he's got his boots set on land that'll be his own, not in quicksand, like I had.*

Tall and sauntering in a blue shirt and brown bull-hide chaps, Rex Starrett had the black hair and blue eyes of his Irish immigrant mother, the unrepentant chin and wide jaw of his father. He smiled at Starrett as he stood there, flipped a coin, and said: "I've been waiting for this ever since we

89

moved over here. Sooner or later, one of you was bound to give the other an order."

"That wasn't an order." His father chuckled. "That was just a suggestion."

"Suggestion? That girl never made a suggestion in her life. 'Saddle my horse!' 'Bring the rain water, Maria, I'll wash my hair now!' That," Rex assured him, "was an order."

Starrett poured water from a gourd. As he rinsed his face, he glanced at his son. Rex was gazing up at Susanna's window. Starrett, who knew every expression of his face, saw the lines of disillusion beside his mouth, and he voiced a thought he had had frequently in the past few days.

"Seems to me you've been mighty rough on that girl lately. What happened between you two?"

"Nothing," Rex said in surprise. "Why?"

"I was looking for a quick wedding, for a while there. Every time I needed you, you were off riding with Susanna."

"I just lost interest," Rex said, "after I found out she thinks she's a cow-country queen."

"But if you marry a queen, it makes you a king, don't it?"

"Maybe . . . with a crown half the size of hers." Abruptly Rex changed the subject, reaching up to take a match from the snakeskin band of his hat. "So you're going to fire Markley?"

"What do you think? It'll be the surprise of that young rooster's life when I fire him."

Dropping razor, soap, and brush into a buckskin sack, Starrett let anticipation of the scene warm him. It was not often life presented revenge in so neat a package as this. Markley, who had spoiled the deal that would have made Starrett a partner with Susanna Dalhart's father on Spade Ranch last year, was now coming home to find the father dead and Starrett running Spade.

Rex's enthusiasm for the firing of Markley did not match his father's. "Seems to me Markley's got a point, too. He was only trying to protect Dalhart's interests when he scuttled your deal with him. Everybody knew about your fight with Chief Jack. Markley figured if you'd swindle a Comanche. . . ."

"All right. I swindled him like he tried to swindle me. I used his range, sold my cattle, and didn't give Chief Jack a three-cent nickel. Why? Because his bucks had been hitting our horse herd and slow-elking our steers whenever they felt like it."

"But if Markley didn't know that, could you expect him to sit by while Dalhart signed up with you?"

Starrett's forehead reddened. "He could have found out before he opened his mouth, couldn't he?"

The fury of that day rose in him again. He remembered bitterly how he had come here with his plan to rebuild Spade to its old power — this great ranch that a bungling owner and an inept foreman had dragged to the edge of bankruptcy. To breed into the Spade herd the rare Brahma cattle Starrett had been collecting for years — those heat-loving, tick-resistant curiosities a few Texans had begun to experiment with — that was Starrett's plan. The little capital he had would go to buy cheap pasture for the longhorns, while the better cattle got the prime pastures. Every spare dollar would be sunk in land — and more land. Starrett, who all his life had leased, borrowed, and begged range without ever owning an acre of his own, knew the value of land. But just as Dalhart was ready to shake hands on it, in had walked Markley.

"That's the fellow who cheated the Comanches out of their lease money last year," he announced. "He'll rob you blind."

So Dalhart had backed out, disappointed and suspicious, and Ruel Starrett went back to the brush lands, where a man could lease a few thousand acres of stone and fescue grass, work himself gaunt, and never quite make a profit. He went back, then, with this outsize ambition of his fit to devour him. And only for blind luck — the luck of selling his cattle last summer a week before the stock market collapsed — only for that, he would still be ranching the brush and breaks.

Rex shrugged, still cool under his father's anger. "I'm only saying it wouldn't hurt to give him a chance," he argued. "He's not the first man who's figured us wrong. They seem to think that to make a living in the Nations, you've got to be a little more bloodthirsty than the Comanches."

"Well, that's no lie," Starrett grunted. "Just the same, Markley's not my choice in ramrods. He goes."

He strode toward the bunkhouse. Sometimes it seemed to him that Rex didn't even know what the two of them had been driving toward all these years. Ambition — its seed might lie dormant for years or it might sweep a man like wildfire, coaxing him on forever with its whispered promises, as it had done with Starrett. He went shoulder-first into the chilly gloom of the bunkhouse with its smells of damp gyprock plaster and liniment. At the far end of the room a bachelor stove squatted in a sandbox. He threw his shaving articles on a cot and raised a rifle from a wall rack by the door. A cheesecloth door clattered and he glanced out. Susanna Dalhart had halted on the steps of the ranch house as if to reconnoiter the yard.

Then she called: "Rex! Saddle . . . will you please saddle my horse?"

"All right," Starrett heard Rex say. Then he watched the girl cross the yard, her boots flashing in and out from under the long gray skirts. Her movements were graceful — collected, a horseman would say. When she passed through the bleached sunlight, her dark hair glistened. She had caught it up with a black velvet ribbon. She was high-bosomed and carried herself so proudly that she looked tall. Her skin was tawny, and with her dark-lashed gray eyes she seemed to Starrett the most beautiful, if the most unpredictable, woman he had ever known. Susanna stopped just short of the door, and Starrett moved into the portal and leaned against the jamb — tall, mustached, smiling down good-naturedly.

"Rex is saddling my horse," she said. "I'll ride ahead and prepare Zack a little. After all," she protested, with a smile, "it would be quite a shock to work on a ranch for ten years and then be fired without warning."

Starrett began polishing the lead nose of a cartridge against his trousers. "You don't suppose," he said, "that I'd have a man around who'd called me a grass-stealing Injun Nations drifter?"

"I . . . I don't recall his saying any such thing," Susanna argued, but her gaze failed.

"I recall," drawled the rancher. He lounged from the door. Susanna hastily moved aside, as though he might run her down. Reaching his pony, he lifted blanket and saddle onto its back. In the corral, Rex was bridling Susanna's black.

"Maybe Markley was your father's taste in foremen," Starrett said. "He isn't mine. Spade hasn't made a nickel in years. Or maybe it was your father's fault. The story in Spanish Ford is that he always sold when he should have bought, and bought when he should have sold."

"My father," Susanna flared, "was one of the most successful commission men in New Orleans before we came to Texas."

"But this isn't a commission house, ma'am. This is a cattle ranch. Why in Tophet did he ever buy a ranch, if he had a good trade?"

"I don't know. I wasn't very old then. But if the war hadn't come, and then the blackwater fever that year. . . ."

A look of sympathy reached Starrett's face. "Miss Susanna," he said, "I've got my own ifs scattered all over Texas. I've been ranching twenty-five years, and this is the first acre of land I've ever owned. I've hide-an'-tallowed, broke horses, and God knows what. I've had to take my graze where I found it . . . in the back alleys most ranchers wouldn't dare go into. But I never," he said, "ranched the kind of brush patch I had to fall back to last year, after Markley killed the deal with your father."

"I heard," said Susanna, with a sparkle of malice in her gray eyes, "that you couldn't go back to the Nations because you hadn't paid Chief Jack for the range you leased from him."

"Did you hear about him stealing horses from us?"

"You've never proved that, have you?"

"No," Starrett said, "and he never proved that I promised him half the increase for the use of his tribe's graze, either. So we came out even steven."

He laced his rifle scabbard in place. Glancing into the girl's face, he saw the haughtiness he knew so well — the sheltered person's disapproval of the man who had to roust for himself. "Well, they're tough times,

Miss Susanna, no denying it." He sighed. "I can't take credit for being partners today with a well-bred young woman like you, on a fine ranch like Spade. It was my luck to sell my cattle the week before the financial panic hit. It was your hard luck that Markley reached the railroad a week too late. So I had the money, and you needed it. It seemed to me it was a square shake all around. I held Spade in one piece. I took controlling interest because I'm the one who'll be managing things."

Rex was heard leading the pony from the corral. "And because you wouldn't take less than control," Susanna declared.

"Of course, now," Starrett speculated, "I could back out, and buy the place at auction next month for half what I paid. I could have done that before, you know."

She caught her breath — startled and a little surprised, as though at something which had not occurred to her before. "Oh, I didn't . . . really I didn't mean to say. . . ."

Starrett's haughtiness softened. He smiled in the way of a man who knew himself and others, and had the sense of humor that self-knowledge brought. "I know what you meant," he said easily. "You think you should apologize for going pardners with a man your father and his hand-raised ramrod wouldn't touch. So I'll tell you what I meant, too. I saved this ranch. I paid off the notes. And I'm going to make it the kind of Texas ranch the capitalists will hear about clean to New York City. And the first step in that direction will be throwing Markley off."

Starrett started to mount, but found he had left his rifle in the bunkhouse. Rex was carrying Susanna's silver-mounted side-saddle from the harness shed. Gazing at him, Starrett all at once was struck by an inspiration. He removed his hat and studied the boy, scratching the short, tough hairs above his ear. Suddenly he replaced his hat.

"Come inside a minute," he told Rex. He left the silent girl and went into the bunk-house. Rex entered and stood by the door, slender as a rifle. "I've been thinking," said Starrett, "that you ought to be the one to fire Markley."

"Why? Markley's nothing to me."

"But you'd be something to him and the rest of the 'punchers if you did the firing. I want them to understand that when you say *frog,* they jump."

"Why act like I'm giving the orders when you're the boss man?"

"But you're going to be. You're taking Markley's job."

Rex straightened. "Me ramrod Spade?"

"Why not? You know more about cattle raising than Markley ever will."

"What about Tom Goss? He's been range boss here for years. He's in line for the job, isn't he?"

Starrett's reply had the snap of a military reprimand. "I'm giving the jobs, not Tom Goss. And believe me, if there's one thing this ranch is going to have, it's the Starrett trademark."

"Goss is a good man," Rex insisted. "He's worked for the job. I'll be hanged if I'll be one of those ramrods who walk into the bunkhouse and everybody stops talking."

Starrett's impatience reached his face. "I said you're taking Markley's place. You can't run a ranch like a church."

"Then run it like an army. Advance the next man in line."

Starrett turned his eyes to the ceiling in an agony of bafflement. "Will you try to understand? Nobody ever gave us anything, Rex. By heaven, I've dug post holes and plowed winter wheat for other men. And if the good Lord hadn't let me sell my cattle this year before the banks closed, I'd be digging post holes again. That much was luck. But it won't be luck that I stay on top. It's going to work the same way for other men, now, that it used to work for me. They'll earn every nickel I pay them, and the ones that give me trouble will get it back. That means Markley, to start. Goss can keep his old job or quit."

The bunkhouse became silent. They faced each other with belligerence in their eyes. They were of a size and of a look — rough-built, large-boned, with the hewed-down hardness of horsemen. The difference was in their faces. Rex had his mother's Irish eyes, and Irish eyes were dreaming eyes. They had argued methods before, but only recently had their tempers come into it.

Looking at his father's stubborn face, Rex said ironically: "I suppose you'll grind the Spanish Ford merchants down to a penny's profit on a dollar now. And you'll want the wagon swept out when they deliver a load of hay."

"Why not? Dalhart was soft. Look where it got him."

"And you'll try to buy old Ledbetter out for a dollar down."

"If he's hungry enough."

"Why?" Rex exploded. "Why the sweat to run this up to the biggest spread in Texas?"

"Sweat? I've been twenty-five years scrambling for a piece of land."

"But you've got it now. You can ease up, can't you?"

Starrett said bitterly: "For the first time in my life I own something bigger than a horse. I'm sitting on a piece of land like I never dreamed I'd own. But I've only got a foot in the door. The fight's just started."

"How do you figure that?"

"Because I've only got a few hundred dollars in the bank, with winter coming on. I'll spend every nickel Markley brings back from Wichita before the week is out. Cash is king . . . that's why we're on Spade, but it also means nobody will give us credit. But prices won't stay down long, not with railroad freight and hard goods costing as much as ever. This country will bounce back fast . . . and I want to be on top when it stops bouncing, not underneath. We've got to work like fools, Rex," he said desperately. "We've got to get the last hour's work out of our men and the last acre of hardship land we can get hold of."

"Spanish Ford's going to love you."

"They don't have to love me. They've just got to keep out of my way."

"You don't give men credit for much, do you? You seem to figure the only men you can trust are dead ones."

Ruel Starrett walked to the door and stared out at the girl who was trying to saddle the big black horse in the yard. His face was dark. "How long has this stuff been in your mind?"

"Quite a while. Maybe it started when you swindled Chief Jack out of his lease money last year. That kind of trading's too sharp for me. You know as well as anybody that horse stealing is just a game with Indians. If they win, fine. If they lose, no harm done. But you used their pilfering to rob them, because you needed money to buy those Brahma cattle of Casement's. A dollar's worth of revenge for a dime's worth of provocation . . . is that the way it works?"

"Yes. And that's the only way it's ever worked. I'll tell you something about men, since you don't seem to know it . . . you can trust them just as far as you can see them."

"How do you know? You've never tried trusting them."

"I tried one, and I'm regretting it this minute, Clyde Tilford, that little pip-squeak of a banker. I could have had that last note against Spade canceled, if I'd held out for it. But you talked me out of it."

"Tilford doesn't own the note," Rex said. "The bank does. If he'd canceled it, the depositors would have been that much closer to going under. I'll make you a bet. Ten dollars he keeps his promise and holds it till you can pay it off."

"I'll make you a bet." His father grinned. "That I don't leave an inch of hide on him if he sells that note."

At that moment Susanna Dalhart's voice called from the yard: "Rex! Will you help me?"

Rex was glad of the interruption, sensing that the situation could only grow worse. "Sure," he murmured. "I'll saddle him for you . . . with a burr under the blanket."

"Now, go easy," Starrett advised. "You'll catch more flies with sugar than with vinegar."

"But I'm not trying to catch this fly."

Starrett watched him saddle the girl's horse, and he thought: *There's something wrong there.* He knew his son's mind well enough to recognize that he was in love with Susanna. Yet for days Rex had treated her almost like a stranger. Something had come between them. *I hope the young idiot didn't rush things with her,* thought Starrett. He went out and rammed his rifle into the boot. Without a look at Susanna, he swung onto the horse.

He heard her exclaim desperately: "Mister Starrett, I insist that you wait for me."

"Insist? What's that mean? Find out from the lady what insist means, Rex." Starrett grinned. He put spurs to his horse and left the yard.

"Help me stop him, Rex," Susanna pleaded.

Rex saw that her eyes were glistening with tears of exasperation. "I can't stop him," he said. "He's his own man."

"But you could hold him until I've told Zack. Zack's as hot-headed as your father. I . . . I'm afraid, Rex."

Her helplessness touched him; she stirred him now as she always did. It was hard for Rex to believe that in a few short weeks she could have taken over his mind and heart until she was an obsession with him. Looking into her face, he saw beneath the bright varnish of her independence. He found a girl who was uncertain, one who might abandon her haughtiness to come into a man's arms and say: Oh, help me. But he set himself against the impulse to let down his guard, and looked away and said: "All right, I'll try."

He lifted her into the saddle and got his own horse. They rode out through the trees to the trail that struck north over the gray-soiled hills. Rex pulled ahead of her. Across the long slope of post oak and blackjack, he could see the chocolate bluffs of the river. A quarter mile ahead, Ruel Starrett racked along easily under the autumn sun.

Susanna held tightly to the leaping head of the saddle, her dark hair ruffled by the wind. "Rex, I'm here, too, you know!" she called.

He glanced back, unsmiling. "You'd better keep up, if you want to stop Dad."

Unexpectedly she reined in her horse. *It's a trick for attention,* Rex thought, and he wanted more than anything to make her come to him. But it was he who turned back. In the dust they gazed at each other. Her gray eyes, fringed with black, moved over his face.

"Rex, what is wrong?"

"Nothing's wrong. Why?"

"Oh, stop saying that!" exclaimed the girl. "Something has been wrong for a week. Are you just a lady-killer who needs a new girl each month . . . or has something really happened?"

Rex smiled. "One thing that happened was that you slapped me the last time we went riding."

"You know why I slapped you. Besides," she said, "a man shouldn't be so easily discouraged."

"I wasn't discouraged. It was something else. You see, I heard something about you in Spanish Ford last week."

Color tinged her face. "I suppose you heard that I'm engaged to Zack Markley? Well, perhaps I am, in a way. But it's never been a ring engagement."

"That wouldn't have stopped me. . . . What about Markley's interest in the ranch?"

Her eyes seemed to rush from his. "Who told you he had an interest in the ranch?"

"Marshal Bennett. He kept quiet about it until last week. Then he told me he'd heard there was some kind of arrangement between your father and Markley. Is it true?"

"It's none of Marshal Bennett's business," Susanna declared. "But . . . yes, he does have a claim on Spade. A very small one. Do you know Barranca Roja?"

Rex nodded. Barranca Roja was a small, overworked pasture from which his father had recently pulled all the cattle to rest the land.

"Well, when Zack came to us . . . that was ten years ago, during the war . . . Dad promised to leave it to Zack when he died. We needed more than just a foreman, you see . . . someone who could take over. Times were bad, and Dad wasn't much of a rancher. So he promised Zack the land, a foreman's salary, and let him keep a few cattle of his own."

"Why didn't you tell us this before?"

"Because it's such an unimportant piece of land. I didn't want a lien to frighten your father off. What's so wrong with it, Rex? I meant to reimburse Zack for the land."

"Suppose Markley tries to claim more than he has coming?"

"If I'd thought he'd do that," Susanna declared, "I wouldn't have sold the ranch as clear."

Looking into her face, Rex realized how little he actually knew about Susanna. He knew her reputation for independence and extravagance, her pride and self-possession, just as her father was known for his expensive cigars and his grand manner, while everyone knew he was mortgaged to the eyebrows. But something else he had learned, when Marshal Bennett told him about the lien on Spade, was that Susanna regarded no sacrifice as too great to protect her position as mistress of the biggest cattle ranch in Salado County — so long as she did not make the sacrifice herself.

"I'm telling you the truth," she insisted.

Rex kept gazing into her face. "I hope so."

"I don't have to explain to you or anyone else, Rex Starrett," Susanna flared. "I could have cut my land up into town lots, if I chose."

"Maybe there'd have been less fuss if you had."

"You don't think much of me, do you?" she asked.

"Depends on how you mean that."

He looked ahead. He was remembering, with a joyless feeling of kinship, a man who had sold a profitable feed business and moved away from Spanish Ford because he had fallen in love with another man's wife. At the time, it had seemed weak and foolish. But now Rex knew it was possible to interlace your life with a woman's so hopelessly that you could never untangle them. A clean cut was the only way to free yourself. And so, though he had not told even his father yet, Rex was leaving Spade Ranch tonight.

He overtook his father as he was crossing a creek that brawled down to the Red under a tattered canopy of water oaks.

"I'll take you up on it," Rex told him. "I'll pass the word to Markley that he's out."

"Good. I'll wait here," Starrett said. But as Susanna rode up, he spoke sharply: "He won't need your help, missy."

"What's the difference?" asked Rex. "I'll do the talking anyway."

Starrett slapped a mosquito on the back of his hand, frowned at the smear of blood, and finally nodded. "Go ahead."

A quarter mile farther, Rex motioned Susanna to go on, and he pulled off the trail to wait. Susanna rode breathlessly until she reached a sandy bluff above the river. She looked down into the wide bosque of the river to find the Spade trail crew. Between broken shores, muddy rivulets of water lapped silvery snags of cottonwoods. At once she saw the horsemen pulled up beneath her. They had evidently just crossed from the north shore. Some were smoking; others were adjusting cinches soaked by the river. She recognized most of the men who had taken the beef herd to Kansas, but for a moment she did not see Zack Markley, and she had a guilty hope that for some reason he had not returned — that she would be freed from the chore of facing him.

She was confused and frightened by what Rex had said. What if Zack refused to sell his claim, slight as it was? She clenched her fists. *He can't refuse,* she thought, *if I insist.*

A big man in a buckskin shirt, his hat hanging by the thong, strode from behind a wagon. "Well, the ranch is still here," he declared. "They haven't rolled it up and sold it for taxes."

It was Zack. He moved forward, inspecting the lashings of the wagons, his blond hair worn as long as a trapper's. Susanna was seized with uncertainty. She had a blind urge to ride to the ranch and lock herself in her room.

Then she heard Markley say: "Don't bed down for the night, boys. This is still a trail crew. Let's go."

At that moment his face turned up. For an instant he stared. Then he cupped his hands about his mouth: "Susanna!"

Without using his stirrup, he hit the saddle and rode up the bluff trail.

All at once Susanna swung her pony and started back to the ranch house. But after a moment she turned back to the river. Her face became firm. After all, who was the owner of Spade Ranch — she or Zack? On this land she was queen. Thinking this, she felt better. With a stiff little smile, Susanna waited for Zack Markley to join her.

She was standing by her pony when Markley arrived. He leaped down, flinging a cigarette aside — as full of energy at trail's end as he had been at the beginning, strong and tall and unbelievably energetic. The foreman was a big, compact man. Clean-shaven, but looking weathered, he strode to her, lifted her off her feet, and kissed her. After a moment, she pulled away, hiding her guilt in embarrassment.

"Zack! Is this something you learned in Wichita?"

He laughed, but continued to gaze at her in that hungry, smiling way. "The only thing that's been right about this trip yet" — he sighed — "is coming back to you, Susie."

"Has it been a hard trip?"

"Haven't had breakfast in bed since we left."

He took her face between his hands and kissed her again. His skin was smooth and leathery-warm and he smelled of sage. When he leaned back to look at her, she remembered every line of his face and the quick, testing expression of his eyes. He turned suddenly to his pony.

"Look here."

From a canvas roll tied behind his saddle, he began to set out articles on the thin fescue grass. "Something gold and something blue," he said. "For a winter bride."

He handed her a box containing a string of blue enamel beads. Watching her face, he chuckled and produced a second box, which she knew at once contained a ring. But Susanna put her hand on it before Zack could open it.

"Zack, I've some bad news."

"What's so bad that it can't wait an hour?"

"Dad died last month," Susanna said.

Markley's shoulders sagged. "Will died?"

Tears were in Susanna's eyes. She nodded and turned away.

"But he was strong as a horse," Markley said, almost in complaint. "What happened?"

"A riding accident. He was training that big gray, and it . . . you know the old water oak near the river?"

Then she could not finish it, but she could hold his eyes and dare him even to think that her father's death had been anything but accidental.

Markley blinked thoughtfully, and Susanna flared: "At least don't criticize the way he died."

Smiling, Markley shook his head. "I never criticized him, Susie. Not me."

"Oh, not with words. Just with smiles. Like everybody in Spanish Ford. They laughed at him, though he was worth ten of any of them. And then when the financial crash came and. . . ." But when the foreman merely watched her coolly, she pressed her hand against her brow. "Forgive me, Zack. I'm just . . . it's good you're back," she finished.

Markley grunted. Then she saw his eyes, sage-gray and quick, travel the land behind her — the hills of Spade, the good Cross

Timbers range of Texas. And suddenly she discerned a harsh joy in them. *Mine, now,* he was thinking, and she was afraid and bitterly resentful.

"Zack, did you and Dad have an arrangement of some kind?"

Markley's glance tested hers. "I was to have a piece of land when he died. Why?"

"What piece?"

"What's the difference?" countered Markley. "It'll all be the same when we're married."

For some reason, she feared to press it. But she was piqued, and asked: "Why was it that you missed out on the good prices, Zack? Ruel Starrett left a week later than you with his herd, but he got to Dodge City before the crash."

The long line of Zack's jaw locked. "Don't be comparing me with Starrett, unless you're joking. . . . Lisandro, dang his ancient bones, came down with the fever and I had to lay over four days."

"Fever or overwork? Dad told you to take more men."

"Why pay three men to do the work of two?" he demanded. Then, his gaze crisp, he asked: "Why all the questions? Do you think I sold for six thousand and reported two?"

"Of course not. I . . . I was just interested. Because it has a bearing on . . . on what I had to do."

From below, shod hoofs roused a dry clatter. Susanna kept her gaze level with his, determined not to let him find her fearfulness.

With cold calm, Markley asked: "What have you done?"

"I sold an interest in the ranch to Ruel Starrett."

Markley's lips pulled over his teeth as he seized her arm. "You sold to Starrett?"

She backed away, her eyes flashing. "Whose ranch is Spade?"

"Ours!" he snapped. "It was going to be ours, wasn't it? Why didn't you wait until I could work something out?"

"I hadn't time. Clyde Tilford's bank almost went under when the railroads stopped building. The stock he'd bought in them was worthless. He held four of our notes, and everything had to be paid up."

"Nobody will ever take Spade!" Markley shouted. "Didn't you tell him that?"

Her gray, oblique eyes smiled at him. "That's just sentiment, Zack."

"But . . . but that pirate, Starrett. Why in heaven's name did you sell to him, of all people?"

"Because he was the only man in Spanish Ford with cash. He paid three of the notes and got Tilford to carry us on the other."

Markley picked up a branch and hurled it savagely into the gorge. "He's getting out," he declared. "He's packing his brand-blotting irons and trade-whiskey-for-Injun-bellies and getting the devil out."

"Why, Zack," Susanna said sweetly, "I thought you only worked for us. Here you are giving orders."

"Sweetheart," Zack said, his smile brittle, "I'm going to have to take a leather to you one day. Yes, I work for you. But I also own part of Spade."

"What part?" asked Susanna.

"Mission Creek," Zack Markley said, smiling straight into her eyes.

Susanna's lips parted. They stood on Mission Creek land, the heart and soul of Spade Ranch, a full third of its best range. It ran south, east, and west from where they stood at the ranch's northern boundary, gray with cured summer grasses, bountiful with water. She had feared this, and now that she heard him say it, her terror rose.

"You're lying, Zack. He promised you Barranca Roja."

Zack's voice was gentle but vicious. "You don't get a ramrod in war times for a brush patch like Barranca Roja. I wouldn't have risked my scalp for it."

"You'll be reimbursed for anything you can prove you had coming."

He grinned, comprehending. "Anything I can prove? Sure, I've got a paper in Clyde Tilford's safe."

"Is it a will? We thought he died without one."

"No, it's a deed . . . effective on his death."

"I set aside three hundred dollars to reimburse you for anything you had coming," Susanna declared. "If you think you should have more than that. . . ."

"What kind of a fool do I look like? Mission Creek's worth five thousand dollars, even in these times. I might take four, just to please you." Then his grin came, stiff and assured. "You know what I think? I think you figured you'd sell to Starrett and let him bluff me out. You thought I'd be afraid of him, didn't you?"

"No. I think you're lying."

"You haven't changed one little bit since you were fourteen years old," Markley drawled, "and I told you to stay away from a horse and you got yourself thrown. You're the spoiledest filly in Salado County, but Zack's just the buckaroo to tame you."

He took her arms in his grasp, but Susanna struck him on the mouth — with her right hand, and then with her left. He laughed and brought her against him and kissed her. Then he shoved her away and turned to mount his horse.

"Where's Starrett?"

"He's on the trail between here and the ranch. But don't try to handle him the way you do a woman."

"You ask Starrett, tonight, how I handled him."

II

When Rex heard Markley coming, he rode back to where his father waited. Starrett glanced sharply at Rex. "Where is he? Did you hang his hide on a fence?"

"I let Susanna talk to him," Rex confessed. "There was something I couldn't explain to you. She's rigged you . . . you or him, I don't know. So I let her tell him her way."

"Rigged me!" Starrett exclaimed.

Rex tilted his head. "Here comes Markley."

Starrett, his stunned face beginning to flush with anger, rubbed his hands against his trousers and worked his boot heels into the earth. Then he waited — a powerfully framed man with bright, angry eyes scanning the trail.

As Markley loped into the oaks, Starrett's eyes picked at him. Markley's carbine was in the scabbard and his hands were both in sight. A coil of maguey lay about his big Mexican horn. He appeared to see Starrett, now, and slowed the pony. Starrett did not stir, though the horse almost rode him down.

"Mister Markley." He smiled.

"Mister Starrett," said Markley with a flash of white teeth. "Mister Injun Nations Starrett. I hear you've bought a piece of Spade Ranch."

"Mighty big piece," said Starrett.

Zack Markley's face glistened with perspiration. "There's a special piece of equipment that goes with the ranch. This rope." He held up the coil of hard-twist maguey.

"Yeah?" said Starrett, frowning.

"So I'll just turn it over to you right now." The rope hissed down before Starrett could lurch out of range. The thick, hard plaits caved in his hat and knocked it from his head. The rope slashed again, and a cut appeared on the bridge of his nose. He was falling back, warding off the rope as Markley began to cut and chop at Starrett's head. There were three cuts on his face and a cut in his scalp. The pony was crowding him

118

against a tree. Starrett's curses were a profane bass roar. He suddenly ducked under the horse; as it kicked at him, he moved into the dust behind Markley. He drew his Colt and snapped a bead on the middle of the ramrod's back.

Rex lunged his pony into him. Starrett's .44 thundered. Zack Markley shouted in pain, and Starrett fell and rolled over and got up.

Rex was shouting: "God's sake, Dad! He didn't throw down on you!"

Starrett was breathing like a cut stallion. He looked at the smoke seeping from the gun barrel. He turned his eyes to Markley again; Markley was grasping the biceps of his left arm. He had twisted in the saddle to gaze blankly at Starrett. Starrett cocked his arm and hurled the Colt at the foreman. It caught Markley in the shoulder. He grunted and tried to draw his carbine, but Starrett dragged Markley from the saddle.

The foreman bore Starrett down with him, but, as they came up, Rex's voice cracked: "Look out, Dad! Here come the rest of them!"

Breathless, bone-white, Starrett stepped back. He snorted through his nose, clearing it. There was blood on his face. Then he turned his back on Markley and walked away. Markley stared at the rancher's back with a respect distilled and purified to a clear, murderous hatred. He walked the few yards to the stream to cleanse his wound.

When the Spade cowboys arrived, led by Tom Goss, the range foreman, Starrett stood hipshot by his horse, his expression confident. Rex sat his pony by his father as Starrett met the gaze of the cowboys.

"Little disagreement," he told Goss cheerfully.

Goss dismounted and pushed past him. The range boss was a lean, middle-aged cowboy with a long brown face and a Mexican cast to his features. He stopped by Markley, who had stripped off his buckskin shirt to cleanse his shallow wound in the stream. "What's a-matter, Zack?"

"Ask Starrett," Markley said tersely. "He says there's going to be some changes on Spade."

"I've bought control of Spade," Starrett cut in. "Markley's fired. Any of the rest of you that wants to can stay. My son, Rex," he added, "will ramrod for me."

Rex's anger clouded his eyes. He felt the cowpunchers' contemptuous gaze. *The boss' son licking the cream,* it said. But at this moment he could not fail to back up his father, so he was silent.

An old Mexican cowboy thrust forward, ropy-looking and sad with years. He spoke earnestly to Ruel Starrett, who remembered him as Lisandro Garza, a horse breaker on Spade. "This is wrong, *amigo.* You know the girl's father would not have wanted it."

"The girl's father is dead."

"So is Spade, then," said Garza quietly.

Starrett ran a testing gaze over the men, recognizing all except one man who had, he supposed, teamed up for safe passage through the Indian country. He said: "I'll pay twenty and found. There'll be a raise after we make a crop. . . . You," he said, staring at the hazel-eyed cowpuncher he did not remember, "what's your name?"

"Titus," said the cowboy with cocksure amusement. "Billy Titus."

"Well, Billy," Starrett said bluntly, "you can look some place else for a job."

"What's the matter with me?" he asked Starrett.

"Any man I ever knew with brindle eyes was meaner than four strands of bob wire in a horse corral. I don't want my cattle fair-grounded by some cowboy that likes action."

Markley spoke dryly. He had pulled on his shirt. "That's fine, Starrett. Titus is with me, anyway."

"What do you need cowboys for?"

"I've got a little land."

"Where . . . six feet in the cemetery?"

"No. I own the Mission Creek section."

Starrett's features did not change. "The Mission Creek I'm thinking of is twenty thousand acres of prime pasture. I've got title to every acre of it."

"So have I. Prior title. . . . Lisandro," Markley said, turning to the old Mexican, "you were the first rider the old man hired. You heard the arrangement when I came here."

Starrett's glance found the puzzlement in Lisandro's face as he gazed back at Markley. He saw him look down then, after a moment, he heard the hesitant words: "The old *patrón* say Meester Zack have Mission Creek when he die. *Sí,* I remember."

Starrett snapped a profane Spanish word and strode after Markley, but a Spade rider dropped from the saddle into his path. It was the brindle-eyed youngster, Billy Titus. He rammed his guns into Starrett's belly.

"Easy, uncle," he said.

Starrett started to grasp the barrels of the guns. But as he stared into the tawny insolence of Titus's eyes, he hesitated.

"You orry-eyed little wolf. Put those things away and tackle me."

"These things," said Billy Titus, "are what

122

make a little wolf like me as big as an ox like you. Now, just flax down to listening instead of talking."

Starrett gazed at the guns, unafraid, yet shaken by an instinctive understanding of the situation. The terrible anger in him was bridled — bridled by a man he could have broken with his naked hands. Yet Titus's guns were on the distant edge of his consciousness.

Markley walked forward and stood beside Billy Titus, who crouched, bristling against Starrett like a terrier challenging a timber wolf. "All right, Billy."

Titus moved away. Markley was face to face with the rancher's wrath.

"I don't know how it was in the Nations, Starrett," he said, "but I'll tell you what goes here. Laws and papers. I've got prior right to all the pastures along Mission Creek, and I've got proof of it. That means you get off."

"Papers? Sure, I've got a paper locked away. Where's yours?"

"In Clyde Tilford's safe, at the bank. It's a grant deed Dalhart made out ten years ago. It was to be effective when he died."

"A deed ain't a will," Starrett rapped.

"It's as good as a will sometimes. There was a case in Trinity four years ago, fella named Saville. . . ."

"Sounds to me like there's a fella in Spanish Ford who's been nosing around some lawyer's office already."

Markley did not reply, but turned and mounted, waving off Titus when he tried to assist him. "I'll compare papers with you before Judge Waggoner any time you say. It looks like a plain case of prior rights, doesn't it?"

"No. It looks like a blamed fool is trying to stampede me. What about the herd money you're carrying? Have you got a deed to that?"

Markley gave him a bland smile. "Wasn't much left, after paying shipping charges and wages. Check at the bank and see how much I deposit. While we're checking on things, what have you done with the cattle I've been grazing on Mission Creek?"

"Put them off," Starrett snapped. "Low-grade mosshorns. What was the matter with Dalhart, letting a ramrod keep a brand without paying for the graze he used?"

"Where are they?" Markley's face stiffened.

"On the community pasture outside town. I left some men to watch them. One of them said he was taking care of them while you were gone. I suppose Dalhart paid his salary, too, eh?" he said dryly. "You're a smart ramrod, you are. But the smartest thing you can do now is to keep them off my land. I don't want those ugly brutes breeding in with my Brahmas. And the last time I was through, some of them were looking pretty poorly. Don't let any of those cows stray back."

"Stray?" Markley said with a slow grin. "I'll put them on Mission Creek as soon as I'm ready."

Starrett's big fists cramped and his face turned dark. "I've got a Fifty-Six-Fifty shell for every one of them that comes across the line."

Markley laughed, and Billy Titus drew up beside him with the air of an aide-de-camp. Starrett was furious, but inwardly shaken. He shot at Titus the gall of his anger for Markley. "This is a big range for little wolves, Titus," he sneered. "Look out we don't hang your hide on a fence."

"I'm pretty good at cutting fences, uncle." Titus grinned.

Starrett watched the Spade men ride up the oak-stripped hillside toward the camp at Comanche Spring, where Markley's cattle were held. Then he turned to Rex. "I'm going to have a talk with that girl," he told him fiercely. "If she's rigged me, I'll take a horsewhip to her."

III

Reaching the ranch yard, Rex went directly into the bunkhouse. His father, observing that Susanna's black crossbar buggy stood at the stoop with a Mexican boy tending the horse, jogged over to the ranch house and angrily entered. Yet awkwardness crept over him when he felt the room close around him. He had hardly been in a parlor since his wife died, and the mossy feel of rugs under his boots, the odors and distant sounds of housekeeping, made him uneasy. Standing in the silent coldness, he rapped on the door frame.

"Miss Susanna?"

He heard her heels on the upstairs floor, and her voice floated down, calm as a spring sky, pretty as a bar of music: "In a moment, Mister Starrett."

Presently she descended, wearing a gray riding dress with a dark-blue cape over her shoulders. "You want to talk about Zack Markley." She smiled.

"Correct." Starrett's jaw muscles rippled.

"The facts are simply these. Mister Markley is entitled to some land or an equivalent amount of cash. I set aside three hundred dollars for him out of the money you paid me. That should be more than enough. I didn't tell you of it, because, although it was a small thing, it might have frightened you off and we'd both have been the losers. But I'm going in town now to see my attorney and straighten it out."

"Do you have this deal with Markley in writing?"

"No, but I'm sure witnesses can be found to. . . ."

"Markley says he's got a witness . . . Lisandro Garza. Garza claims the Mission Creek pastures belong to Markley. That's almost a third of the good land on the ranch, ma'am."

"Yes, I know. I didn't know Lisandro had turned against me, too, but . . . but I hope to have everything straightened out shortly."

Starrett closed one fist. "Would you say this came under the heading of larceny or embezzlement, Miss Susanna?"

"Bad judgment." She sighed. "A Dalhart talent, you know. But I defy you to prove wrong intent."

As she passed him, fragrant of sachet, he turned to follow her. She went lightly down the steps, crossed to the buggy, and prepared to mount. Starrett, exasperated and yet somehow unable to dislike the girl, went to assist her. She glanced at him in surprise, and he saw that the gesture of taking her arm made a change in her — softened her, uncovered something uncertain, as though she had been trying to regard him as an enemy and he had destroyed her defense against him.

"Miss Susanna," he said quietly, "I wish you'd tell me one thing. How does a nice woman like you ever stir up a mess like this?"

"Well, I can try to tell you. I don't suppose you'd understand. Do you remember the day I agreed to sell you the interest in the ranch?"

"Yes, ma'am. It was the day after your father was buried."

"Yes, and the day he was buried I was still afraid to go ahead because of this little lien that Zack has blown up so big. I wasn't sure of him even then. But I heard a woman make a remark at the funeral that made up my mind. This woman whispered . . . oh, she meant me to hear, all right . . . 'Suicides shouldn't be buried in the same graveyard with other folks.' "

Starrett had, of course, heard the suicide talk. Somehow it fitted his sketchy impressions of Will Dalhart. Though he had not known Dalhart well, he admitted to smiling now and then at the lofty little Louisianan with his imperial, his big cigars, his grand

128

manner, and his whispered insolvency. Everyone cheated him, and it was a wonder to Starrett how anyone so incompetent came to be operating a ranch as big as Spade. And then, after the financial panic struck, when it was learned that Clyde Tilford was putting pressure on Dalhart for payment of his obligations to the bank, it was not surprising to hear shortly that Dalhart had suffered a fatal riding accident.

Gazing at the girl, Starrett frowned. "Why should that remark have changed your mind?"

"Do you think I could let the ranch that had killed my father go to the men who'd made him ridiculous? I had to sell to you or lose it. And Dad hated them so . . . old Cortland, selling him a ton of rocks in the hay he bought one year! And Ledbetter selling him blind horses and sick cattle, and Joe LaPorte, that worthless little tinhorn gambler. . . ."

And that legend, too, Starrett recalled. How Will Dalhart, drinking more than usual because he held a draft for a more than usually profitable sale of cattle, had been taken by LaPorte for $7,000. It was said that in the next week, Spanish Ford lost three fleshy citizens who succumbed to apoplexy after prolonged fits of laughter.

Starrett heard Susanna saying bitterly: "He came home at sunrise and said to me . . . 'I've just lost the year's profits.' And he locked himself in his room and didn't leave it for a week. Oh, don't you see why I couldn't let everything be lost? Why I had to prove that we weren't beaten yet? I . . . I had to show them, Mister Starrett. Don't you understand?"

"Tell me this," Starrett demanded, "do you know for sure what your father promised Markley?"

"Would he have left his foreman more than he left me?"

"Everybody else took advantage of him. Why not Markley?"

"Because Dad wouldn't have consented to it. I'm going in town now and start proceedings to turn down Zack's claim."

"What do you reckon Markley figures his claim in Spade is worth?"

"He set a price of four thousand dollars. Ridiculous." She added: "And yet I'd pay it for your sake, if he couldn't be scared off any other way. But, unfortunately, 'most all the money you paid me went to retire the notes against the ranch."

Starrett stood back. "I wish you luck, ma'am. Otherwise a war may be fought over your bad judgment . . . as you call it."

■ ■ ■ ■

In the bunkhouse, Starrett found Rex laying articles from his trunk onto a slicker spread across the straw tick of his cot. Still tasting the lees of his violent scene with Markley, Starrett lifted a bottle of Mexican brandy from a shelf of patent medicines and slumped onto a cot.

"She admits Markley's got a claim," he growled. "But, by heaven, he'll write his own epitaph if he steps onto that land." A wild emotion stormed through him. "I've got two-thirds of a damned tough lifetime invested here, Rex."

"Then you'd better work out a settlement with Markley."

"Understand me," Starrett said, thrusting the bottle at his son. "Right or wrong, we're here to stay. And here's something else you'd better chew on. Susanna's supposed to be engaged to that bull. If she marries him, we've got *him* for a partner."

"What am I supposed to do about it?"

"Marry her first." Ruel suddenly grinned.

Rex stared. "You're putting me up for collateral? Honest?"

"You love her," Starrett insisted. "So what's funny about beating him out? My

131

Lord, if I were your age. A girl . . . a gamble . . . what more do you want?"

"To pick my own gambles. And my own girls."

A stormy power rang in Starrett's voice: "We've got everything sunk in this ranch, Rex. But if she marries Markley, he'll buck us every step of the way."

The bittersweet memory of the girl's face tantalized Rex. "If I love her," he said, "I've got the sense to leave her alone. A girl who'd cheat a man the way she cheated you . . . where would she stop in cheating her husband?" He finished rolling the slicker. "I reckon this is as good a time as any to tell you, Dad. I'm getting out."

Starrett gazed at him blankly. "Out of what?"

"Out of the ranch . . . out of the fight. You've seen that Ranger company camped south of town?"

His features under iron control, Starrett said: "Yes. I reckon every unemployed cow prod in Texas will be joining the Rangers, now that they've been reactivated."

"So here's one of the first," Rex said. "Captain McNelly swore me in yesterday. I've got all the qualifications . . . a horse worth a hundred dollars, a saddle, and two guns. We take off tomorrow night."

He waited for the storm. It did not come. Starrett turned and walked to the door. As he stared into the sun-dappled yard, he was motionless. "You made up your mind in a terrible hurry, didn't you?"

"I suppose. But I've been thinking about it for a long time."

"Why?"

Rex hesitated. How did you make a man like his father understand something purely of the heart? "Well, I want some action, for one thing."

His father chuckled. "Liable to be some around here."

"But the wrong kind. I want to know I'm fighting on the right side."

"Your old man's side ain't the right one, eh?"

"That's what I don't know," Rex said shortly. "I don't know whether Markley's lying or not, and you don't care. If he's sunk ten years running this iron for a boss who didn't know a steer from a butter mold, thinking he was going to get a piece of land for it, then he can't be frozen out."

"Blast it, I can't give up everything I've fought for just because a girl has tricked me."

"Then your fight's with the girl. Suppose the judge rules for Markley. Will you compromise with him?"

"I can't. I can't, Rex. It ain't in me to take a shoving around."

"If it's not in Markley either, then what's going to happen?"

Starrett set his jaws and shook his head, despairing of making his son understand him. And Rex, giving up the task of making his father comprehend why he could not join his fight, shrugged.

"Anyway, that's part of it. And I don't want the name Spanish Ford's going to give us when you start firing old employees like Goss and starving out ranchers like Ledbetter."

"Ledbetter's a fool. He's overgrazed his ranch for years. If I give eight hundred for his spread, it'll be a godsend for him and a favor to the state of Texas for saving the land. And I'm not going to fire Goss."

"But you'll put somebody in the ramrod spot over his head. So he'll quit, if he's the man I think he is."

Starrett's face was rough with emotion. "The fact that I need you don't make any difference, eh?"

"You don't need me." Rex smiled. "I stayed with you while you needed me. You're set now. You can get satisfaction out of Markley or compromise with him. You don't need me to do that."

Starrett's eyes darkened. "A man don't need his son just for the work he can get out of him, Rex. I need you now more than I ever have."

"Why?"

"Because the things I've fought for I'll never live to collect. I wanted to be the biggest cattleman in Texas. I wanted to do something for Texas as well as myself . . . bring up this Brahma breed of cattle, as a starter. Cross 'em with Herefords and Angus for a tick-proof steer they'll never quarantine out of the stockyards. I wanted to be . . . I don't know . . . important. I've done things I'm ashamed of, but what man hasn't? But now I know the only Starrett who'll profit by all I've done will be you. That's why I need you, Rex. You're going to be the Starrett I wanted to be."

With a twinge of guilt, Rex looked away. For he knew he was leaving Spade as much over Susanna as the conflict of his ideals with his father's. Yet it was as impossible to liberate himself from his love for Susanna while living so close to her as it was to adjust ideals with his father, and at last he said: "I wish I could stay, Dad. But I can't stay any more than you can quit. I've got my reasons, believe me. I'll be back some-

135

day. Well. . . ." He smiled, extending his hand.

Starrett abruptly turned away. From his trunk he removed some greasy rags and gun oil and set about cleaning his rifle. He was breathing hard. His face was the color of suet. Rex hoisted his slicker and blanket roll onto his shoulder.

At the foot of his father's cot, he paused, hesitated, and then said earnestly: "You savvy what I mean, don't you?"

Starrett squinted down the barrel of the gun. He plugged a shell into the empty chamber. Rex dropped his hand and walked out. But after he had left, Starrett's hands clenched on the rifle until his fingers mottled. He sat there without stirring in the dark bunkhouse.

For some time after Rex had left, Starrett remained slumped on the cot in the bunkhouse, his rifle lying across his lap, but the hand grasping the oily cleaning rag having fallen motionless. His gaze, fixed on the smoky wall, contained the dull anguish of the eyes of a stunned fighter. In the gloomy atmosphere of liniment and leather, he heard Rex ride from the yard, and afterward a lonely silence throbbed in the room.

He felt old and broken. God had not given him many things to love — a woman who had died too young, a trade that ill-returned his affection — but this strapping son of his had made it all up to him. This clear-eyed lad whose name meant "king" and whose destiny was the destiny Starrett had picked for himself, but would never live to enjoy.

Rising in a torment of disappointment, Starrett placed himself in the doorway. *He's just testing me,* he thought. *He'll come riding back any minute now.*

But Rex did not reappear on the $100 horse that was to carry him to glory with the Rangers. Starrett felt as though he stood at the center of a huge emptiness. How could this boy who looked so much like him possess the baffling mind of a stranger? His thick fingers groped over the breech of his gun, as he beheld for the last time the dream he had carried so long — the vision to which he had sacrificed every luxury, even, once or twice, the luxury of honor. His mind lost itself in visions of additional ranches pasted onto the expanding map called Spade — the legions of cattle, the army of cowboys, the trains of freight rumbling in with supplies.

The vision tore like a rotten hide. Suddenly a sense of having been cheated assailed him. His gusty emotions seized him and the drums of resentment began to thud in his brain.

Looking down at the rifle in his hands, he thought grimly: *If he were anybody but my son.* He juggled the weapon in his hands, feeling the good heft of it. Slowly the tense lips under the mustache softened. He pushed his hat back. So a Ranger had to have a $100 horse, did he?

Turning quickly, Starrett lifted the bottle of Mexican brandy from the medicine shelf and uncorked it, but on second thought he replaced it. *No,* he decided. *Not for the kind of shot I've got to make.*

IV

The gash that Ruel Starrett's shot had opened in Markley's arm was becoming feverish, and, while its angry inflammation radiated, his mind flushed with anger. His sleeve was stiff with blood and he kept his mouth tight against the pain. But once, when he caught his biceps in pain, Tom Goss, the old range foreman, was instantly at his side.

"Best rest a spell, Zack. The camp ain't going to move before we get there."

"I'm all right," Zack snapped in the testy manner of a man who considered weakness a moral failing.

They were crossing a corner of the big Mission Creek pasture — 20,000 acres of fine northeast Texas graze. They had seen few cattle in the hilly, oak-dappled grassland, but just before they reached Mission Creek, at the western border of Spade Ranch, they approached a small herd of curious-looking, humpbacked cattle.

Billy Titus chuckled. "He calls himself a cattleman . . . and look at those critters. Gray as wolves and humped like camels."

"Freaks," Tom Goss grunted. "I hear they're breachy and full of fight. Come from India, fella told me. Brahmas. Some such name. Don't never rope one alone, he said."

"He was right," Markley said. "But you'd all better nail this up where you'll remember it. Brahma cattle may be the only ones that get through to Kansas before long. They're immune to ticks. There's no Texas fever in a Brahma herd, and the farmers up north are beginning to find it out. One of these years they're going to quarantine us right out of the shipping pens, if the fever gets any worse. But they'll always let a Brahma herd through. And heat . . . it don't come too hot for a Brahma."

The cowboys accorded Starrett's humpbacked curiosities a more respectful attention as they passed.

Before long they crossed Mission Creek. Soon the trees and brush thickened, the graze began to starve out, as the country slid off toward the Red River. The earth, scoured by rains, supported a fuzz of dry fescue grass and stunted grama. It was community graze, a little wedge of worthless land near the river town of Spanish Ford, where hogs, goats, and cattle had long been pastured awaiting the riverboats, and where now there was little left but stone and moss-hung oaks. But here was where Starrett had thrown Markley's cattle when he took over Spade.

They turned up a shallow cañon in which a fog of wood smoke lay. Almost at once they caught an odor that nauseated them. Markley told Goss: "Garth must be keepin' camp like a Basco sheepherder. Man!"

The range foreman, riding beside him, glanced up the rocky hillside at their right. He pointed, and Markley's gaze found a dead steer. As they rode closer, a quartet of buzzards flapped slowly from the ground. The animal's belly was swollen, but it was apparent to a stockman's eye that it had not been dead long, for the legs had not been forced to that grim sawhorse angle.

"Starrett wasn't joking, Zack," Goss said

quietly. "There is some sick cattle over here."

"If Garth had been on the job," Markley snapped, "the brute wouldn't have been poisoning itself on oak shoots on this starved-out range."

Goss's long face regarded him carefully. He resettled his straw sombrero. "Who you trying to hooraw, Zack? Ain't no oak shoots this time of year."

Markley shrugged. "Rattle weed, then."

But it was Billy Titus, the little Wichita gunman, who finally gave a name to it. He dismounted and ran a hand along a stiff foreleg of the longhorn; a faint crackling of gas could be heard. Titus turned away, took a handful of earth, and washed his hands with it, and, looking up at Markley soberly, he said: "Blackleg, Zack. You just thought you had a herd."

"Blackleg," Markley retorted. "There hasn't been any blackleg here in twenty years. If it was blackleg, Starrett would have used it for an excuse to quicklime the whole herd."

Goss continued to stare at the dead steer. "Starrett ain't been over lately or he'd have known in a hurry. He pushed them out of Mission Creek, them being yours, and because there was sick ones in the herd, even then."

Markley pressed a sharp look on him; he turned in the saddle and stared at the others.

"Now, all of you listen to me. There may be some sick cows in my herd. I don't know. But a man's herd is his own, even if it only tallies a couple of hundred cows, and it's his business what he does with them. Mission Creek is mine, too, and, if I want to put them on it, there's no law against it, is there?"

"No law," said Goss, "but it would be plain foolishness. Why infect all your land, when it's been confined?"

"I'll send Horse Ledbetter out to look at them. If he says it's serious, I'll keep the cows here. If it ain't, I'll move them when I'm ready."

He turned his pony back up the cañon. Leading the silent cowpunchers, he reached the little cow camp at Comanche Spring where Clay Garth and his two helpers were headquartered. A string of skinned jack rabbits hung from a line between two trees; odds and ends of harness sprawled about and a branding iron hung from a tree branch. There was a deerskin shelter near the fire ring in the heart of the camp, and Clay Garth stood beside it with a smile on his face, but a saddle gun in his hands.

"Heard you coming, Zack," he said, "but I wasn't sure who it was. How was Wichita, boy?" Garth had rude Scandinavian features, with milk-blue eyes, long, widely separated upper teeth, and cheek bones like stones under the flesh.

"Rough," Markley grunted.

"Hear you got your tail in a crack when the banks closed." Garth grinned.

"Sold four cows for less than we got for one last year."

"Yeah, we got your letter. Reckon you heard about the old man killing himself?"

"Who says?"

Garth winked. "Man his age ought to know better than to ride under low branches. He was no cattleman. Ought've stayed in Noo Orleens."

Garth fired the inevitable questions about the trail, the Wichita girls, and Markley answered tersely, with his mind swerving to Ruel Starrett and blackleg. He was shocked to realize that there was blackleg in his herd. It would mean destroying the small nucleus of a cattle herd he had been building so long. For all his casualness with Tom Goss, Markley would as soon have slept in a penthouse as put sick cattle on good land. He had feelings about land — almost religious feelings. He had brought Spade along through the years, while he watched its fumbling owner sink into debt and bungle everything he attempted. But all the time Markley had kept the range clean and the herd healthy, and always there was the thought: *mine someday.*

And now he was back and Starrett's name was written across the land and the star of success hung over the wrong man's head — the bull of the Nations, the shouting, two-fisted brush-popper, Ruel Starrett.

Markley ripped off his shirt and looked at his wound. To Garth's question, he said: "Tree branch. Got any bluestone?"

Garth bluestoned the wound for him. "Heard about Starrett, I reckon?"

Markley grunted. Standing there with the bloody shirt in his hands, he decided this was as good a time as any to count noses. "How many of you boys want to work for me?" he asked.

Titus shrugged. "Why not?"

But the others were silent, until Markley shot at Goss: "Well, Tom? You're kind of quiet."

Goss rubbed the side of his nose. "You want it straight?"

"When I get it any way but straight, I'll hand you a quirt across the nose."

144

"Well, I reckon I'd like to live longer than a man's like to do working for you. I've worked for worse men and better, but nobody ever asked more of me than you."

Markley stared at him. Glancing at the others, he saw the same embarrassed expression Goss wore. He was angry, and yet puzzled, for Goss was a seasoned cowboy, and not a careless man with his opinions.

"Tom, I never asked anything of you boys that I wouldn't do myself."

"But you've got the energy of a bull, Zack. Maybe you don't know it, but it was your own fault we hit the pens too late for the good prices."

"Watch out, Tom," Markley said levelly.

"I mean you like to killed Lisandro with work, that's all. He's an old man."

Markley glanced in dull wonder at the Mexican cowboy, who, embarrassed, sat gazing across his coffee cup. He saw something he had never observed before — Lisandro was an old man. He looked as juiceless as a winter apple.

"Why, he lost those stragglers, not me. So why shouldn't he go back for them?"

Markley's temper was rising, but now, with his quick instinct for the mettle of men, he closed his mouth. Against the luxury of a blow-off, he decided to come back to this later, when he could level with Goss. He brought a smile to his mouth.

"I didn't know I was such a roughneck," he said. "Well, there ain't any hurry. Make up your minds later. We'll go on in and I'll pay you what you ain't already drawn."

As he drew on a fresh shirt from the roll behind his cantle, the pain in his biceps keen, but no longer feverish, he experienced an obscure satisfaction in what Goss had said. He had never considered himself a tough ramrod. He had never been near the end of the leather himself, while working stirrup to stirrup with his men. It gave him confidence to know that he could outstrip the average man without effort. It furnished him with some sureness for the coming clash with Ruel Starrett.

Markley spoke to Clay Garth: "Has Starrett been over here lately?"

"Not since he run your cows off. He told me that he'd shoot any of your brand that wandered onto his range. I've got Red and Milt riding line."

"Many of the cows got this oak-shoot poisoning, whatever it is?"

Garth's pale eyes regarded him queerly. "Most of 'em. Don't you know what it's called?"

"I'm not going to guess. I'll send a man

146

out to look them over. In the meantime, start bunching them. I may decide to move them."

"If I was you. . . ." The flat menace in Markley's face stopped Garth. "OK, boss," he said, in two words accepting leadership and a job.

Markley turned to Goss. "Tom, it'd help me if you were to stay out here with Clay. He'll need another man, and you know how to handle this Starrett as well as I do, if he should show up. Just don't take any shoving, you know? Those Starretts run about nine parts wind to the bushel. I'll send somebody out to relieve you in a day or so."

He headed off without letting Goss, who had a wife living in Spanish Ford, make his refusal.

Markley led the men to the juncture of the side road with a road coming boldly through the tall hackberry growth. This was the Central National Road of Texas. In dry seasons it was pounded to dust, in wet it degenerated into chocolate mire. At all seasons, it carried a crushing burden of horses, oxen, and wagons from the coast to the river town of Spanish Ford.

They swerved right on this road and came to the heights above the village. Half hidden by leafless trees, the sandy brick buildings and sheet-metal roofs of the town braced against a slope that ran to the bank of the river. The buildings were of uneven height; a dozen cross streets slashed at odd angles across the wide main street of Spanish Ford, which had a steepled church at this upper end and wharves at the lower.

As they entered the village, Markley was impressed by the number of men lounging about — sure token of hard times — and he touched the heavy money belt under his shirt. These days a man with money was king. Money and land — a man could imbibe them and go to glory. Markley seemed to feel vibrating in the air a hairspring, the delicate timing of everything he must accomplish in the next few hours. He glanced at Lisandro Garza and knew things must be squared there; he looked at Billy Titus and recognized the strength he could provide.

"Billy" — Zack smiled suddenly — "can you handle those guns or do you only carry them to scare the girls?"

"Spot me a target."

Markley nodded at the brown hulk of the livery stable. "That weathervane," he said. "Five dollars if you drop it."

Billy Titus drew his right-hand Colt. The Spade men, beginning to ease out, trail-

proud as homecoming warriors, made a commotion as they ringed up to watch Titus shoot. And while this went on, Markley drew Lisandro aside.

"Thanks for what you did this morning. This'll make it right, eh?"

The Mexican frowned at the gold piece Zack offered. "The lie was not for pay."

Markley slapped the old man's back. "Come on, *hombre*. That wasn't a lie."

Raisin-brown and grieving, Lisandro's face confronted Zack's. "I heard the old *patrón* say you should have Barranca Roja when he died, Meester Zack. That is what I heard. I only say Mission Creek because I . . . I was sorry that I slow you down on the trail."

Markley's face hardened like muscle. "You keep on saying that, Lisandro, and you're going to believe it. From now on, anything's a lie but this . . . that Will Dalhart promised me Mission Creek."

"But you say you have a paper, no?"

"Yes, but . . . suppose I lost the paper? Then I'd only have your word."

"You ask me to stand with my hand on the Bible and tell that lie? Meester Zack, I wish to go to confession tomorrow. But I cannot confess a lie I mean to repeat."

Suddenly Titus's gun crashed. The weathervane atop Kohl's livery stable spun reck-lessly.

A man with a pitchfork appeared angrily in the door, saw Titus unlimbering his second pistol, and ducked back. The Spade men laughed.

Markley's face quickly firmed. "That's one lie you'd better repeat, old man, or don't show up at the hearing. You'll be the sad-dest Mexican in Spanish Ford if you cross me up."

Billy Titus's second gun snapped the weathervane. Titus came over to collect his money. Markley good-naturedly paid him. "So you're with me?"

"You bet," Titus said. Then he looked over the street. "Going to go hard with the girls in this town tonight."

Markley suddenly discerned a big, lower-ing figure in the portal of the marshal's of-fice, next to the bank. It was Spanish Ford's one-armed law force, Marshal Charlie Bennett. His face was angry as he called to Titus: "Cut that out, you fool!"

"What's the trouble, uncle?" Titus winked.

"Come here," Bennett said. "I'll check those things for you."

Titus derisively gave the marshal a hand salute, turned his pony, and rode upstreet along the saloon fronts.

Bennett called to the foreman: "Who is that fellow, Zack?"

"I don't know. He slung in with us a few miles back. I reckon he felt like blowing off steam."

"Well, he won't blow it off in Spanish Ford. Tell him for me that I want his guns in my office by sundown or else he gets out of town." Then, abruptly, he smiled. "As for you, welcome home."

"Thanks," said Markley. He turned his back on Bennett.

He saw the surprise in the faces of the others, who liked and respected the marshal. But Markley understood what perhaps they did not. Sooner or later, he might be pitted against Bennett, and he did not want to be deterred by motives of friendship.

When they rode off to the saloons, he discovered that Marshal Bennett was still waiting in his doorway. A big, thick-limbed man with cropped hair and powerful shoulders, Bennett had taken to wearing silver-rimmed glasses at times.

"How were the Indians?" asked the marshal.

"Scarce."

"Dodge City still full of tinhorns?"

Zack flipped his reins about the rack. "I didn't go to Dodge. I went to Wichita."

151

"Well, how was Wichita?"

Markley turned, but his gaze ascended the street instead of honoring the marshal. "OK," he said.

"What's the matter, Zack? Did I speak out of turn?"

"No, but I've got a lot to do. I can't waste all day."

The square frame of Bennett's face came through the flaccid flesh of middle years. "I sho' won't keep you then, man. I wouldn't waste your day for anything. It's not asking too much to deliver that message to that fellow about checking his guns, is it?"

Markley shrugged. "Not if you really mean it."

"I mean it."

V

Within Clyde Tilford's bank the spirit of dejection was as palpable as dust. Markley passed down the aisle between the metal wall covering on his left and a series of brass wickets on his right, a brown-skinned, blond man who walked like a tiger. He reached the curtained corner where Tilford had his office. He sauntered in and closed the door.

Clyde Tilford glanced up from his untidy desk. At once he smiled and rose. "Well, ain't this good news."

Tilford was a plain little man with a dissatisfied mouth and eyes. Markley inspected him with a faint smile. Little men took their troubles so pathetically hard. He looked tight and driven.

"Hello, Clyde," Markley said. "Lost weight, ain't you?"

"Ain't had much reason to get fat. Man, you just don't know." Tilford quickly cleared his face. "I suppose you heard about Dalhart."

"Kill himself, you think?"

"Well, he had plenty of reason. Spade was getting away from him. Maybe he couldn't face people."

"Never could. Always hiding behind a big cigar and a diamond stickpin. But he was scared. And the scareder he got, the more money he and Susanna would spend."

"I guess you know what happened to Spade."

"I also know Starrett's getting off Mission Creek."

Tilford blinked. "How so?"

"Will Dalhart left me that land. Didn't you know that?" Tilford started a grin, but it faded as Markley said angrily: "Now, don't give me that! You knew I was to be mentioned in his will, didn't you?"

"Well, sure, Zack, but . . . well, Mission Creek."

"You didn't think I'd risk my scalp for a goat pasture?"

Tilford moved a paper on his desk, then he took two cigars from a box, handed one to the foreman, and both men lighted up. With the rising of the smoke came a thoughtful quiet. Tilford's harried eyes brightened.

"I don't know about you," he said, "but I wouldn't want to be the one to chouse Starrett off the land."

"I handled the Indians in 'Sixty-Three. I can handle Starrett."

"And you mean Susanna sold a partnership to Starrett with a lien against it?"

Zack's gray eyes chilled. "Leave Susanna out of it."

Tilford shrugged. "You really plan to put him off?"

"How else am I going to get the land?" Markley puffed the cigar. "So things have been rough, eh?"

"Oh, we'll make it," said Tilford staunchly. "I've always watched my investments, so the bank is really. . . ."

"How much railroad stock did you buy?" The foreman grinned.

"Only a little. I never went overboard."

"I'm glad to hear it. We saw a lot of rusty rails up in the Choctaw country. Clyde," he said abruptly, "I want to buy a note. There were four notes against Spade when I went away. How much is still outstanding?"

"As a matter of fact . . . ," Tilford began stiffly.

But Markley interrupted heatedly: "Hang it, if you can only pipe the banker's song and dance about being sound as oak and never talk about a customer, you can pipe it alone. But I'm telling you this. I'm in business, and the ones who help me now will be the ones I'll help later. Starrett couldn't have bought up all those notes. And if there's anything outstanding, I want it."

"He owes thirteen hundred."

"I want the note," Markley said.

"I promised to carry him till the herd money was in. What kind of a banker would I be to betray a trust?"

"What kind of a bank is a busted one, Clyde?"

"You aren't talking about buying notes with Spade money, are you, Zack?"

"Don't you worry about where the money comes from," Markley snapped, but quickly swerved to surer ground. Taking a folded paper from his trousers pocket, he said to Tilford: "Got an envelope?"

Tilford watched him seal a smudged paper in the envelope. "What's that?"

"It's a legal paper. I want to leave it in your safe. It's the only hold I have on Mission Creek, and I don't want Starrett knocking me over the head to get it before the hearing."

Tilford locked it in the little Salamander safe in the corner. Markley was ready to leave now, but the banker spoke hesitantly: "Better deposit that herd money, Zack, before something happens to it."

"It's in a safe place right now, Clyde. My private safe . . . a money belt around Billy Titus's waist. Nobody'll tamper with that safe. What's the matter? Is the bank so hard up you're soliciting contributions?"

"All banks are hard up," retorted Tilford grumpily.

Markley returned to the street, and, standing on the walk, he put a cigar in his mouth and gazed up the road. He grinned. He savored the taste of importance. He had been a big-ranch ramrod for years, and liked the prestige, but it would be nothing to the weight he would carry as the boss man of a ranch like Spade. A big buyer, a free spender, a director in the bank.

Starrett called himself an ambitious man; he did not know what the word meant. He did not comprehend this feeling of a force in you stronger than you yourself, this power that could take hold of you and direct you — this massive hunger, this wild horse in the heart. Markley struck a match for his cigar and walked briskly up the street.

Rex Starrett halted for a smoke under a locust tree. He shifted his weight to one stirrup, and stretched a free leg to rattle a spur and frown at it, his mood in his face. He felt guilty and dissatisfied at running out on his father. He had not said one word to him that he did not mean, and yet he knew that the force that had really pushed him from Spade was Susanna. He began to anticipate almost desperately the action, the places, the girls he would encounter with the Rangers. The dangers and privations did not trouble him; self-denial had been an end in itself in the Comanche country, toughening your mind as well as your body. The one pleasure he had ever clung to was his love for Susanna. He had the guilty conviction that love was for women. This softness of desire shamed him. But there was something in this girl — so headstrong and proud, so extravagant that she would risk another's money to satisfy herself — which flagged him off. There were women like that, women as dangerous as an unfamiliar weapon.

A sound in the hackberry grove at his right caught his attention. Above the thin metallic clicking of insects, he heard a horse moving. He had ranched too long in arrow-and-lance country to let it pass unnoticed. But the distant horse scuffed along as though it was merely grazing, and he rode on.

When he had gone a few rods farther, he heard a sound on the road before him. He started to pull into the brush, for Markley's men were on this road, then he saw a buggy parked on a rise a hundred yards beyond. A girl in a dark cape was working with the harness. With a stroke of excitement, he realized that it was Susanna. For just an instant he considered detouring around her. He knew exactly what a good bye would do to him, and yet he was unable to deny himself this last encounter with her.

Susanna glanced around quickly as he rode up. Recognizing him, she dropped the rein she had been working with.

"Thank heaven! You don't happen to be carrying a pocketful of rivets, do you?"

Rex smiled. "You're lucky the rein didn't break while the horse was running. Let's see."

Susanna began brushing her hands together to remove the dust. "A girl should

never go driving without a man, anyway."
She was turning it all over to him, Rex saw,
and he was pleased. Standing there, he
looked at the leather that had parted.

Suddenly he heard Susanna exclaim: "Are
you going somewhere? You have your blankets."

Rex nodded, but kept frowning at the rein,
wondering why it should have broken.

"Well, where?" Susanna persisted.

At that moment he discovered the knife
cut in the leather and he glanced at her —
not really surprised at the trick, merely
confirmed in an opinion. Yet her face did
not betray her. Whatever trick she was
perpetrating, she always had her look of
pure youthfulness. The dark-blue cape she
wore distilled a pale blue in her gray eyes;
her skin was blushed by the cold. She
looked young and cared for, and it was hard
for him to recall the complicated things he
had seen in her only a short time ago.

"I'm leaving Spanish Ford," he said.

Then he began doubling back the leather
plait to make a temporary fastening.

"Just like that, Rex . . . without even good
bye to anybody?"

"I told Dad," he said. "I wasn't sure
whether I was going or not until today."

"Why are you going?"

"Change of scenery, I expect."

"Is there anything wrong with this scenery?"

"No, and there wouldn't be anything wrong with this rein if you hadn't cut it with a knife."

Color flooded her face. "I . . . I wanted to be sure you stopped."

He shook his head, marveling. "If all women are like you," he said, "it's a bachelor's life for me. I'd never get one figured out."

"Do you have to figure her out?" she asked. "Can't you accept a thing you don't understand?"

"Maybe. But I wouldn't have much peace of mind." He slapped her horse. "OK?" He helped her into the buggy. He rode beside her as she started on toward Spanish Ford.

"What about your father?" she asked him.

"He'll make out. He can handle Markley or anybody else."

"No, Rex," she said. "I don't think he can handle Zack . . . not if Zack has made up his mind to cheat us out of Mission Creek."

Rex flicked her a smile. "*Us?* Anything Zack gets will be yours when you marry him."

"Who said I was going to marry him?"

"Just a notion I had."

"As a matter of fact . . . ," she said, but stopped. "It happens," she concluded, "that I don't love Zack."

He said the thing that was bound to hurt, but it expressed the great doubt he had of Susanna. "But you'd marry him anyway, if you had to, to save the ranch, wouldn't you?"

"That's a contemptible thing to say!" she exclaimed. "You . . . you can ride by yourself, if that's all you think of me!"

She slapped her horse with the reins and it went ahead in a high trot. Rex watched her drive up a long swale leading to a ridge. He decided he could only catch up and apologize, though he knew he was right. But before he could spur his horse, he heard a sound like a hand slapping the withers of his bay. A tuft of black mane hairs flew, and he felt the convulsive lurch of the pony. A moment later the giant crash of a rifle came to him from a bois-d'arc tangle a hundred feet from the road. Stunned, Rex felt the pony giving way under him, falling straight forward. He made a frantic motion to draw his carbine, but the horse went down fast. Its knees struck the earth, and he sprawled forward, hearing far-off echoes of the shot, and Susanna's voice calling his name. It was too swift for him to feel fear. He thought of

Zack Markley, crouching there with the stock of a carbine to his cheek, and he wondered at an ambition that would send a man into the brush to snipe at his enemies. The earth smashed against him as he rolled, shocked and breathless, into the shallow ditch beside the road.

VI

Somewhere a man was ripping through the brush. Rex crawled back toward the horse, which lay scarcely moving, and pulled his carbine from the boot and rolled into the ditch. He fired a shot into the bois-d'arc thicket and the running ceased. But suddenly he remembered Susanna. He peered up the hill and saw the buggy swerve into the brush, lurch onto two wheels, and topple over. The horse, thrown onto its side, lay kicking as it tried to extricate itself.

"Susanna!" Rex shouted.

To his relief, the girl crawled from the wreckage of shattered bows and torn fabric, her cape whitened with dust. Her black hair fell loosely over her shoulders. She groped from the brush into the road and stood there, bewildered. Then she saw Rex and, catching up her skirts, began to run toward him.

"Get down!" Rex shouted.

A shot roared from the brush, dynamiting a small crater in the road dust as Susanna came on, but she did not stop. Rex brought his carbine up to his shoulder and fired into the thicket. There was another shot from the thicket. The pocket in the hills rocked to the echoes of the shot. Susanna came, falling once, and rising again and running on. Rex sprang up, caught her with one arm, and dragged her into the ditch. She clutched him as he turned back to the road.

From the brush came furtive cracklings. Rex sprawled against the bank, his cheek dented by the gunstock. He thought of Billy Titus, Markley's little brindle-eyed cow-puncher, who his father disliked. He thought of Markley, possessed of an irrational ambition, and wondered whether Markley thought that killing Ruel Starrett's son would stop Starrett, or did he mean to take them both? Then a horse crashed through brush and hit a trail and began to lope. It was going away from them, and Rex fired at the sound. The echoes cascaded over the hills. Rex let the shell slip from the breach, waited another moment, and rose. Silently he helped Susanna up. He smiled as she looked disconsolately at herself — dusty, her clothing awry, and with a small tear in her gown.

"This almost makes it worthwhile," he said. "The proper Miss Dalhart with dirt on her face."

She refused to smile. "Someone meant to kill you, Rex."

He gazed into the thicket. "Maybe he figured I'd scare out. Let's see what's left of my horse," he said.

The pony still laid on the road, although the wound was shallow, a raw notch across its neck. Susanna gazed pityingly at the animal. "Will he die?"

"No. He's just been creased . . . the way you might clip a man with a singletree. He'll come around, but nobody will ride him for a couple of weeks." He was silent, a muscle in his jaw tensing and flexing. "I'll see about the buggy."

He took his saddle and blanket roll and walked up the road, knowing this might be the end of the Rangers for him. Unless he could wheedle a $100 cavalry-trained horse from someone, he was out of it. The fine cavalry mounts left from the war were growing scarce. He began figuring his chances, but the only angle he saw was borrowing the money from his father. Of course he could not do that — he couldn't take it even if his father offered it.

Rex extricated Susanna's horse from the shafts, righted the buggy, and harnessed it again. Susanna came up the road to watch him work.

"I didn't distinguish myself, did I?" she said. "I suppose whoever fired at us is saying . . . 'Those Dalharts scare like chickens.'" As she began to recover her poise, anger snapped in her eyes.

Rex put his saddle, carbine, and blanket roll in the back of the little sidebar buggy. "Tell you one thing about those Dalharts. You're so prideful you ought to be under glass. What's the difference how you looked? You're alive, aren't you?"

"Maybe it was a joke," she said angrily. "They used to play tricks like that on Dad, so they could laugh about him in the saloons. Once they put a handful of shoeing nails under his saddle, so he'd be pitched off." She clenched her fists. "Oh, Rex, Rex! I'll show them yet! I'll show this town!"

He gazed at her. "Show them what?"

"That we aren't the easy marks they've always said. From the day we came here, they've been watching to see us go under. Everyone took advantage of Dad . . . cheated him, played tricks on him . . . and now that he's gone, they're playing tricks on me."

165

Rex wanted to say — "This was no trick." — but, if it eased her fear to think it had been, he decided, let her believe it.

"There's so much of us here, Rex," she said earnestly. "My mother is buried here, and my father . . . all our money and most of our pride."

"So, that's one place where you've doubled your capital. You've got enough pride for a whole town."

"Who wouldn't have, the way everyone has tried to make fools of us?"

"Not everyone. Just the few who'd have tried it with any outsider. But most people liked your father. And they like you, when you aren't being the cow-country queen."

"Queen? What do you mean, Rex?"

"Not many people like taking orders."

"Why, I don't give. . . ." But she colored under his smile, remembering, perhaps, the trains of maids in her home, the times she had called from the gallery — "Saddle my horse, please!" — to whomever happened to be handy. "Well, I don't mean anything by it."

Rex chuckled and lifted her by the waist to the seat of the buggy. "I'm just telling you so you'll know, in case it gets to bothering you."

And because there was kindness in his

tone, tears suddenly glistened in her eyes and she gripped his hand. "Don't leave Spanish Ford, Rex. I need you."

"For what?"

"As . . . as a friend. You know I wasn't trying to cheat your father on the ranch. You should know I wouldn't cheat anyone."

All the tenderness Rex felt for her rose in him and tried to blind him to what he knew. But nothing had been changed by a shot fired on the road.

"You don't need me any more than I need you, Susanna," he said. "But, you see, I don't trust you."

"Rex," she said, pouting.

"I mean that when the going gets hard, you'll do what you have to do to save yourself. Because you're bound to show people. If it looks like Markley's going to beat my father out, you'll marry him, if that's the only way you can stay on as mistress of Spade. Isn't that true?"

"How does anyone know what he'll do until he does it?" she said miserably.

Rex smiled and mounted the buggy. "Maybe what you need is a year in a dirt-floored shanty to get acquainted with yourself."

"Perhaps I'd rather not get that well acquainted, Rex," she said archly.

■ ■ ■ ■

In midafternoon they reached Spanish Ford. Rex halted the buggy before the National Road Hotel. He held Susanna's hands for a moment before he lifted her down.

"Don't let anybody stampede you into anything," he told her. "If they try to put the pressure on you, send them to me."

"I'd love to" — she smiled — "but you won't be here."

"I will until I find a horse," Rex said ruefully. "A hundred dollars' worth, cavalry-trained. I may be around a while before I track down a mount like that."

"I hope you are, Rex. I hope you never find him."

"I'll leave the rig at the hotel barn," he told her.

Susanna stood forlornly on the walk as he drove down the alley to the rear of the hotel. She wished she could have given him the answer she knew he wanted. But what was ahead seemed so confused that no one could be sure of himself.

As she approached the hotel, a small, sharp-eyed man in a gray frock coat and stovepipe hat emerged and held the door for her. Susanna recognized him. Her mouth firmed as she saw him smile at her. She tilted her chin and started past.

"Miss Dalhart," he said. "A nice surprise. I've just been asking after you."

"What is it, Mister LaPorte? Did you want to invite me to a game in your badger pit?"

The thin mouth smiled. "No. I hoped you might do me the honor of having something . . . coffee, a sherry . . . in the dining room?"

Joe LaPorte was the gambler who had fleeced her father of $7,000. All her dislike for him lay in her eyes. "What do you want?" she asked.

He hesitated. "Why, I thought you might be interested in selling your interest in Spade Ranch. Naturally I didn't want to ask sooner, with your father so lately gone."

"Did someone say it was for sale?"

"No, but I thought it might be."

"Why?"

LaPorte smiled. "I'm like a doctor. Nearly everyone comes to me, and most folks talk. Maybe you like legal trouble better than most ladies. I don't suppose you do. So I thought you might be interested in a quick sale for your land."

"How much?"

"Two thousand dollars."

Susanna laughed. She was almost as tall as the gambler, and she gazed straight into his eyes with the finest contempt of which she was capable. "You miss the price by five thousand, Mister LaPorte. And what is more, any price I quoted you would have to include the seven thousand dollars you fleeced my father out of."

"Fleeced?" LaPorte protested.

Susanna passed him to enter the hotel. She thought with desperate anger: *If I had a hundred thousand dollars, I'd spend half of it to run him into jail.* But now she had scarcely $100.

Yet she might have owned all of Salado County, as she swept to the desk and said: "I'd like a nice sunny room for a few days. And please send a hairdresser up. I've had a most uncomfortable ride."

VII

Ruel Starrett, having finished the harrowing work beside the wagon road, let the hackberry groves along Mission Creek swallow him. He had eluded Rex successfully without having been seen. He stopped by a deep, murky hole, drew cleaning rod and patches from his rifle, and cleaned the gun.

The action had knocked all the bounce

out of him. He could crease a range horse ten times without missing, but to fire at one with his son riding it was another story. Yet it had been worth it. Rex would not ride to the Rangers on that horse! Nor, if he figured it properly, could he find another $100 horse for what pocket money he might have.

Starrett's schedule prevented him from riding on to town. He wanted Rex and Susanna to go in, and at the proper time he would come in, leading Rex's wounded horse, which he would have found straying by the road as he himself came in. He lounged beside the stream, hearing the jays scold, watching a red fox slink from a clearing and disappear into the brush. He smoked a cigar, pondering the run of this rotten day.

His eye picked out buzzards wheeling in the sky. It was some time before its significance pricked him. Then he rose slowly, staring across the hills — over the community pasture of Spanish Ford, this worthless sprawl of trees and brush where he had dumped Markley's cattle. He suddenly threw his cigar in the stream and strode to his horse. He started for Comanche Spring, where Clay Garth, Markley's man, had his camp.

With the afternoon wearing thin, he found

Garth and Tom Goss preparing an early evening meal at the camp. Squatting silently by the fire, they watched him ride up. Starrett's eyes picked out the rifles in their laps, and the small day herd of cattle on the hillside behind the camp. And now he slowed, and put his anger away like a cartridge in a bandoleer. Raising his hand, he greeted them.

"Hello, Goss . . . Garth. Seems like Markley's put you fellows to work, eh?"

Tom Goss resumed crumbling herbs into the jack rabbit stew.

Garth's bony features stayed with the rancher. "Just passin'?"

Starrett nodded. "Goss," he said, and the range boss looked up. "I had a talk with my boy, Rex, this morning. He won't take that ramrod job I was figuring him for. He claims you're in line for it."

Goss's eyes had a slow but thorough intelligence. They examined critically every line of Starrett's countenance. "That what he says?"

"How about it? Sixty a month. You can keep a brand of your own, if you want to pay for the graze."

Temptation whetted Goss's eyes. He was a married man, and married cowboys were notoriously ambitious, for two could not

172

live well on a cowboy's salary. He frowned and rubbed the last of the herbs off his hands. "Sixty," he said.

"Little shack of your own . . . married, ain't you? Heard your wife lives in town."

Goss picked up a branch and broke it. "I don't know. I told Markley I might go with him. I'll have to talk to Phoebe first."

"You'll have to see who's going to win, first, eh?" Starrett snapped, irked at Goss's reception of his offer. "Suit yourself. This was Rex's idea anyhow. . . . I saw some buzzards over this way," he said. "Losing any stock?"

Garth snapped a look at Tom Goss and shrugged. "Who don't, now and then?"

Starrett rode past the fire and circled the day herd, held in a large stone corral. They heard him shout — "Moses and Aaron!" — and come loping back. He gestured with his saddle gun. "Those brutes have got the blackleg! Why ain't they been quicklimed?"

Garth rose with his rifle in the angle of his elbow. "Because we ain't sure of it yet. Zack's sending a vet out."

"Ain't sure!" Starrett raged. "What do you want . . . buzzards on their backs? Those cows have got to be slaughtered, and the sooner the better."

"Not today, they ain't."

"What are you gathering them for?"

"To treat," Garth said, showing his wide-spaced teeth in a smile. "The other boys are bringing in the rest."

Starrett felt a core of panic begin to spin in him like a Kansas cyclone. The presence of these slavering, diseased cattle of Markley's, so close to his herd, terrified him. Blackleg, the nightmare there was no wakening from. It ran its course from health to death without fail. He pointed a forefinger at Clay Garth.

"I'm going to tell you something, pardner. If anybody moves those cows across Mission Creek, I'll not only kill the cows but the men who moved them. Savvy? That means you, or Goss, or anybody else." He shook the rifle in his gloved hand. "I'll drive a slug right through his belly, and I won't mince around getting started."

Garth sucked his tooth, standing with his legs planted widely and his eyes derisive. "You better talk to Markley. I just work here."

Starrett wheeled his horse and rode out.

Late-evening shadows lay like ruts on the road as he approached Spanish Ford. He jogged past the slaughterhouse in the hack-berry woods, where fires blazed under hog

174

caldrons. Frost clinked in the air. Starrett's black horsehide jacket was fastened at the neck, and with one gauntleted hand he gripped the lead rope of Rex's horse. He had found the animal grazing near the road. Riding on, he read sign along the street. A few horses stood at racks. A gang of bull-whackers shouldering into the Indian Head Saloon paused to glance at him. Behind a window of the bank, an alpaca-coated man on a high stool, working by rock-oil light, glanced out at him like a prisoner. As he rode on, he felt the glances trailing him. This town knew the whole story, he reflected. Like as not they were nudging each other and saying: "Old Starrett's in for it now!" *They just don't know me,* thought Starrett.

He cut to a hitch rack before the marshal's office, his mind still churning with the sight of Markley's plague-ridden cattle. Looping the reins over the pole, he ducked under it and stepped up on the walk. Then he saw movement in the alcove of a building next to the marshal's. The building was shuttered. Above the door was the emblem of the defunct *Kansas and Gulf Railroad.* Starrett halted, peering into the shadows. At first it had looked like a bale of blankets heaped against the wall, but now he saw it rise to man height and recognized a familiar high, thimble-shaped hat. It was Chief Jack, the Comanche from whom Starrett had leased range a year ago.

He raised his hand, and Starrett acknowledged the gesture and said: "How is it, Chief?"

"Tohe-chit!" said the Indian. "Bad year for Indians. Much hunger."

"Bad year for white men." Starrett smiled, searching the raisin-brown face.

"Much sorrow among my people."

Starrett handed him a gold piece. "Buy the tribe some stick candy, Chief. It'll cure anything."

He would have passed on, but the Comanche grunted: *"Wohaw!"*

Starrett's face set. "Now, understand me. You had all the *wohaw* you're gonna have out of me. Free beef, hell. Stop stealing beef in good times, Chief, and people will give you beef in bad."

The flinty eyes watched him move on to the door. "You owe tribe money. Why you no pay?"

"Because it don't work that way. When you rob a man, you're lucky he don't shoot you. Next time you lease range to somebody, don't hit his herds all year and you'll get paid."

"My heart turn bad toward you," warned the chief, thumping his chest.

"How was your heart when you were robbing me?" asked Starrett.

He rapped at the door of the marshal's office. Someone spoke, and he opened it. Bennett was sitting at his desk in the small, overheated room with its tow-sacking floor. Starrett glanced at the one-armed marshal, who was reading a newspaper through silver-rimmed spectacles.

"Where's Rex? I found his horse on the way in."

"Out back," Bennett said.

Starrett opened a door on a lot littered with bottles and cans. At the back of it stood a small adobe jail in a thicket of dead weeds. In the cold twilight, Rex stood beside a corral flanking the jail, one foot up on a bar as he looked at a horse. Starrett strode out.

"What the devil happened? I found your horse as I came in. That bay of yours has been shot, boy."

Rex walked from the corral. "I know. I was on him." He went into the building.

Starrett had the shocking thought that Rex might have learned who had done the shooting. But he clenched his jaws and trailed him inside. Bennett indicated a blackened pot on the stove.

"Coffee. Think the horse will pass muster?" he asked Rex.

"I don't know, Charlie. Don't know whether he'd assay a hundred or not. Captain McNelly's got an eye like a hawk."

Bennett glanced at Starrett. "Well" — he shrugged — "it won't hurt to try."

Starrett scoffed. "That jack-legged brown out back wouldn't assay twenty-five dollars, if that's what you're talking about. Listen, will you? I find Rex's horse dogging along half dead, and no sign of the boy. All the way in I've been wondering if he'd crawled off in the brush to die. What in thunder happened?"

"Somebody shot him," Rex said. He put one boot on the low window ledge and gazed across the street at the National Road Hotel. "I didn't get a look at him."

"And you can't cipher out who it was?"

"We could guess," said Bennett. "But you can't swear out warrants on guesses."

"Who else would profit by Rex being shot but Markley? It was him or that tin-plated gunman of his."

"Or maybe Chief Jack. He's still sore over the trimming you gave him."

Starrett emitted a scornful grunt. "Have you talked to Markley?"

"Not yet. First I'd like to find some

evidence. I suppose that means a ride out there to find the sniper's footprints, or see if he left his rifle shells."

Starrett, feeling a deep throb of alarm as he remembered the copper shells he had left, unusual in caliber, veered suddenly. "I suppose Markley's been blowing off about all he's going to do to me, eh?" Bennett nodded. "Well?" Starrett prompted, and the marshal got up and went to the window to stare into the darkening street.

"He hauled me over to the judge's office and made a deposition and asked for a hearing. He claims all the pastures along Mission Creek. Says he's got some kind of legal instrument entitling him to the land, and that Lisandro Garza will back him up."

"When's all this going to happen?"

"Eleven A.M., day after tomorrow."

"Just as a guess, Marshal," Starrett asked seriously, "what do you think's going to happen?"

A buggy rattled past. It was a familiar one, and Starrett's neck hairs bristled when he saw that it was Susanna's, with Zack Markley holding the reins. The girl sat beside him. He heard Rex move, and saw him rise stiffly beside the window with his face queerly tense. The buggy went on, and Bennett, who had not seen it, answered the rancher's question thoughtfully.

"I think Judge Waggoner will throw you off the land," he said.

Starrett's rage came up in his throat like bile. "The man ain't been born yet . . . ," he began.

"You wanted my opinion," retorted Bennett. "All the evidence is on his side. If you were in Markley's boots, you'd be as sore as he is. Seems to me your quarrel's with Susanna."

"I don't have a quarrel with anybody," Starrett said sharply, "as long as they leave me alone. But I've got a quarrel with the first man who don't."

"Are you going to the hearing?"

"Sure, to see if that Mexican can lie as good on the witness stand as he can in the saddle."

"What if he can?"

Starrett glared at the marshal and at Rex, but, even armed with his fury, he felt futile. *If Rex were still with me,* he thought bitterly, *there'd be no question about it.* But now he felt indecisive, and his doubts underlaid his voice.

"If he can, it still won't make any difference. I stay."

"You don't make much of a case for yourself."

"All right," Starrett said, his face suddenly heating, "I'll make a case against Markley, if not for myself. I'll show you the kind of swine you're standing up for. Do you know he's running a herd of cattle out there on the community graze that are rotten with blackleg? Do you know he's threatened to move them onto Mission Creek?"

Even Rex was jarred from the preoccupation he had been placed in by the sight of Susanna with Markley. "How do you know?"

"How would I know if I had smallpox, if I had it? By the symptoms." Then he stabbed hotly at the marshal: "So what is the law of Spanish Ford going to do about it?"

Bennett pursed his lips. "If it's really blackleg. . . ."

"It won't be hard to find out. Where's Horse Ledbetter?"

"He's in town, all right," Bennett said, his face troubled. "But even if it is blackleg . . . well, it'd be up to Markley whether he wanted to slaughter them or try to treat them. Though everybody knows. . . ."

"Everybody knows," said Starrett hotly, "that one diseased steer can kill all the cattle in ten counties. There's two things we've got to do, and do them quick. Send Ledbetter out to diagnose the trouble. Then kill

181

the cows for Markley, if he won't do it himself."

"By what right?" Bennett shrugged.

"By right of force, if we have to!" Starrett shouted.

Bennett pulled his heavy body up out of the desk chair. "No use getting heated up before you know what you're fighting over. Come on. Ledbetter may still be at his place. He's been spending most of his time in town since ranching began to seem like work. Rex," he added, "you might as well bring your horse down and let him take a look at it."

Horse Ledbetter's place of business was a brush-and-adobe shack halfway between the town and the river. Starrett, Rex, and the marshal walked down in the early night. At the wharf, the lights of a river packet rocked gently.

"Been tied up there two weeks," Bennett commented. "Captain can't sell the freight he brought up, and ain't got money to buy the hide 'n' tallow this town's got to sell. Hard times."

Hard times, echoed Starrett's mind, *and until this morning, I was set to make a killing out of hard times. The biggest rancher in Texas.* He felt the fabric of that dream begin to tear in his grasp. Horse Ledbetter's little ranch west of town had been part of it. But Ledbetter, whose part-time trade of treating sick animals gave him his nickname, had turned down Starrett's first offer for his land. It was poor land; he maintained it like a slatternly wife. It had produced too many cattle and needed a rest; it cried for saltlicks and boxed springs. These were the things Starrett planned for it, when Ledbetter got over the notion it was a cow heaven of Kentucky bluegrass and set a reasonable price.

Leaving the road, they picked a way through a litter of decaying harness and ironware in the yard. Rex's horse scuffed along on its lead rope. At the last moment they saw the buggy parked beside the adobe cabin, and Starrett knew that this had been Markley's destination, also.

Markley had left the buggy, but Susanna sat in the darkness with the hood of her cape over her head. Her voice came softly to them. "Good evening. I see you brought in Rex's horse, Mister Starrett."

Starrett grunted a reply. "Ledbetter inside?"

"Yes, Zack is talking to him. Why don't you come back in a few minutes?" she suggested, and Starrett laughed.

"I'm not afraid of Markley, missy." He

struck the door. A man of middle height with thin gray hair and a ruddy face with full cheeks, like a 'possum's, opened it.

"Come in, boys, come in," Horse Ledbetter said with uneasy good nature. "What you got there, Rex? Sick horse?"

"Shot horse," Starrett retorted.

"Don't say!" Ledbetter exclaimed. "Well, let's have a look at that shot horse."

He turned back into the cabin, found a lamp, and brought it out. Behind him came Zack Markley, big and relaxed and silent. He went over with the others to look at the wound on the withers of Rex's pony. Starrett felt his anger coming up strong in him, thinking of all this man represented — menace where there had been confidence, treachery where there had been trust. He observed that Rex, too, was staring at Markley with something cold and savage in his eyes, and he thought: *Now, that's funny. He was taking his side this morning.*

Ledbetter hummed as he examined the cut. He had the face of an affable failure, a good-natured drunk, a manner of blinking as though trying to see through a fog.

"Well, sir, I reckon a little creosote will keep the screwworms out of this wound." He creosoted the wound. He asked jovially: "Going to make me another offer on my land? About due, ain't it?"

"Every month you're on that land it's worth fifty dollars less to me."

"What's the matter with how I ranch?"

"I've seen feed lots that didn't pack in as many cows as you do. That land will have to be rested a year before it's fit to use again. I wouldn't give over eight hundred."

Ledbetter hit Zack Markley with his elbow. "How do you like that? Eight hundred."

Markley drew quietly on his cigarette and smiled to himself. He strolled over to the buggy. He took Susanna's hand and said something, and Starrett was aware suddenly of Rex's breathing.

Rex spoke tartly: "How long before the horse can be ridden?"

"Ten days, two weeks."

"All right. . . . Dad, I'll take him up to the stable."

"Go ahead and take care of your other customers, Horse," Starrett told the veterinarian. "I'll dicker with you afterwards."

"Oh, Zack ain't in a hurry."

"I'd be," said Starrett. "I'd be in a hell of a hurry, if I had blackleg in my herd."

Markley came from the buggy. "Who says it's blackleg?"

"I say. I came through today. Every cow

in that bunch will have to be shot."

"I think you ought to get there first thing tomorrow, Horse," Marshal Bennett declared. "If it's blackleg. . . ."

Markley's face was rude and sure and impatient. "If it's blackleg, I'll have Horse start treatment."

"Treatment! You know the treatment for blackleg!"

"Now, there's been many a cattle saved," Ledbetter soothed him, blinking importantly. "I've got some medicine I picked up in Houston a few years ago. . . ."

Starrett came in angrily: "If Markley ain't got the guts to kill his own cattle, I can find men to help him."

"Can you?" Markley grinned, and at last it struck Starrett that he was completely alone in this fight. Only a man next door to blackleg would go out on a limb to fight it, and, since Spade Ranch and the river lapped the community pasture on three sides, there was only Horse Ledbetter to worry about transference of the disease to his herd.

He glanced with cool scorn at the marshal. "Are you with me, Bennett? Or will you make your fight with your feet on the desk?"

"You've always thought you could bull this town into liking you, haven't you?" Bennett snapped. "And now that you need help, you're alone. Personally I don't give a sheepherder's undershirt what happens to you, but I've got an obligation to the town and the county to keep the range clean. . . . Zack," he said, "you're going to leave those cattle where they are. And if they've got to be slaughtered, you ain't going to try and stop us."

"A man can handle his cattle how he wants," Markley stated. "If I want to move those cattle to cleaner range, I'll do it."

"You move those cows and you'll soon learn how I keep the peace. You come into this town with a tin-plate gunman and start telling me how the place is going to be run and there's going to be trouble."

Markley dropped his cigarette and rubbed it out. "Billy Titus wouldn't like being called tin-plate, Charlie."

"Yes, and Billy Titus and his big guns are going to part company tonight or Titus leaves town," Bennett reported. "I gave him till sundown to check them with me. What kept him?"

"I reckon you'd better ask Billy." Markley smiled.

"I will, right now," Bennett said. Then he hesitated, and it seemed to Starrett that it gave him away. He had not been laying down the law so much as protesting a situation he was incompetent to handle. After a moment, the marshal turned and left the yard. There was nothing left to say. Starrett followed him.

Markley watched Ruel Starrett disappear into the darkness, and afterward the yard was silent and an edged wind whipped across the ground and the buggy horse stamped. Markley's eyes were on Ledbetter.

"You know, Zack," Ledbetter said uncomfortably, "if it is blackleg, like Starrett thinks . . . well, you don't want the whole county down on you. . . ."

Markley moved a few paces from the buggy, where Susanna had sat silently through all the conversation. He spoke quietly. "Horse," he said, "I've got a feeling for land and cattle. I don't aim to move those steers, but you don't need to tell Starrett. I'm going to be ranching Mission Creek myself, and I want it clean. I always kept it that way for Dalhart, didn't I?"

Ledbetter nodded, fascinated and dominated by the mixture of aggressiveness and good nature in Markley.

"So don't worry about what I'm going to do. All I want is a little time. I don't have to tell you how Starrett operates. You've had him putting the clamps on you for that land, haven't you?"

"It's good land, too," Ledbetter complained. "I ought to have two thousand for it."

"You'll get it," Markley assured him, "if I have to pay it myself. Now, listen. I want you to ride out to Comanche Spring with me in the morning. But you're not going to find any blackleg in my herd. Just blackwater fever. Bad, sure. But it's not going to spread until tick time, and that gives me till spring."

"Yes, but. . . ."

"But nothing! Believe me, Horse, if you change your diagnosis in a week or two and decide it is blackleg, I'll dispose of the cattle myself. Time. A little time," Markley emphasized.

Ledbetter chuckled and dug Markley's arm with his thumb. "Old Starrett will sweat, eh?"

"Sweat?" Markley said. "He'll die."

Markley mounted the buggy and drove out. They began to rattle up the steep road. Susanna spoke tensely: "Zack, you're not going to move those cattle?"

Markley laid a hand on her small, clenched fist. "I can't be telling you everything till I know whose camp you're in."

"Why did you ask me to drive down here

189

with you?"

"To talk a little."

Her eyes snapped. "The only talk I want from you, Zack, is the truth. What did Dad promise you?"

Markley tooled the buggy along over the soft ruts. "Why go over that again?"

"I'm going to talk to Lisandro," Susanna declared, "and make him tell me the truth. You're lying. You know you're lying. I should think you'd hate yourself."

"I'd hate myself if I let a bull like Starrett scare me out."

Susanna bit her lip, her eyes despising him. "How much money do you want to withdraw your claim?"

"I told you I wouldn't take less than four thousand for my part of Spade. That doesn't mean it's for sale, though."

"But you would take four thousand?" Susanna said scornfully, lifting her chin.

"You can do a lot with four thousand cash these days. But you aren't apt to dig up four thousand, Susie. Not a Dalhart. You could spend it in two days, but you could never raise it."

"Will you ever forget I'm a Dalhart? Will you ever forget to make fun of the name?"

Markley halted the buggy. His smile was gentler; his eyes had ceased to joke. "Sure.

190

When your name is Markley."

She thrust his hand away. "Oh, how can you be so . . . ?"

"How can I be in love with a girl who hasn't the business sense of a sparrow? I don't know," Markley said soberly. "Maybe that's the whole thing. Maybe you're the softness I need. Whatever it is, I want you. No," he said, shaking his head as she started to speak, "I'm not thinking about land. I'm thinking about you and me. I've been in love with you for years, but there never seemed to be a right time. But this is the right time."

"Zack, you must be as crazy as you say I am. To try to rob me of what my father left me . . . and propose to me the same night."

"I'm not trying to rob you of anything but trouble. You need me as much as I need you."

"I can't talk tonight, Zack," she said. "I'm tired."

He let the horse move out, smiling, feeling sure of something of which he had been gravely in doubt before.

VIII

Rex Starrett stabled his horse at Stockdale's. He was on his way up the street when he saw Susanna and Markley drive past. He was seized by an ague of jealousy. He had seen Markley take Susanna's hand at Ledbetter's, and that small act, coupled with the fact that Markley was actually the whole source of the girl's trouble, told him that she was doing exactly what he had predicted — she was keeping her fences mended with Markley.

Rex saw them go into the hotel. He stopped at the alley beside the large building and lighted a cigarette. He was scarcely aware of the heavy evening traffic or the mellow striking of the church bell above the town. He said to himself that, if Susanna would make such a marriage, she was not worth breaking his heart over.

In a few moments Markley came out. Rex hesitated. It was none of his business, he knew. But the shooting of his horse that morning had been, and it gave him an opening. As Markley put his foot on the step of the rig, Rex called loudly: "Markley!"

He saw Zack Markley turn fast — a tall wedge of a man with broad shoulders filling a fringed buckskin shirt, and narrow hips, and his hat on the back of his head. His body seemed to key itself as he recognized Rex, but still his hard-fleshed features bore, like a fading photograph, the expression he had worn as he had looked at Susanna. His mouth seemed disdainfully confident.

"Hello," he said, and smiled.

"I want to talk about that horse."

"What horse?"

"You ought to know." Rex crossed the alley. "The one you or Titus shot today."

Markley watched him stop a few feet away. "You talk like a bigger fool than your father."

Rex's anger was rising. "Where were you about noon?"

"I haven't given an accounting of myself since I got out of knee pants," Markley said.

Rex breathed deeply of his cigarette and tossed it away. "All right, I can check with your men. But this is between you and me. Leave Susanna alone."

Markley stared at him. Then he laughed. "Well, for Pete's sake. What are you . . . her father?"

Rex was aware of the unreasonable stand he was taking. He was too angry to care. "I'm telling you to leave her alone till this is over."

Markley raised his belt an inch, his eyes mild but watchful. "That'll be hard to do, Starrett, seeing as we just got engaged."

"That's a lie," Rex said. He felt the cold shock of it in his belly. He searched the flat, rawhide-tight features.

"Check it at the courthouse in a couple of days."

Markley turned to reënter the buggy, and Rex seized his arm.

"You're lying!"

Markley turned then, with unexpected violence, and at last it was unsheathed in his eyes — the bright, malicious savagery he had hidden like a knife. Markley's mouth stretched over his teeth in a tough, taunting grin, as he tilted forward in a balanced shift of his body. His fist flashed. Rex tried to block it with his shoulder, but the blow, with all the strength of Markley's powerful back muscles in it, smashed into his chin.

He scarcely knew he was falling until he sat heavily on the boardwalk. As he attempted to rise, he slipped over on his side and seemed to feel the walk tilting under him. He thrust his hand out to keep from sliding into the street. He was faintly conscious of pedestrians surrounding him and Markley in a tight, shouting ring.

Then his head cleared and he saw the ramrod standing over him. Markley's eyes shone with a brittle joy. Rex pushed himself up. His rage filled him as he went into Markley. He swung furiously and missed, and hooked with his left and missed again, and heard Markley say something taunting and some men in the crowd laugh, and somewhere his father seemed to lecture him disapprovingly with his time-worn advice: *Let the other fellow get mad.* But when he slowed and tried to pace himself, Markley was plunging into him again, big and brutal as a wild horse, crushing his jaw with a roundhouse swing, hurling him into the street with a hook to the ear, poising above him for a moment with the raw and bloody pride of a bare-fist boxer, but even more than the expectation of pain was the thought of Susanna — a sad and wistful regret. Rex flinched and tried to roll away as Markley's foot struck his ribs.

Rex could hear men hurrying to join the crowd around him and Markley. A buggy stopped beside the ring and its yellow carriage lamps gave a weak light to the scene — Rex, lean and dark-haired, gasping with pain on the ground, the big, buckskin-shirted form of Markley looming over him. There was blood on Markley's fists and his face had twisted like rawhide. He watched while Rex painfully came up again, his back against the yellow spokes of the buggy. The pain in Rex's chest was sharp as a knife.

Markley waited, and Rex lunged at him again, swinging a blow to the foreman's head, loosing a roundhouse right at his ear.

But Markley was strong and untouched. He stabbed Rex's belly and slashed his eye. Then he slammed a fist into his chest again, and the night turned black and Rex was drenched with weakness. He fell again, turned over, and hunched with his knees drawn up.

Then he heard a girl cry: "Stop it, Zack!"

He knew it was Susanna — as he knew instinctively that Markley was coming in again to kick him. But after a moment he looked up and saw her on the hotel steps. Markley had turned to frown at her. She ran down the steps and came through the crowd toward them. Markley pulled away as she tried to clutch his arm.

"Susanna, get away," he said.

Rex rose again, but had to hold onto the buggy wheel, a cold and desperate vacancy in him. He glanced at Susanna. Her hair had fallen in dark waves about her shoulders, as though she had already unpinned it when the noise called her from the hotel. She was attempting to bind Markley's arms to his sides, but he flung her off and approached Rex again.

Rex ducked his first swing and smashed at the foreman's face. Markley's head rocked. Rex halted him with a blow to the ear, and, when Markley stumbled, he caught him clean and hard on the mouth. Markley fell against the step plate of the buggy and crashed to the ground. He came to his hands and knees, shook his head, and spat blood. Then he came up savagely and tore the buggy whip from its socket. He doubled the lash and gripped it as a handle, making a bludgeon of the weighted stock. He started for Rex with his lips stretched tightly.

But Susanna was after the foreman in a silent fury. She caught his arm and pulled him away. "Do you have to snipe from the brush and fight like an animal?" she cried.

When Markley turned on her, his face dark with wrath, she brought her fingers down his face from the cheek to the jaw line. A pinkish cut opened on his cheek. It filled with blood, and the blood ran down and dripped onto his fringed shirt. He flung the back of his hand against Susanna's cheek. Suddenly she began to weep.

Rex started after Markley, but a man caught him and said roughly — "Now, cut it out." — and it was his father's voice.

Markley's shoulders slumped. "Susanna, I . . . I didn't aim to. . . ." Susanna turned away, but Markley clutched her arm and said: "You shouldn't have busted in. It was between him and me."

Susanna tore away from him and hurried

back to the hotel. After a moment Markley faced Rex, who stood there, his head clearing. Markley seemed scarcely to remember him. His eyes were confused. Then he shook his head.

"I didn't shoot that horse, Starrett. Ask Billy Titus where I was all afternoon."

IX

In the barbershop of Vern Bricker, who cut the hair, shaved the jowls, and minimized the facial injuries of Spanish Ford, Rex sat on a stool while Bricker surveyed him, critical as a horse buyer. Ruel Starrett slouched in the high red-plush barber chair, chewing a cigar while the barber worked.

"That ear'll be thicker'n a plug of tobacco if it ain't leeched," Bricker said. He was a small man with blond hair and a small, worried face, his forehead perpetually wrinkled, his eyes sapphire blue and merry. He conjured a lively black leech from a drawer and placed it on Rex's puffed ear.

Starrett shifted in the barber chair. "Did you get it out of Markley about the horse?"

"He said he didn't shoot it."

"Then what were you fighting about?"

"Why does a man ever fight? Because he wants to."

Starrett grunted. A small man in a high-crowned derby and gray suit entered the shop. He nodded at Bricker and was about to hang his hat on an antelope prong when he discovered Ruel Starrett, smoking his cigar in the second chair. It was Clyde Tilford. Starrett gazed at the banker as he exhaled a mouthful of smoke. Tilford, his skin looking whiter than ever, glanced at the barber.

"How long?"

"Five minutes. Just finishing up,"

Tilford glanced at Starrett. "I thought you might be down to see me today. Step outside a minute, will you? There's something you ought to know."

Starrett sauntered after him. In the chilly drive of the wind, the banker thrust his hands into his pockets. "I need that money, Starrett," he said desperately.

"You'll get it just as soon as I get it from Markley."

"Markley hasn't got it," Tilford blurted.

"He must have. He didn't give that beef herd away."

Tilford peered tensely at him. "I didn't mean that. I meant Markley personally hasn't got it."

"Who has?"

"Billy Titus, in a money belt. Zack told

me this morning. I asked him to deposit the money so you could pay the note, and he said he wasn't ready. I told him he ought to put it in a safe place, and he said it was in one . . . in Titus's keeping."

Starrett felt warmth coming up his limbs, throbbing and racing. "Is this straight?"

"Straight as a string." Tilford put a hand on Starrett's sleeve. "I want to play fair with you. I said I'd wait until Markley was back before I called in that last note. And he is back."

"You'll give me all the time I need. That was the deal."

"But I can't gamble, Starrett. I've been audited and passed, but all the money's still going out. Nothing ever comes in. And the first time anybody asks for a thousand dollars cash . . . and there's one or two like Bob Graves that still can . . . why, I'm in a fix. And if I'm in a fix, Spanish Ford's in a fix."

Starrett's eyes dreamed. "Markley says Titus has the money, eh?"

"Yes, but go easy. They say he's a wrong Injun. Marshal Bennett's ordered him to turn in his guns over some loose gun play this morning."

Starrett's eyes had a brazen shine. "He's dangerous like a cur dog." He glanced at

200

his pocket watch. "Bennett will be making the rounds pretty soon. I'll have a word with Titus before he takes his guns. I'd hate to have anybody think I was afraid of that little buzzard."

"All right, but go easy," Tilford counseled again.

Starrett did not mention to Rex what he had heard from Tilford. He felt a greater satisfaction than he had all day. He knew where Markley was keeping the ranch money, and he was certain that he had kept Rex from going with McNelly's Rangers for another day or two. The longer he could keep him here, he reasoned, the less chance there was of his leaving at all. He himself would be too deeply involved in the conflict with Markley to leave. He put his mind to the business of Titus, figuring that Bennett would tackle him about 9:00 P.M., when he hit the Indian Head.

He told Rex at dinner: "You might as well bed down at Bennett's place, since you've got your blankets."

They walked to Bennett's office, but the marshal was not there. Starrett was uneasy, having planned to catch him before he left. Suddenly Rex said: "He's taken the manacles."

Starrett glanced at the wall behind the

desk, where a shotgun was racked, together with a rifle and some souvenirs of forgotten badmen. The manacles were gone. But wanting Rex out of it, he said: "Well, what's that prove? This is a big night, with the Spade boys back. See here," he ordered sternly, "that rib of yours may be cracked, where Markley kicked you. You'll do yourself no good parading around. Spread your blankets here and get some sleep. I'll talk Bennett into forgetting Titus tonight."

To his surprise, Rex did not debate it. He knew then that Markley had hurt him worse than he had admitted.

Rex told him earnestly: "But get to Charlie before he tackles Titus. He's no match for that Kansas gunslick."

X

Starrett drifted up the street, visiting a couple of saloons patronized by teamsters and boatmen. He moved to the Indian Head and stopped outside the saloon. Transparent paper glued over the windowpanes gave an illusion of frosted glass. Inside, a piano clattered and there was a muted clamor of men laughing and talking. Starrett passed the stage lamp beside the door and was about to enter when he saw a man approaching from above. Even in the dark, he knew the heavy-shouldered form of Marshal Bennett, and he felt quick relief.

"Big night, Marshal," he greeted.

"Big enough." Bennett's jaw molded into a hard line.

When the marshal pushed the slatted door aside, Starrett said: "Titus is in there, I think."

Bennett gazed at him with sad anger. "Do I look old and incompetent enough to need help, Starrett?"

"I didn't say that. But I've got a score to settle with Titus, too. Suppose you get in line."

Bennett gazed off over the dark roof tops of Spanish Ford. "This town has never had any real trouble in the twelve years I've marshaled it. I've drawn my pay for serving notices on people who couldn't pay their taxes and locking up drunken cowboys. Titus is here to make trouble. It's my job to dehorn him. I've never needed a wet nurse before, and I don't need one now."

"Oh, I never said . . . ," began Starrett.

But the marshal had entered the saloon. Starrett followed and took the first heavy breath of air cautiously — the tobacco smoke, the dust, the fumes of bullwhackers' sweat and liquor. Bennett stood just ahead of him, at the end of the long bar that ran down into the congestion and smoke of the room. Game tables filled most of the room and the walls were covered with colored lithographs of Indian fights and fat nudes, with a rogues' gallery behind the bar of dead outlaws lying rigidly in undertakers' back rooms. There was a door at the rear that led into the dance hall, from which came the stringed disaster of a mechanical piano and the slightly tipsy laughter of Joe LaPorte's girls. LaPorte was talking to Bennett.

Starrett followed their gaze to a table where Zack Markley sat with Billy Titus and two other men. Tilted back in a chair, Titus was playing solitaire while the others talked. His hat was on the back of his head; his blond hair fell forward onto his brow. He was smiling to himself. Starrett saw that Markley had a bruise under his eye and a long scratch on one cheek. He was surly-eyed and restless, and the hand lying on the table by his drink was cramped into a fist.

"He ain't making any trouble," LaPorte said. "Why don't you leave well enough alone?"

"I told him to check his guns with me by sundown."

"Going to give you some advice, Charlie.

Billy won't take any sass. He's a tough boy. A good boy, but tough."

"Good, hell! I'll give you some advice too. Keep yours for people who want it." Bennett started through the tables.

LaPorte saw Ruel Starrett then. He gave him a stare of dislike. "Something?"

"Whiskey," Starrett said.

He saw Titus's eyes come up to find the marshal and begin to burn with a wicked pleasure. Suddenly he wished he could stop it. He could see no end for Bennett but catastrophe. *I could horn in,* he speculated. But this was Bennett's party, and no one in the world could help him.

Bennett stopped at Zack Markley's table. The ex—Spade ramrod glanced up with a taunting expression. Titus rocked on the back legs of the chair, waiting.

"Pretty good with those guns, ain't you, Titus?" Bennett snapped.

"Been told so."

"You know who doesn't appreciate your sharpshooting? Bob Stockdale . . . the man whose livery barn you shot up. He signed a complaint this afternoon for malicious mischief."

"Can't he take a joke?" Markley cut in.

"Not when it costs him nine dollars and forty-six cents. I want your guns," Bennett stated bluntly.

Titus's small mouth with its crowded gopher teeth grinned. "No dice."

Starrett saw the red creeping up the back of Bennett's neck. He looked at the empty sleeve and the thick, old-man's fingers of his right hand, and turned his back on the scene.

"Markley, does this fellow work for you?" Bennett asked.

"He will, as soon as I'm in business."

"Then you'd better tell him to turn in his guns. You don't want the reputation of hiring a bunch of bad actors, do you?"

"I don't care what people think, just so my boys can rope a steer."

"Rope a steer," the marshal retorted, "or handle a Colt?"

"I don't hold any skill against a man."

The room had begun to quiet. In the hush, the mechanical piano rang strenuously and in the far room a girl called something in a shrill voice.

"I want your guns, Titus," the marshal said.

Balanced on the rear legs of his chair, Billy Titus held his grin — a glittering-eyed lynx on a branch, poised and impatient. "Better take 'em, then, uncle. I ain't giving them up."

Starrett turned quickly from the bar. There was an expanding force of fury in his head. He stared at Zack Markley with poisonous contempt for permitting this shaming of a one-armed old man by a banty rooster of a killer.

Bennett's voice came at last. It was baffled and truculent. "I . . . I'll give you till ten o'clock tomorrow night then to leave town. That's the last. I won't have trash like you cluttering Spanish Ford while I'm marshal. Do you understand? Ten o'clock . . . or jail."

When Bennett came back through the tables, his eyes were stony with the heat of an anger that had been turned in upon itself. Suddenly Starrett's pity and rage exploded. He shoved away from the bar and started across the room.

"Stick around," he told Bennett as he passed.

"Cut it out," Bennett said tensely. "I'll do this myself or quit."

"No, I'm setting them up this time. Watch."

He kept his eyes on Titus's face, waiting for the instant when the gunman knew that he was coming after him. He could see the tension suddenly run through Titus. He observed him straighten and come to an edge like a fleshing knife. Starrett flicked a glance at Markley and caught the relish in his eyes, and he thought: *He didn't plant that money on Titus for nothing. This is a trap.* But no trap was stronger than its spring, and Titus was the spring of this one.

All at once Titus rapped: "Hold it, uncle!" He laid his hands on his thighs near the grips of his Colts.

Starrett walked on through the tables with his teeth gleaming in a smile. He stopped behind Markley's chair, a stride from Titus's. He rested his hand on Markley's shoulder and felt the ramrod tighten.

"Seems to me the toughest things about you," he told him, "are a herd of sick cattle and an apprentice gunslick."

"What do you want?" Markley asked.

"The money Titus is carrying," Starrett said. "It belongs to Spade."

"What the hell are you talking about?" Titus snarled.

"The gold in your money belt. I'll get a court order for it someday, but as long as I'm here. . . ."

"Get out," Titus snapped.

Starrett moved as though to advance. Titus's eyes flinched. "I told you to get out. If you fool with me, you'll go out a tame Injun."

"Temper, Billy," cautioned Starrett.

"Stand up, now, son, and pull out your shirt tail."

Across the room, a man chuckled, and there was a rustling of men craning to watch. Titus's face flushed. In bafflement, he flashed a glance at Zack Markley. "Do I have to kill this fellow to show him I mean something?"

"Maybe you better, Billy," Starrett said. "You know what I think? I think you shot a mangy dog somewhere and thought it was Billy the Kid. I think you're yellow as a sunflower. You wouldn't have the guts to shoot me if you had those Colts in your hands right now."

Only the muscles in Titus's jaws gave him away. They flicked like whips, and then he let the chair drop onto its four feet and his guns were halfway out of their holsters. Someone shouted a warning and a chair crashed. The men behind Starrett began to sprawl out of line.

Starrett jumped like a cougar. He landed on Billy Titus. He clutched both Titus's guns, and, when they came from their holsters, one of them blasted into the floor. The bullet struck a table leg and scattered sawdust and the lamps flickered. Men scuttled away like crabs. Starrett wrenched the guns from Titus's hands and tossed them aside. Then he seized Titus's hands. Titus bucked and tried to tear away, but Starrett roared his laughter into his face and held him there.

"Hey, Billy!" he shouted. "Is that the way you tamed Wichita? Why, I had a sick 'possum once that was faster than you!"

Titus was sweating pure venom. His eyes were cold as a snake's and he was the color of suet as he twisted and pulled, but his hundred and thirty pounds could not stir Starrett's bulk. Starrett began to squeeze the slender bones in his grasp. He saw the quick pain twist Titus's face.

"All right, cut it out," Titus gasped.

"No, no," Starrett protested. "If I let you go, you might bite. I don't know what they do up in Wichita, but I reckon they don't use guns. At least, Billy," he said softly, "I reckon you ain't going to use your guns around here, if that's what Mister Markley was counting on."

Titus cried out and smashed his knee into Starrett's groin. Starrett groaned with pain, and his rage flooded out of his heart and into his hands, and they convulsed as he crushed the gunman's fingers. Titus went to his knees, crying out once and then slumping. Starrett released him and stood back, his hands over his groin. His face had gone sallow.

"Get up," he snapped.

Titus looked at his guns and turned his hands over and inspected them. He tried to move his fingers. Then his eyes came to Starrett with pain and fear and hatred. After a moment, he arose, his features white.

"Pull out your shirt tail and give me that money belt," ordered Starrett.

Markley rose, now, and looked at Titus with cold contempt as the gunman pulled up his shirt. The white, skinny midriff was bare. Disappointment came sourly into Starrett.

"I should've known," he snorted, "that nobody would trust you with a rusty beer token, let alone fifteen hundred dollars." He stared at Markley. "I'll have that money, and quick. Hang around this town a while and you'll learn things about Ruel Starrett."

Markley's hands clenched his gun belt. His emotions were in hand like the reins of a wild team, but they were there — taut and dangerous.

He told Starrett: "And if you ever come at me like that, you'll learn something about Zack Markley."

Starrett turned his back on him to face the room. "How many of you men know

211

Markley's running blackleg on the community pasture?" he asked. In their faces he read that they had all heard it, but no one answered him. "How many of you will go with me tomorrow on a quicklime party?"

No one replied. A rancher named Bob Graves picked up his drink and sipped it, gazing mildly at Starrett. Anger whipped through Starrett. "What's the matter with you? Do you want this plague to sweep you all into the ash can?"

Graves shrugged. "That's quite a distance from me, Starrett. I'd just as lief wait a spell. No sense in ruining a man if it ain't called for."

Starrett glared at the rancher's back as he turned away, and swept the other half-amused faces with his wrath, but he held his outburst, thinking oddly of Rex's warning that, if he ever needed a friend, he would not find him in Spanish Ford. *Well, damn them,* he thought, *Starrett never crawled for help before, and he won't start now.*

He started out. At the bar he recognized the familiar lean shape of old Lisandro Garza, the Spade cowboy. Garza's raisin-brown face was drawn, rake-thin, and yet somehow aristocratic.

"Ain't you been to confession yet, *hombre*?" asked Starrett ironically.

"No, *señor*."

"What's the matter . . . didn't you commit any sins on that trail drive? Didn't you get wicked up in Wichita?"

Garza's thin fingers turned his glass. "No."

"Or tell any lies? You can't go to Mass if you told any lies, can you? Tomorrow's a feast day, ain't it?"

Garza looked at his liquor. "I make my own peace, thank you."

"But if you mean to repeat the lie Markley paid you for," Starrett persisted, "you can't take the Sacrament, can you? You're getting to be a purely old fellow, Lisandro. What if you die after lying about my land?"

Garza turned and walked down the bar. Starrett laughed and walked out.

A few minutes after Starrett had left, Markley stood up. "Let's go, Billy."

Billy Titus, sickly with pain, had been anesthetizing himself with whiskey. Wild deeps of anger burned in his face. He took the half-finished bottle of corn whiskey and shoved it in his coat pocket. As they passed out of the saloon, he glared challengingly at anyone who looked at him, his hands on the butts of his guns.

Once on the walk, he turned on Markley, shouting: "Damn him, Zack! I could have

213

given him two seconds and beat him to the draw."

Markley started down the street. "He could give you two minutes and beat you now, Billy. I thought you said you could handle those things."

He glanced in scornful amusement at the cowboy. He knew that all Titus had was his gun prowess; he was merely a half-shaped man with great vacancies in his soul, of which no one was more aware than Titus. His guns were all he had to make up for them.

Titus began recounting what he planned to do to Starrett — gut-shoot him as he came from the stable; ambush him on the range — but Markley drawled: "And get yourself hung? Billy, if you're going to work with me, you'll have to play it smarter than that."

"How?" Titus begged, full of pain, whiskey, and chagrin.

"I'll come to that. The thing to do now is to get your hands looked at. Then you ought to get some sleep."

"What about Starrett?" Titus demanded.

"Well, let's just say we'll hit him where it hurts worst. His land."

"You really figure you can whip him out of it?"

"With a little help from the right people," Markley said. "You're one of them, Billy. We'll get you squared away now and fix you up with a hotel room. You can pay me back tomorrow night."

He had Titus's hands treated by a doctor. The middle finger on his right hand was broken and a knuckle on his left was badly dislocated. Afterward he installed him in a side-street hotel with his bottle of whiskey. Then he walked back to the main street. He stood beneath a wooden awning and frowned up at the windows of the hotel. One of them would be Susanna's. He felt a pang of guilt as he recalled the way she had looked at him after he'd slapped her.

Well, it would not influence a thing. When he wanted her, she would come, yet his guilt and dissatisfaction lingered, taking the edge off everything. For she would come with contempt and a heart closed to him. He would never have her in the way a man wanted a woman; always it would be there between them — the knowledge that he had broken her like a horse.

Markley had a mounting awareness that this ambition of his was like a spoiled mistress — wheedling, coaxing, demanding — but never to be denied. And he reflected ironically that only one man in Spanish

Ford could understand such an ambition —
Ruel Starrett.

XI

Late the next morning Susanna left the
National Road Hotel. It was a day of cold
wind, sharp shadows, and leaves rattling
along in ruts. She had risen early, read in a
little prayer book, and then, needing something to break the mood that was on her,
walked down to Grooms's Emporium and
selected material for two new gowns. She
picked out patterns. She asked that the
charge be made to the ranch account, and
carried the material and patterns to her
dressmaker. After leaving instructions, she
walked back to the main street, twirling her
parasol.

Walking to the hotel, she caught the
glances of several women directed at her.
One of them she recognized as Mrs. Tompkins, wife of the new physician in town. She
resented their attention. *Slapped her in front
of everyone,* they would be whispering.
Fighting over her. Can you imagine?

She wished desperately there were something she could do, some gesture, to show
them she wasn't frightened by it all. Of
course they would soon know she was hav-

ing two gowns made of the dearest material in Spanish Ford. But what she needed most, she began to realize, was friends. But the women had never made overtures to her, and in retaliation she had not joined in their church doings and sewing circles. As she approached the hotel, she saw that the women had halted on the walk.

To her surprise, Mrs. Tompkins spoke with a quick, warm smile: "Good morning, Miss Dalhart. I hope you're well?"

"Very well, thank you. And you?"

Awkwardly they passed the time of day. Then Mrs. Tompkins said, her fair skin flushing: "We think something should be done, Susanna. It was shameful."

Embarrassed, Susanna faltered: "You mean . . . ?"

"Scandalous," the other woman said. "Why don't you bring charges against him?"

Susanna smiled. "Why, it would take someone bigger than Mister Markley to enforce the charges, and it would be hard to find anyone. And I really think he acted entirely on impulse."

"Yes, but . . . right on the street," said Mrs. Tompkins. "Why, if one rowdy goes scotfree, it would soon come to the point where. . . ."

"If I could settle all the ranch's difficulties

with a slap or two," Susanna told her, "I'd consider myself fortunate."

It was the first time a Dalhart had ever admitted that things were less than perfect with the ranch, she realized, and she was instantly sorry she had said it. Yet the women seemed genuinely sympathetic.

"Everyone's having his difficulties, I suppose," Mrs. Tompkins said. "If we can do anything . . . anything at all." She smiled.

"Thank you," Susanna said. "You're very, very kind." She watched her walk on with the others. *Why, I think she meant it,* she told herself. She liked Mrs. Tompkins's smile. *I should have called her Missus Doctor Tompkins,* she thought. *She would have liked it.*

As she turned to start up the hotel steps, she saw a Mexican cowboy jogging in from the alley. She recognized him with a small thrill of excitement.

"Lisandro!" she called.

Lisandro Garza shot her a sidelong glance and swerved his pony up the street. Susanna raised her voice angrily. "Lisandro, come here at once!"

Lisandro returned, dark-skinned, shy-eyed, guilty. He sat above her with his hat against his belly. " *'Uenas días, señorita.*"

"Good morning? Is that all you can say, after being away for months?"

He dug at his ear. *"Saludos,"* he added. "I hope you are in good health, *señorita.*"

"Not very good, Lisandro. I worry so much about what will happen to the ranch. Have you heard about the terrible quarrel Zack and Mister Starrett are having?"

In the cool morning, he began to perspire lightly, nodding and chewing his mustache all at one. "A pity."

"Such a pity. And one that is all based on a lie. Your lie, Lisandro."

"Mine, *señorita*?"

"Lisandro, tell me the truth . . . mind, I said the *truth.* What did my father promise Zack Markley?"

Lisandro pondered. "Well, you know I am pretty old man, Mees Susanna. Sometimes I don't remember so good."

"Oh. You aren't sure about it, then?"

"Yes, I am sure . . . that is for saying, I try hard to remember, and . . . and it seems like. . . ."

Susanna let silence pile up on the cowboy's head. "I hope," she said, "that you'll remember better than this before the hearing tomorrow. Will you do that for me? It would be a great pity if men were killed because you had lied, wouldn't it?"

Lisandro bowed his head. "I don't tell a lie, *señorita,*" he muttered.

Walking thoughtfully into the hotel, Susanna told herself that he was lying. Faithful old Lisandro was lying. But a Mexican of his caliber never lied. An honest Mexican was more trustworthy than an American six days of the week. Why should Lisandro lie?

With a vague hope of finding an answer, Susanna sat down by a window with her prayer book again.

Marshal Bennett did not visit his office until late. Rex had risen, breakfasted, and returned to the office before he appeared. Rex heard him dismounting in the rear. He wondered how he might bring cheer to the marshal, who had been humiliated before his town. The fact that Billy Titus's fangs had been drawn would be little comfort.

Bennett approached the door. For the matter of that, thought Rex, he was not the man to bring cheer to anyone. There was the steady, grinding misery of recalling Markley's words: *We just got engaged.*

Let her go, Rex told himself. *You knew she'd do it anyway.*

He wished that he knew how to fight it — this obsession with a girl, this irrational need for her. She would marry Markley, and Markley would break her, not understanding her and not caring why she did the illogical things she did.

He gazed out the window into the raw daylight. Behind Stockdale's barn he could see his horse eating hay. It reminded him that McNelly would be taking his Ranger company out today, deserting the camp south of town, and he wished desperately that he were going with them. Why couldn't he lead the horse until it was ready to ride, using whatever he could stir up as a mount until then?

Bennett came in, grunted a hello, and pulled a pair of manacles from the pocket of his coat. He hung them on the wall with a sour smile. "The fighting marshal of Spanish Ford."

"Cut it out. You never claimed you were a fighting marshal. But you've kept the peace here all these years. If Dad hadn't tamed him, you'd have taken him yourself today."

"Would I? I doubt it. I'd have given him till tonight, and tonight I'd have given him till tomorrow."

"He's just a four-bit gunslick, and now we know he isn't even much good with his guns. Let it go. Charlie" — Rex smiled suddenly — "I think I've got this horse thing licked."

"How's that?"

"Will you lend me that brown of yours for

a week?"

"Sure, but how will that help you? He's weak in the paster' joints and too old for anything but straight ridin'."

"Straight riding's all I want out of him. My bay will lead for a week, and by that time I can ride him again."

The marshal began to nod. "That's it, Rex. That's it." Then they were silent, and Rex grinned at Bennett, and Bennett nodded.

"Gonna miss you, though," he said.

"I'll miss you, Charlie. Wish you were coming along." Rex glanced into the street. "I'll have to move. The bay's got to be shod. I can leave your horse with your relatives in Trinity, can't I? One of them will be coming up before long."

Bennett watched him kneel and quickly roll his blankets. "You know, you never quite made it straight to me why you're leavin'. Just can't hit it off with your father, is that it?"

Rex hesitated. "That's part of it."

"What's the rest?"

Rex sat back on his heels. "Ever love a girl you couldn't get, Charlie?"

Bennett smiled — the smile of an older, understanding man for a young one suffering a malady of the young. "I reckon there's

222

a woman in every man's life that he thinks about once in a while, long after he couldn't even tell you what color eyes she had."

"This girl's are gray, Charlie. She's beautiful. And sweet, most of the time. It's the times she's not that bother me."

"Why don't you marry her, then, and sweeten her up? Maybe marriage is all she needs."

"I haven't got a dowry, and this girl comes high. She wants Texas for a ranch and heaven for a buck pasture. If she ever marries for love . . . well, it will just be coincidence." He knotted a rope about the bedroll and stood up. "I suppose it seems mean, walking out on my father this way. But I can't even buy the kind of fight he's going to make. If I knew Markley was ringing in marked cards on him, it would be different. But the main thing is, I've just got to get out. If I stuck around here till Susanna married Markley, I'd probably kill them both. So I'm getting out."

"Good luck," Bennett said. "See you before you go?"

"Sure, Charlie. And don't worry about Titus. Nobody else thought anything about it at all."

He went out. The weather was turning. Horses at hitch racks humped their backs and a dog slinking along the walk had his tail between his legs. It was a day for departures, a day for pulling your hat brim down, and saying good bye to towns you didn't like. Rex started across the street.

Near the foot of the road, a horse jogged in from the east and came up the street. The wind whipped its dust away. The rider had wrapped a scarf around his head to protect his ears and had anchored it with a high-crowned gray derby. It was Horse Ledbetter, the veterinarian. To the cantle of his saddle was tied a linen sack of instruments. He turned into the livery stable ahead of Rex.

Rex was intrigued, for it was early for Ledbetter to be coming in from a call. He thought of the diseased cattle at Comanche Spring, and quickened his stride to reach the barn. In the straw-littered gloom of the livery stable Ledbetter was dismounting, while Bob Stockdale held his horse.

"That's too early a ride for this child, Bob. Out to Comanche Spring and back already."

"What'd you find?"

"Not a lot, Bob, not a lot. Sick cattle, all right. But I figure I can save most of them."

"What are you calling it?"

Rex moved into the barn and stood listening near the door.

Ledbetter chuckled. "I'm like a doctor, Bob. Never give a thing a name till the patient dies of it." Then he asked: "Tom Goss in town?"

"No. Goss is running Markley's range camp, ain't he?"

"Not no more, he ain't. Zack fired him this morning. Didn't like how Goss was running things. Thought Goss might have rode in."

"Oh, Zack went out, too?"

"Him and me rode out together." Now he heard Rex cross the floor. He drew his mouth into a grin. "Hello, son."

"So you won't give a name to it," Rex said.

Ledbetter spread his hands. "You never know at this stage. Little fever, gassy pockets . . . could be lots of things."

"Could be blackleg, couldn't it?"

Ledbetter picked up the stained sack of instruments. "Could be 'most anything, but. . . ."

"This state," Rex said, "would just about lynch a man who let a plague wipe out half its beef herds. Is it blackleg?"

Ledbetter's muddy features fumbled. "I ain't a-goin' to say till I know, Rex."

They heard footfalls approaching from the street. The sunlight was cut off by two men who entered quickly. One was his father,

225

Rex saw, and the other was Tom Goss.

Goss peered into the gloom and grunted: "There he is."

Rex watched his father walk forward, catch Ledbetter by the shirt, and throw his palm against the veterinarian's cheek. Ledbetter tried to pull away, but Starrett slapped him with the back of his hand, and then with the palm again, and kept this up until Ledbetter covered his face. Finally he hurled him against a stanchion and let him stumble away.

He turned and faced them all. "This louse-bitten fool isn't about to ruin me while I can still fire a rifle. Rex, are you going with me?"

"What's the matter?" Rex asked.

Goss said: "Zack gave orders this morning to move his cattle across Mission Creek. They're moving them right now."

"But not onto my land," Starrett snapped.

"What are you going to do?" Rex asked.

"I told Markley before. I'd quicklime any cow he moved onto me. And I told Garth something he seems to have forgotten, too."

Rex looked into his face and knew he meant it. He would kill Garth if he tried to prevent his slaughtering the cattle. He had a long, yearning thought about the Rangers, knowing that if he went with his father, it might be too late to catch up. But these were the marked cards he had told Charlie he would fight over. He made his decision. He asked Stockdale for a rent horse, and the liveryman took a saddle and blanket from a rack and walked to a stall.

Starrett thanked him with a surprised glance. Then he told Goss: "That job's still open."

Goss stood with his straw sombrero on the side of his head, a poor man who wore his independence proudly. "I'd like it, Mister Starrett. But not starting now."

"It's now or not at all."

"All I know about you is hearsay. What I've heard hasn't all been good. I'd take the job, because, if it got rough, I could always quit. But I couldn't quit being dead if this carbine roundup of yours goes wrong."

"You're still looking for work, then, cowboy." Starrett glanced at his son. "Is Bennett at his office?"

"You're not going to drag Charlie into this."

"Drag, hell! He's the law, ain't he? He told me last night he was with me if Markley tried to cross Mission Creek."

"Charlie's the law, but the law doesn't say a man can't move cattle onto his own land. And if the ruling goes against you tomorrow, then Charlie's lost his job. Leave him out."

Rex saw him weigh it in his mind. The possibility of taking Bennett along, against the certainty that Rex would drop out. In the end, he said: "All right. I'm going up and order a wagonload of quicklime sent out there. Ready in ten minutes."

Starrett strode to Grooms's Emporium and gave his order. He bought a box of .56-50 cartridges, broke it open on the counter, and stuffed the shells into his pockets. He wished Rex had been willing to let Bennett go along. Yet even more than Bennett's badge, he wanted Rex with him. It was working out as he had hoped. Markley was showing his hand. And now he had only one vague worry about Rex's leaving, and that was three copper shells lying by a cow trail on Spade, at the spot where he had made the shot that had dropped Rex's horse. Of course there was little likelihood of their being discovered, but Bennett had stated his intention of investigating the shooting. A .56-50 was not an ordinary caliber, and it might look bad.

He got his horse from the hotel barn and rode back to the livery stable. Rex was waiting. Up and down the street the word had gone; Starrett saw the curious eyes watching them. He loaded his rifle in full view of everyone, rammed it in the boot, and said: "Let's go."

They took the river trail, followed it a mile, and cut south on a deer trace to the heart of the community pasture. Comanche Spring was an hour's ride. He and Rex did not converse. In a little over an hour they came to the ridge above Garth's camp.

"They've taken off, all right," Starrett declared.

The camp was deserted. Except for three cattle in the corral, too sick to drive, the herd had vanished. Starrett felt an uprush of mortal fear. In his mind he saw his Brahmas and the Spade mother herd rotting with plague. As they passed the camp, he angrily threw his rope over Garth's deer-hide tent and dragged it and all the haberdashery of Garth's living into the brush.

After that, he headed straight for Mission Creek, pushing the horses hard. The trail was plain enough. Across the range with its exhausted meadows the cattle were driving toward Spade. Starrett swung onto a long ridge that paralleled Garth's line of march. Finally he pointed with his rifle, and a half mile ahead Rex saw the herd stringing down a rocky valley that emptied out in the creek. Starrett's face was sallow with rage.

"Take it easy," Rex counseled him. "If there's going to be any shooting, let Garth start it."

Starrett quirted his pony. When he came abreast of the herd, Rex was a hundred yards behind. Starrett glared down on the scene. Swinging ropes unhurriedly, Clay Garth and two other cowpunchers drifted in the rear of the cattle. Garth had a limp wheat-straw cigarette in his lips. He rode, erect and high-shouldered.

Starrett glanced around as Rex came up. The hillside was rocky. "Light down and get set in those rocks. Cover me while I go down. I'll lay the gad to the cattle. If Garth gets in my way, that's his own look-out."

Rex swung down. He placed himself in the rocks and laid his carbine in position. Starrett bucked down the stony hillside. He saw Clay Garth's head suddenly turn toward him. The tall cowboy's cragged face stiffened. Garth dropped his coil of rope over his saddle horn and pulled his rifle. He shouted at the others, and came loping along the flank of the herd to cut Starrett off. Starrett surged ahead of him and turned the point of the herd. He could see the gaunt heads of the infected cattle — their mouths swollen, strings of saliva trailing.

Garth's voice cracked like a rifle: "Get

away from those beef cattle!"

Starrett snapped his gun to his shoulder and began firing into the herd. A big roany longhorn went to its knees. Starrett fired at another steer, and it crashed down. The herd broke. Starrett lunged his horse at them and got the herd turned back on itself. Then he veered toward Garth, and that was when he saw that the man had dismounted and stood by his pony with his saddle gun raised to his shoulder.

A jolt of fear shook him. Garth, his long, stony features expressionless, stood perfectly still, like a hunter in the final instant before his shot. Starrett swung his rifle, rushing to catch up. Yet he knew it was too late, and he stiffened himself against the tearing impact of the bullet, thinking: *This is how Rex covers a man.*

Then he saw Garth stumble forward, dropping his gun and reaching toward the earth with both hands. Garth's head hung. He looked like a very tired man falling to the ground. But at that moment the rolling crash of a carbine reached the valley floor. Starrett saw the dark smear of powder smoke against the hillside. Garth fell and rolled over and lay on his back with one knee drawing up. High in the rocks, Rex came to his feet. His gun was directed now

231

at the two cowpunchers coming along the foot of the hill.

Starrett turned his horse broadside and covered the men with his rifle. "Party's over, boys! Hold it right there!"

The men halted and held a consultation, staring up the hill at Rex.

Starrett shouted again: "Take your man and get!"

The men reined up beside Clay Garth and stared down at him. He lay still now on the henna earth, under the heatless winter sun. His hat was beside him. The muzzle of his rifle lay near his outflung hand. One of the cowboys dismounted to examine him. He looked up, gazing at Starrett silently.

"Is he dead?"

"Dead as a tick." The man's face had a yellow tinge under its sunburn; he wore a short reddish beard and long sideburns.

"I hope you noticed," Starrett said, "that he threw down on me before I fired."

"You didn't fire. It was the fellow up the hill."

"He was shooting into the herd. I shot Garth when he threw down on me."

"His gun ain't been fired."

"If it had been, I'd be dead instead of him. I told Garth. I told Markley, too. Where's Markley?" he demanded.

232

"Went back to town after Ledbetter left."

On the hillside, Rex was still standing with his carbine ready. Starrett's jaw muscles tensed. *I wish I'd been the one to kill Garth,* he thought. *Maybe they really believe I was.* "Load him onto his horse," he said.

The cowboy shrugged and glanced at his companion, who dismounted and went to unsaddling Garth's pony. Starrett observed them loading Garth across the horse. The horse fought as they worked. They controlled him in grim silence.

When they were ready to leave, Starrett said: "Take him to town. What's your name?" he asked the man with the chestnut beard.

"Milt Howard. You're Starrett, eh?"

Starrett grinned. "See you in court, Howard."

Rex came down the hill as the men left. He looked sick, and Starrett thought of all the green recruits he had led into battle in the war. Rex stared at the dark, soaked earth where Garth had lain, until his father cleared his throat.

"Look at it this way. I'd be dead if you hadn't shot him. Now, let's get that herd back where it was."

But Starrett's guilt rode him. There would be a hell of a row over the killing. He wished he had not dragged Rex into it. He was not sure what to expect when he returned to town. A warrant for his and Rex's arrest or an ambuscade on Front Street. It disturbed him, until at last he told Rex: "There's no sense in your staying around. It would be a good time for you to take off with the Rangers, if you're still bound to go. I'll square this with Bennett. They think I shot Garth anyway."

"If I take off, there'll be a posse after me in an hour. We've got to face this down. Why did you tell them you'd shot him?"

"This is still my fight. Now, you keep your mouth shut when we talk to Bennett. There comes the wagon with the quicklime," he said. "Let's get these brutes in the corrals and go to work."

XII

The rumor that Starrett and Rex had left Spanish Ford came to Susanna as she was eating lunch in the hotel. Three men — two merchants and Clyde Tilford — were having cigars and brandy near her.

"It's no different legally than if they were to shoot your horse in the street," Tilford declared.

"Legalities be damned!" another man

said. "If somebody don't dispose of those cattle, they're going to spread the plague all over Texas."

"Maybe not. Cold weather comin'. Markley could argue that, anyway."

Susanna dropped her napkin and approached Tilford's table. The men started to rise, but she smiled and begged them to be seated.

"Forgive my listening. Do I understand that Mister Starrett has gone out to destroy Zack Markley's cattle?"

"Yes, ma'am. Think he'd consult his partner first, wouldn't you? Or are you a purely silent partner?"

"That's beside the point. It seems to me that Marshal Bennett's order not to move his cattle would put Mister Markley in the wrong."

"That's a nice theory. But what if Markley puts up a fight when Starrett hits the herd?"

Susanna's heart thumped. "I thought Zack was in town."

"No. He rode out with Horse Ledbetter this morning."

Susanna felt sick and suffocated. "Good day, gentlemen."

She hurried down the hall to her room. Once there, she lay crumpled on the bed, wanting to weep, but finding only dry, choking terror within her. "Rex, Rex," she gasped. Her mind tried to elude the horror that sought to close it in, but she kept seeing a wagon rumbling into town with a man lying under tow sacking. When they pulled the covering from his face, it was Rex. She thought desperately of ways to prevent the violence that lay like a shadow over Spanish Ford. But there was nothing she could do but wait.

About 4:00, with the sun throwing its last gold rays into her room, she heard a commotion in the street. A man shouted and there was a murmur of voices and the hard strike of boots on the walks. Susanna hurried to the window. Then, shocked, she leaned against the frame of the window.

A small crowd of men had formed before the marshal's office. Three horses stood there. The body of a man was lashed across one of them. Two men were untying him, and she could hear shouts running up and down the street. Susanna turned away, covering her face.

At last she heard a name called distinctly, and, hearing it repeated several times, she knew Clay Garth was the man who had been killed. Relief poured over her. Yet all the sinister echoes of the scene remained.

She walked to the armoire and took down her Bible. She sat on the bed and tried to lose herself in the words. But all she understood was what her mind kept saying: *If it weren't for you, he wouldn't have been killed.*

When she gazed down on Front Street again, it was dusk. Lights burned along the steep street. There was a great traffic in and out of the Indian Head Saloon. She could see several men before the marshal's office. Still the Starretts had not returned.

Directly across from the hotel a man stood in the alcove of the gun shop. She saw a rifle leaning against the wall beside him. Then she made out the white blur of a bandaged hand, and, as surely as she knew that it was Billy Titus, she knew that Zack would be standing on this side of the street. Suddenly she knew what she must do. She felt almost calm. After rubbing her cheeks with a towel to bring the color, she went downstairs. She asked the clerk to send for Zack Markley.

"Why, he's right . . . sure, ma'am, I'll fetch him myself."

Susanna waited in a chair by the alley window. Markley could not have been far. He came in a moment, carrying a carbine and looking sober and intent. He wore a short canvas jacket and chaps, as though he had been riding, and an unlighted cigarette was tucked over his ear. His hat was tilted forward and to one side. When he saw Susanna, he took the chair beside her.

"Heard the news, I expect."

"Yes. Zack, what are you going to do?"

"That's up to Starrett."

"Then what's the gun for?"

He turned his stolid gray eyes on her. "Why did you send for me?"

"Because I have something to say. But you must tell me first what happened."

"Starrett shot Garth when he tried to save my cattle. Milt Howard and the other fellow backed down to him."

"Were you moving the cattle onto Spade?"

"No. I gave orders for Garth to move them to a new spot on the community graze, after Ledbetter said it was only blackwater fever. But I told Garth not to take them across Mission Creek, and Milt says Garth didn't."

"Zack, that wasn't fair. You tricked Starrett into killing them."

"Into wiping out the herd I'd been building for years? That joke would be on me."

"But you knew they had to be destroyed. You planned this whole thing to put him in a bad light at the hearing."

"Maybe there won't have to be a hearing."

"If you mean to remove your opposition by killing it, you'd better be careful. Suppose they find that Garth fired on Starrett first?"

"Is that all you wanted to say to me?" Markley squinted down the barrel of his gun.

"No. I want to buy you out. Will you still take four thousand dollars?"

Markley turned his head in surprise. "Where did you get four thousand dollars?"

"I haven't. But I know where I can raise it."

"Where?"

"From Joe LaPorte, at the Indian Head."

Markley tilted his head back and laughed. "All the gamblin' Dalharts aren't dead, after all. You mean you're going over there and try to fleece that fox out of his brush?"

"No. I'm going to ask him to come to the game room here. I don't mean to gamble, exactly. Just to cut cards with him. I'd have as much chance as he would."

"Susie" — Markley chuckled — "LaPorte will walk out of here with your interest in the ranch . . . that's what'll happen." He smiled at her determination. "There's an easier way to save yourself, if that's what you're thinking of."

Susanna rose. She gazed down stiffly.

"Will you take four thousand?"

Markley rubbed his chin. He seemed to gaze into a darkness he could not quite fathom; he shifted in his chair.

"I reckon I'd be tempted beyond myself. But don't forget what I said last night." He reached for her hand. "Forget LaPorte, Susanna. Forget Starrett. Think about you and me. You know what I said, though. If we get married, it will have to be pretty quick. I don't want people saying you married me just to save yourself."

"If I ever do marry you, Zack, that's exactly why it will be. You may as well understand that."

Markley's head turned. He tilted his ear to the window. Susanna heard the horses then. As Markley stood up, she clutched his wrists. "Zack, don't!"

He thrust her aside. A harsh vitality flooded his face. "Zack!" she cried. She started to follow him to the door, but halted, and after an instant hurried to her room.

XIII

Markley stopped on the porch of the hotel to reconnoiter the street. It was not quite dark. A hundred yards below him, the Starretts were walking their horses past the livery stable. Both men slouched wearily, like riders who had come a long distance. Markley took his eyes from them and gazed across the street. Billy Titus made a hand signal from the alcove of the gun shop. Markley nodded, and walked slowly down the steps of the hotel and placed himself behind a horse trough. He was ready. A cold stream of impatience flowed through him.

The Starretts came on. Markley could see white smudges of quicklime on their clothing. The muscles of his jaw rippled. So they had completed the butchering of the cattle, as Starrett had threatened. Markley wiped his palms on his chaps and held his carbine firmly.

Suddenly he knew that Starrett had seen him. Though the rancher gave no indication of it, something about him came to focus. Markley saw his lips move, and Rex glanced toward the hotel and saw him behind the horse trough. Then Rex turned his head and saw Billy Titus. He spoke to his father. They came on. It seemed to Markley that Starrett was smiling to himself.

He rehearsed a statement in his mind: *I was standing on the boardwalk when they came in. They stopped at the marshal's office. Then, as he dismounted, Starrett pulled his rifle on me.*

It would be surprising, Markley told himself, if he did not pull his rifle from the boot. Under the circumstances, he would be a fool to leave any of his weapons out of reach. Starrett knew that. Starrett had fought Comanches and had taken the ways of Indian fighters. This particular way would trip him.

They were within a hundred feet now. Bennett's office, on the shady side, was half the distance between them. The sun still burned along the eaves of the buildings on Markley's side. All the foot traffic in this block had vanished, but a buggy rattled in from a side street above him. It halted and a man cursed his horse, and the buggy could be heard turning.

Still Starrett did not make a move. His son, taller and more slender, his unshaven jaws blue-black in the dusk, was watching Titus. They rode on up the center of the street. His knee braced against the horse trough, Markley let the seconds run by. Ruel Starrett swerved abruptly to the marshal's tie rail, crowding Rex over with him. Markley started and raised the gun. They reached the rail. Markley observed that they would have their backs to him when they dismounted. He straightened; his leg trembled a little. Perspiration was greasy on his fingers. *What's the matter with me?* he thought angrily. *Even the Comanches never brought the scare sweat out on me.*

Rex was on Starrett's right, and he dismounted now without warning, pulling his carbine as he did so. But Starrett's horse shielded him. Markley was aware of Titus taking a step forward. Then Starrett dismounted, yanking his saddle gun, also. Markley's heart studded in his throat. He snapped his carbine up, but immediately lowered it, swearing under his breath. Starrett had dismounted on the right side of his horse — away from Markley. While Markley weighed it, Rex Starrett ducked under the hitch rack and stepped into the alcove of the marshal's building. Titus was stalemated. Markley saw him duck back to safety.

A man began to chuckle. It sounded loud in the silent street. It was Starrett. He said: "Markley, you'd better come over here. I want a talk with you."

Markley hesitated, sour with disappointment. It had been a situation as pretty as a straight flush. A man could not be condemned too strongly for taking revenge on someone who had murdered one of his men and slaughtered his herd. But it needed to be impulsive. The setup now was like two armies drawn up for battle. Markley grunted, lowered his carbine, and crossed the street.

Starrett and Rex had already gone into the marshal's office when he reached the walk. He signaled Billy Titus to wait and walked into the office. The air was dense with tobacco smoke, and warmed by the small bachelor stove. Five men were waiting for him. Markley's eye flicked over them. He knew that Marshal Bennett was holding Milt Howard, one of the cowpunchers who had brought in Garth's body. But he did not realize that Tom Goss, the old range boss, was on hand. He snapped a look at Goss, but the man was rolling a cigarette and did not glance up. He looked closely at Milt Howard. Howard was still with him. He knew it by the steady anger in the cowboy's brindle eyes. Markley gazed at Ruel Starrett, who was holding a cigar against the ash grate of the stove to light it. Starrett kicked the ash door closed, and looked around at him. His hard walnut features were tight with satisfaction. Suddenly Zack was furious.

"You've been waiting all afternoon for him to come in!" he raged at Bennett. "Now, why don't you get to work?"

"What do you want me to do?" Bennett asked mildly.

"You've got Howard's affidavit on your desk. Do you need more than that?"

Bennett tapped his desk with a pencil. "I need Starrett's." Starrett removed his gauntlets, which were smudged with quicklime. He smacked them against his chaps.

"Write this down, then, and I'll sign it . . . 'I was given warning that one Markley planned to move his diseased cattle onto my land. Informant was Markley's foreman, Thomas Goss, who was fired for refusing to move the cattle. My son Rex and I attempted to stop the herd from crossing Mission Creek, and were fired on by Clay Garth. . . .' "

"That's a lie," stated Milt Howard. Starrett struck his gloves against his leg, and Howard's eyes sheered to Markley. "Clay never fired a shot."

Starrett placed on Bennett's desk the rifle he had carried in. "Has that been fired? It's Garth's."

Bennett reamed the bore with his fingertip and glanced at the powder smut. "Been fired, all right."

"After we left, then," Howard said.

"So you say. I say I dropped him while he was trying to get off his second shot."

"How far were you from the firing?" Bennett asked Howard.

"Hundred yards, I reckon. But Clay never. . . ."

"You told me earlier that the Starretts were firing into the herd. With all that clatter, how can you say definitely whether Garth fired or not?"

Markley entered savagely: "Are you the county marshal or Starrett's attorney? If Garth was killed defending my herd, that makes the men who killed him murderers, doesn't it?"

Bennett shrugged. "That's in the same category as another question. Is a man justified in killing somebody who's throwing diseased cattle on his land?"

"Correction, Marshal," Zack Markley snapped. He faced Howard. "What were my orders to Garth?"

"To move the cows to the southeast corner of the community pasture," Howard said.

"Did I tell him to move them across Mission Creek?"

"No, sir," Howard said. "You told Garth not to cross the creek."

Markley glanced at Ruel Starrett. With a flush of triumph, he witnessed the sagging of the rancher's jaw. Starrett's head snapped to confront Tom Goss. "You said the order was to move the cows across Mission Creek."

Flushed and angry, Goss stared at Zack Markley. "Them *was* the orders. Are you trying to make a liar out of me, Zack?"

"Tom, I have no use for any man who'd lie to put his ex-boss in a spot," Markley said quietly.

"Then why the devil were you moving them?" demanded Goss.

"Because Ledbetter told me to get them onto new graze. The Comanche Spring area is full of ticks, and it's the ticks that carry this blackwater fever. After keeping that range clean of rattle weed and Indians for twelve years, would I be fouling it up with tick fever when I'm about to take over?"

Bennett regarded him for a long moment. "Zack," he said, "that sounds like dirty poker. You tricked these men into butchering your herd."

"Opinions again, Marshal. I say my herd was destroyed and my ramrod murdered. I say Starrett ought to be jailed."

Between Markley and Ruel Starrett stood Milt Howard and Tom Goss. It came with surprise when Starrett suddenly lunged at them, the hard angle of his shoulder butting Howard into the desk, while Goss hastened to turn sidewise and let Starrett pass like a charging bull. Markley stepped back. Starrett's face was crowded with rage; his fist was cocked. He threw the blow and Zack ducked and felt it explode against the side of his head, and, swerving away, he fell over someone's boot and sprawled on the floor. Starrett came down on him like a hide. He crushed the breath out of him with his bulk and began to chop at his head. Markley felt the skin tear over his cheek bone. He heard the crazy snorting of the man and was suddenly convulsed with rage. Reaching up, he dug his nails into Starrett's face and clawed at his eyes.

When Starrett turned away to protect his face, Markley lurched to his feet and saw Starrett seize the doorknob and pull himself up. Markley began to swing with both fists. He knocked Starrett against the door and, seeing the blood on his mouth, felt something vicious tear loose within him. He felt elevated, drunk with a species of anger that was the purest joy. Starrett was stunned. He propped his shoulder against the door, wincing as Markley cut his face with his fists. Markley turned his fists down as they struck to give Starrett the edge of them, and they brought the blood to his mouth and one tough black eyebrow.

Someone was shouting. The men stood

close to them, but no one appeared ready to step in. In Markley's head was the thought: *I called him to be more of a brawler than this.* He smashed Starrett's jaw with a roundhouse blow and then lowered his fists, watching as Starrett's knees buckled. But the rancher did not fall. He caught himself and gave his head a shake that spattered his shirt with blood. There was a milkiness in his eyes. But then they cleared. They flooded with a brutish hatred that took Markley's breath. Starrett roared as though purging himself of his hurt.

Markley backed up a stride. Starrett's fist caught him on the chest. It thudded like an Indian drum. Braced on both feet, the rancher threw a long blow at Markley's face. It jolted Markley; his vision swam. Then he saw Starrett coming in, and planted himself solidly and swung with him, blow for blow. They were standing that way when the massive thunder of a shot rocked the small room.

Markley ducked aside, his hand dropping to his Colt. But it was Charlie Bennett who stood with the smoking revolver in his hand.

"Now, by heaven, it's a bullet in the leg for the first one of you who swings again!"

His chest heaving, Ruel Starrett glared at Markley. Neither man spoke.

"Listen to me, you fools . . . if I have to use a scatter-gun, I'll tame the man who so much as raises his voice before the hearing tomorrow. What's the matter with you? Are you crazy? Do you want to turn this into a civil war?" He ran out of breath. "Judge Waggoner will go into the matter of Garth's death tonight. Until then, I want you to stay clear of each other. I'll jail the first man who starts another fight."

Markley watched Starrett wipe his face on his bandanna, sweep his hat from the floor, and walk to the door. Markley paused to roll a cigarette, but his hands were trembling too much and he gave it up. It was quiet in the room with a kind of shamefulness. Yet Markley understood, and he knew it was in Starrett's mind, also, that this had not been an end, but a beginning. He and Starrett were too much alike, too stubborn, too heavily mortgaged to their own ambitions, to accept any sort of defeat but one that was complete.

A few moments later, when he left, he saw Starrett entering Vern Bricker's barbershop. Billy Titus was waiting on the walk. He looked wizened and alarmed.

"What was the shot?" he demanded. "I ran down and saw Bennett holding the gun, but . . . what happened to your face?"

"Let's have a drink," Markley said, walking away from him.

In a rear room of the Indian Head Saloon, Markley washed up. Titus talked glumly about how the encounter with the Starretts had gone wrong. Markley used a styptic pencil on a cut across his cheek bone, not listening. He chalked up the forces against Starrett. Lisandro, a live witness to the deal Markley had made with Will Dalhart. The killing of Garth. The cattle slaughter. The paper in Clyde Tilford's safe. But that was unfinished business, and there was only one night in which to finish it.

Markley dumped the blood-tinged water from the wash basin into a bucket. "How about a drink now?"

"Sure, Zack."

Markley regarded the little gunman gloomily. *How could a man change so in twenty-four hours?* he wondered. With his broken gun hands, Titus seemed like a spaniel trying to run with wolfhounds. He was eager to please, where he had been cocky. But walking toward the bar, Markley laid his arm across Titus's shoulders.

"How're the hands, kid?"

"Better." Titus glanced up. "Kid? I'm dry back of the ears."

"As in Billy the Kid." Markley chuckled.

"He was plenty dry, too. But you'll show 'em, one of these days."

Titus grinned, pleased. But then his eyes soured. "I'll sure be glad when these hands heal."

"So you can square with Starrett? Why wait on the hands? What's the matter with tonight?"

Titus's thin fox features glistened. "How?"

"I don't mean with guns. Don't think I'll need guns. That'll just be the frosting on the cake, if Starrett wants to frost it after I whip him in court. There's a paper I've got to get out of Tilford's safe tonight."

"You mean the paper you put in yesterday?"

Markley nodded. He hung back as they neared the bar. "Nothing to it, Billy. There's no watchman at the bank. The hasp on the back door is like strap iron. Use a pry bar and walk into Tilford's office. Use the same bar on that Salamander safe of his. The paper's in an envelope with my signature across the flap. Take it out and leave the envelope on the floor. Bring the paper with you and throw it away."

Titus blinked. "That's a lot of trouble for a paper you don't want, ain't it?"

"It's just newspaper," said Markley reluctantly.

After a moment, Titus grinned. "It wouldn't be the deed you were going to show the judge, would it? This would look bad for old Starrett, Zack . . . the paper being stolen the night before the hearing. Why, the judge might rule against him just on that evidence, eh?"

"Will you do it?" Markley asked.

"Will I do it!" said Titus joyfully.

"Better make it around eleven, then, while there's still people moving around, so you won't be noticed."

"Where you going to be?"

Markley gingerly touched a bruise on his forehead. "I'll be busy," he said tersely.

Milt Howard was at the bar, his foot hitched onto the rail and his hat lying on the counter. He was with some other men who were listening to his story of the session with Marshal Bennett. Markley ruffled Howard's red hair with his knuckles and the cowboy grinned. Markley bought drinks, but remained on the edge of the talk. Finally he winked at Titus. "Easy does it, kid," he said, and sauntered out.

The cold edge of the wind struck him. Above town, the church bell began to ring. 8:00 P.M. *Chow time,* thought Markley, sloping easily down the street against the river cold. Up the street he saw Mexican women hurrying to church, and a few Mexican men drifting their ponies up the hill. A tall cowboy with the red spark of a cigarette glowing before his face jogged by. Markley did not recognize him, but the man wheeled his horse.

"Meester Zack!" he said.

Markley's mind had been too full to worry about Lisandro Garza all day. He said — "Howdy, *amigo.*" — and tried to see the shadowed face.

"Meester Zack," announced Lisandro with soft syllables of pride, "I am on my way to church."

"Goin' to get right with God, eh? Well, don't get too right," Markley added in playful reminder.

"I was today at confession."

A cold draft blew on the ramrod's neck. "Yeah?"

"And I tell the priest . . . 'I have sinned, I have told a lie.' "

It seemed to Markley that his mind was freezing. The critical importance of Lisandro had almost slipped him. With Lisandro against him, he was finished. His mind began to finger the small currency of possibility — bribes, threats.

"By any chance," he asked ironically, "did you give particulars?"

"It was not asked."

"You ain't forgetting we've got a date tomorrow morning."

"The hearing? No, Meester Zack. To get absolution, I must claim true sorrow of heart. How can one be truly sorry for a sin he means to commit again? So I don't be at the hearing. I was today at confession, and . . . and I am clean, like a new shirt."

"You won't testify for me?"

"No."

"Will you testify against me?"

"To say nothing is enough. I return to the ranch tonight to collect my belongings. I cannot work for Meester Starrett, who is *mal' hombre,* nor for you, who are also *mal' hombre.* I work, maybe, on a Mexican ranch."

"Lotsa good people there, eh?" Bright and sharp as a knife, it lay in Markley's mind — the thing that must be done. "Well, good luck, *hombre.* I'll tough it out without you. No hard feelings?"

Surprised, Lisandro reached down to accept Markley's handshake. "No hard feelings, Meester Zack." Then he rode up the street.

Markley was glad now that he had not stabled his horse. It still stood at the Indian Head rack. Thus it would never be noticed that a short time before Lisandro Garza left Spanish Ford to ride to Spade Ranch, Markley himself quitted the town. He mounted in the darkness and rode down an alley, planning to strike the National Road farther south. Thinking of the tremendous risk he was taking, he felt a strong anger against the Mexican. With everything else set up for a strike, this had to happen. Yet somehow it did not seem to him that he had made the decision to kill Lisandro himself. It was already made long ago, waiting for him to pick up his cue. This massive ambition of his was making the decisions almost faster than he could keep up with them.

Starrett had a shave, and a leech put on his eye to reduce the swelling. "One thing about disagreements," Bricker, the barber, commented. "Keeps my leeches from going hungry."

Starrett grunted. Under the hot towel, he gauged the results of this day. He saw it clearly. Markley had suckered him out of position. It had cost him only some cattle he would have had to slaughter anyway. He could cry murder at the hearing, and sue for damages to the herd. If Milt Howard and the other cowpuncher ever recovered from the shock of the killing, they might recall that Garth had been shot in the right side, so that only Rex could have shot him.

Bricker's razor made a silken scraping. Staring glassily at the pressed-tin ceiling, Starrett bit down on his guilt. He had managed everything miserably. Because he wanted to tie Rex to him, the boy might come under a charge of murder. The things that happened to a father shouldn't happen to a mad dog. You loved your son so much that he rebelled when you tried to guide him. You tried to keep him with you and dropped a rope around his neck.

Starrett whipped off the apron. "Let it go."

"But I ain't trimmed your mustache."

"The way this town's going, you'd probably slit my throat." Starrett spoke roughly, then he tipped the man a quarter. He went out. Responsibility lay on his back like a sack of grain. "Damn it all," he said wearily.

Across the street, a man in a thimble-shaped hat with a blanket around him passed the hotel. *Chief Jack is getting an old man's shamble,* thought Starrett. *Well, why not? He had negotiated the leasing of the tribal range to a man who had reneged on payment. His prestige with the tribe must be drooping like a wet eagle.* He felt a twinge of conscience, but thought: *Why did he steal cattle and horses from me, then?*

But it was true that thievery, with an Indian, was little more than a game. Trouble was, Jack had overdone it. So when it came time to divide the marbles, he learned they had been playing for keeps. Still it galled him to see the results of his hard dealing.

"Hey, Chief!" Starrett called abruptly.

The Indian turned his head.

Starrett said: "Come here." He did not quite know what he was going to do until the chief stood beside him. Then he pulled a ragged envelope from his coat pocket and wrote on it with a pencil. He glanced with surprise into the contemptuous stare of the chief's eyes.

"I've been thinking about your village," Starrett told him. "Why should your people suffer because their chief showed bad judgment? Lot of good people in your village. So you pick up some bucks tomorrow and ride over to the ranch. If I'm not there, show this to Vicente. He's running things for me. He'll let you cut out fifty steers from the long-two herd. Sell 'em or butcher 'em . . . I don't care. But this'll square us."

The Comanche turned the envelope this way and that. "You no trick me. You no call me cow thief two time." He jammed the balled paper in his pocket.

Watching the Indian cross the street again,

Starrett muttered: "Fool." He headed for a saloon.

XIV

In the marshal's office, Rex shook the last flakes from a tobacco sack. The cigarette it made was skimpy, but he lighted it and watched Charlie Bennett place his collection of depositions in a folder. He sat with his boots propped on the edge of the desk. Rex had not shaved, and felt no urge for dinner, though he had not eaten since breakfast. A need to tell Bennett about the killing kept picking at his mind. But all at once he realized something. Bennett knew it already. The clue was obvious.

"Aren't you going to ask for my deposition, Charlie?"

Bennett shrugged. "Another time. I've got to meet Judge Waggoner at the courthouse." He rose impatiently and took his hat from an antelope prong.

"Charlie." Rex smiled, and Bennett's gloomy features gradually eased as he looked at him.

"OK, how did it go?"

Rex told him about the shooting. "It was my father or Garth. It happened fast. You knew it, didn't you?"

"Sure. The diagram Howard drew. How could your father have shot him in the right side, if he had his left side to him, aiming the rifle?"

Rex gazed at the cigarette in his fingers. "And now Garth's lying on a board in Ed Rohl's shop. And this morning he was probably thinking he'd have to cut down on the whiskey or wondering if he'd ever make enough money to get married."

"Getting too deep for me. All I know is I'd join the Rangers tonight, if I was you. Judge Waggoner ain't blind, either."

Rex shrugged. "If it goes to a trial, you don't think I'd let my father stand it, do you? But if it makes him feel better to think he's helping me now, OK?"

Bennett grinned sourly. "You Starretts. Fight like shrews and hang together like Dalharts. Wonder how Susanna feels about all this? If it wasn't for her, none of it would have happened. Fist fights, beef killing, and now a man killin'. That little lady's giving a mighty big barbecue." He twisted the door-knob. "Forget about Garth. He was a no-good one, anyhow. So long, kid. Have some dinner and go to bed."

Bennett had been gone ten minutes when a man opened the door hurriedly and stared at Rex, sitting by the stove. He was coatless, had a face like a bull's, and a small mouth. Rex had seen him tending desk at the hotel.

"Where's Bennett?"

"He's gone to the courthouse. What's up?"

"You're a friend of Miss Dalhart's, ain't you?"

Rex came to his feet. "Is she in trouble?"

"She's in a high-stakes game with Joe LaPorte from the Indian Head. I don't know how much she's lost, but she's losing. It don't look good to have guests getting fleeced in our game room. But I can't stop it myself. I thought Bennett. . . ."

Rex remembered the town jokes about Will Dalhart, about his fleecing in the Indian Head. He pictured the sleek hands of LaPorte, the little saloon gambler, shuffling cards. Suddenly he felt a sad kinship with the ridiculed Dalhart family.

"I'll talk to her," he said.

Standing in the door of the game room, he had to stand on his toes to see over the heads of the crowd. At a small mahogany table by a window, Susanna and LaPorte were playing cards. Rex forced a way into the room and reached the table. Neither Susanna nor LaPorte noticed him. LaPorte's tightly curled black hair gleamed under the harp lamp. He riffled the deck and smiled at Susanna. She sat stiffly, her hands clenched in her lap.

"Ma'am, this kind of game could go on forever. Do you play faro?"

"No, and I hardly think this is the time to learn. The same bet. Please take your card."

LaPorte placed the cards on the table, Susanna cut, and the gambler delicately lifted the top card. Nine of hearts. Susanna reached to take her card. Rex felt a desolate sense of pity. The utter nonsense of attempting to make a killing from a gambler! For it was obvious to him what she was trying to do — to win enough to buy out Markley.

Susanna turned a card, gazing at its six black pips with a faint frown. But Rex saw her underlip tremble as she said: "The same bet. A hundred."

LaPorte added a blue to his stack. He flexed the fingers of his hand and covered the pack.

Rex said: "The game's over, LaPorte. Everybody out."

LaPorte's head turned. Susanna gazed up at Rex in astonishment. Then her eyes kindled. "This is a private room! We'll play as long as we like!"

"You and LaPorte stay, then. Everybody else goes."

A rancher with a Robert E. Lee beard gripped Rex's arm. "See here. . . ." But when Rex turned on him, he muttered and went out.

The room began to empty. Joe LaPorte stiffly collected his cards and chips. Rex finished herding disgruntled onlookers from the room and closed the door. He knocked the gambler's gray stovepipe hat from an extra chair and sat down.

"Have a seat," he told LaPorte.

"You said the game was over."

"That game is. We're going to play another. How much are you out?" he asked Susanna.

"Nine . . . nine hundred dollars." Susanna closed her eyes.

Rex took a card from the pack and laid it face-up with a scoring pencil across it. "Write him an IOU for nine hundred dollars."

"I'll do no such thing! My luck's bound to change!"

"Is this how you were going to get off the hook?"

"If I win, I'll have enough to buy Zack out. If I lose, Mister LaPorte will be no worse a partner than I am."

"You couldn't take four thousand from this fellow with a gun. Sit down, LaPorte," he repeated, and LaPorte sat down and waited with a frown. Rex threw the cards at a tall china cuspidor. "I'm waiting for that IOU."

Susanna's stiffness broke. She scrawled the IOU. When she looked up at him again, he knew that she was waiting with a desperate hope that he could get her out of her predicament.

Rex placed the IOU before LaPorte and briskly rubbed his hands. "Here we go. If you win, you take the IOU and another nine hundred. If I win, we tear up the IOU. Ever play First Blood?"

LaPorte frowned. "Arm wrestling, with . . . ?"

"With knives." Rex placed his knife on the table with the blade standing at right angles. "We used to play it in camp. It's like arm wrestling, only if you lose you get pinked. Or you can even get a knife through your wrist. Set your knife up the way mine is."

LaPorte rose angrily. "I'll play none of your Injun games! I didn't start this! She sent for me!"

"I hear you started one with her father, though. Now, maybe I outweigh you a pound or two, but, then, you outweighed her."

LaPorte started for the door. Rex leaped up and struck like a cat. He hooked a blow into the side of LaPorte's head and the gambler fell against the wall. Rex's barely held anger broke over the dam.

"People are going to learn that Susanna's not going to be back-alleyed in this town. No tinhorn gambler will look twice at her after tonight. Sit down."

The room held the echoes of his voice. He was not accustomed to tempers and he felt surprisingly exhilarated. White and silent, Susanna stood by the window. LaPorte stared with frozen hatred. At last he walked to the table. From his trousers pocket he took a pocket knife. Rex placed it on the table. The two blades gleamed like icicles.

"Now" — he smiled — "let's get to the game."

LaPorte placed his arm as Rex showed him. Rex took the opposite chair and linked his fingers with the gambler's. His hand was so large that LaPorte's looked like a woman's.

"Any time you're ready."

At the window, Susanna bit her lip and turned her back to the table.

LaPorte, his eyes small and moist, watched Rex's hand, as though he might detect the impulse flashing to it an instant before Rex drove against him. His coat sleeve fell back from his pleated shirt and exposed the white wrist rising from it. Not far from his elbow lay the clasp knife with its blade spearing upward. LaPorte waited, muscles flicking in his face. But after a full half minute of anticipation, he began to calculate his own attack.

Rex, studying his face, discovered this by the pursing of the man's lips, and he smiled to himself and waited. Suddenly LaPorte lunged. His elbow rose from the table, his shoulder rolling as he threw all his weight against Rex. Rex's hand was driven back and down. The point of his knife glinted below his wrist. LaPorte grunted with exertion, his face glistening.

Susanna whirled from the window at the sound of the scuffling. She stared at the sight of Rex Starrett about to lose the gamble for $1,800. Rex's expression did not alter.

"Elbow on the table," he said.

LaPorte let his elbow come back to the wood. A vein expanded in his forehead. He puffed out his cheeks, straining. But when he relaxed, Rex drove at him. LaPorte gasped for breath. His shoulder was wrenched. But Rex did not spear his wrist on the knife. He halted an inch above it and smiled into the gambler's face.

"Come on! Make it hard!"

La Porte labored. He closed his eyes. The knife was beginning to puncture his white skin. He made a sound in his throat like the whining of a dog. Then, gripping his chair with his free hand, he smashed forward again, but Rex's hand did not budge.

Rex said: "Watch, now."

Suddenly Susanna knocked both knives away. "Rex, this . . . this is cruel!"

"What was it," Rex asked, "when he fleeced your father? What was it when I walked in here and he was fleecing you? This is what he needs. He couldn't palm an ace if that wrist went stiff on him. He couldn't turn a lose into a win the way he's probably done ten times since you came into this room with him."

He leaned over, retrieved both knives and reset them. But LaPorte rose angrily. "Your money," he said. He retrieved his hat and knife, made a stiff nod to Susanna, and walked out. Susanna slipped into a chair and pressed both palms to her cheeks. Finally she gathered herself. She gave Rex a wan smile.

"It's been a long day, hasn't it?"

"The longest day in the year," Rex agreed.

"Thank you for teaching me what I already knew . . . that you can't beat a fox at his own game. But I was ready to try any-thing."

"Another thing you'd better learn, then, is that it's a man's game now. You may have started it, but the men have taken it over."

She shook her head helplessly. "What am I going to do, Rex?"

"Wait. The same as all of us."

"What happened at Comanche Spring?"

"We stopped them, that's all. We protected ourselves, and that meant killing Garth."

"I saw them bring Garth in. I thought . . . I was sure it was you."

"And that upset you?"

"What would you expect, Rex?"

"The last I knew, you were engaged to Markley. I had it from the groom-to-be himself."

Susanna gasped. "Is that what you were fighting over?"

Rex said sheepishly: "That, and my telling him to stay away from you."

She laughed, with a catch in her throat. "And you call me complicated, Rex Star-rett. You tell me good bye, and then come back to build a fence around me. And it isn't even true. It must have been Zack's own idea."

"You mean you're not going to marry him? That's for sure?"

Her eyes faltered. The caged glow of the lamp shadowed her face. She looked sad and confused, and Rex knew that all her doubts were still there. He felt sorry for her, and yet drawn to her more strongly than ever. He went to her and took her chin between his thumb and forefinger.

"Put it another way, then. Will you marry me?"

"Now? While all this is going on?"

"If love is going on, what's the rest matter?"

"Isn't it a little impractical? Getting married when neither of us may have a cent next week?"

"It wouldn't bother me."

She turned her head. "It's nice of you, Rex, to want to protect me from myself. That's what you're doing, isn't it? You're afraid I'll marry Zack as a business venture. You're so sure I'm not strong enough to let the ranch go."

"I'm not saying that. You're saying it."

"But it's what you think. That's why you lecture me all the time about not letting anyone influence me."

Rex smiled. "I'm not lecturing anybody, Susanna."

"But you keep putting me into positions where I have to lecture myself."

She's back, Rex thought, *the other Susanna, putting the blame on another for her own weakness.* "I don't mean to do it," he said. "All I mean is that I want you enough to forget everything else."

"Then wait a little for me. Until everyone isn't hating everyone else."

"All right. I'll wait a little."

"Until after the hearing. Is that what you mean?"

He pinched her chin. "I love you. That's all I mean."

He waited, but she did not say it. She was afraid she might regret it later, he knew, when she had to forget him. Suddenly he wanted to kiss her, and he held her shoulders and kissed her on the mouth. Then he stepped back.

"Now, go to bed, and stay away from tinhorns after this."

"Rex . . . ," she began softly.

But he went out quickly. He hesitated in the corridor, trying to tear his mind from the picture of her alone in that empty room. At last he settled his hat on his head and walked away.

As he was leaving the hotel, he met his father coming up the steps. Starrett, with worry in his face, said: "I got to thinking about that Mexican . . . old Lisandro. Where do you think I found him? In church!"

"That's all right, isn't it? All the Mexicans from the trail crew went, didn't they?"

"Yes, but that old sinner! Going to confession and lying through his teeth! That damns him to hell, don't it?"

Rex was intrigued. "It damns anybody, I guess. Unless. . . ."

"Unless what?"

"Unless he's changed his mind. Maybe he's decided to turn your witness."

"I'll believe that when I hear it."

"Why didn't you work him over after he left the church?"

"Why bother? I didn't wait for the end of it. A man who'd lie to his Maker, would he draw the line at lying to me?"

Rex rubbed his chin. "Either he's damned himself to perdition, then, or he was telling the truth all the time."

"I'll take the angle about perdition," his father grunted.

XV

Markley had ridden hard, due south on the National Road, then east on the ranch road, and now, well inside the borders of Spade Ranch, he cut into a grove of hackberry trees. The pony was soaked with sweat.

Markley checked his carbine. Then he pressed back through the brush and climbed some rocks overlooking a bend of the road. He peered down, his breath frosty in the bitter air. The high pile of boulders on which he stood thrust like a peninsula into the ranch road, forcing it into a horseshoe turn. The situation was perfect. Markley rolled a cigarette and automatically cupped his hand over the glowing tip. He squatted with his carbine across his thighs.

A frown of resentment darkened his face. He knew the risk he was taking, though, when the death of Lisandro was discovered, they would look immediately at Ruel Starrett, who stood to profit most by the silence of the only witness against him. Markley's complaint was that it was unjust for him to be measured by the common yardstick that was used on other men — a man like old Marshal Bennett, say, or that fumbling ex-master of Spade, Will Dalhart. In such men, ambition was a spark that eventually flickered out, unmourned. Men like that could not understand what it was to desire anything besides a woman. They would never believe that the demand to increase in stature, to become important, could be as peremptory as the love for a woman. The only man who could possibly have condoned his motive in coming out here tonight was Ruel Starrett.

Markley shifted position and a spur clinked. He frowned, slipped the leathers, and laid the spurs aside. Across the darkness floated a sound. Markley crushed his cigarette against the rock. Straight up from the rock he came, a dark shadow with glints of metal at his belt. There was a tall buttress of rock at his left. He placed his shoulder against it and put the gun butt to his shoulder. Fifteen feet below, the road was a pale twist of earth through the brush. Ready, now, Markley lowered the carbine and peered at the far entrance to the turn, into which the horse was coming.

He was nervous, yet he felt strong and perfectly steady. A night hawk passed like a bullet. The horse came on; suddenly it was visible on the road, a lean mount striped with shadow, ridden by a lean rider with a serape covering his shoulders and the lower part of his face. The horse halted. Gooseflesh surged up Markley's arms. He raised the gun, but it was too far for a safe shot. As he hesitated, he made out faintly a familiar pattern of actions: Lisandro pulled his tobacco from his coat pocket, opened the sack with his teeth, troughed a paper in

the fingers of his reins hand. Markley relaxed.

Lisandro went through the patient rite of
rolling the cigarette. He dug for a match.
Somewhere between his finding and striking it, Markley shifted. There was a scrape
of metal — as shrill as a scream, it seemed
to him. Then he heard the spurs at his feet
go sliding off the rock.

Lisandro Garza dropped the cigarette.
"Who's there?" he called. He turned the
horse.

In despair, Markley fired. The night shattered like an Indian bowl. The bullet kicked
Lisandro around in the saddle, and Markley
was half blinded by the bright burst of gas-
ses. He began rocking the lever and firing,
taking the recoil of the gun solidly and
bringing the gun barrel back on the target.
When he had finished firing, he stood still
and listened. To his surprise, a shot flashed
up at him. It struck the rock and cried off
into the darkness.

Markley fired again. He heard something
grunt — horse or man, he did not know.
But when the horse began to buck jump
into the brush, he was savagely angry. "I
spoiled it!" he raged, and, staring down at
the road, he prayed to see Lisandro lying
there. But the man was gone. Wounded —

274

dying — grazed? There was no way to tell.

Markley ran back to his horse and returned to lunge into the brush after the Mexican. It was too dark to read sign. He pushed along recklessly. Then he halted to listen. There were only the tiny chips of sound made by birds and insects. Like a wounded fox or a dead one, Lisandro lay quietly in the thicket. Markley scattered his fears with the thought that the Mexican had been hit hard by that first shot. Even if he survived, no one — not even Lisandro — could say who had shot him. In fact — Markley felt the grip of fear suddenly go out of his belly — most men would think it had been Starrett, trying to silence him before the hearing.

He returned to the road to search for his spurs. He found one on the edge of a wagon rut. The other was not visible. He struck a match; the wind pinched it out. Markley flung the matchstick from him. He could not remain here all night; sooner or later he would be missed. He gazed at the spur in his hand. It was worse to go back with one than none. But before he could throw it into the brush, he reflected that it might be found. He thrust it into one of the flat pouches thonged to his saddle. After that he started back to Spanish Ford.

XVI

When the Starretts rode to the courthouse, the tree branches dripped and the boardwalk leading from Front Street to the brick courthouse a block east was black with moisture. Starrett observed that the yard was already crowded with buggies and wagons. The wet saddles of a line of horses glistened. He ran his eyes over the men standing in the bare, frost-rimed yard and on the steps of the courthouse. A few women in black gowns stood on the walk. Starrett and Rex left their ponies beside the building.

"I wonder what this Waggoner's like?" Rex asked.

"Four bits' worth of whiskey nose and black linsey-woolsey," Starrett said. His face was slick from the razor, with a nick on the chin and bruises from his battle with Markley. At the door they passed Clyde Tilford and some merchants. They went into the small courtroom with its gleaming spittoons and new pew-like benches. Starrett took a seat beside Bennett and lighted a cigar. The courtroom began to fill.

The bailiff rose hastily. "Hear ye, hear ye, this court is now in order!"

Judge Waggoner, wearing a black suit and

with his hair parted down the middle, entered from a rear door. Everyone stood up. Then there was a noisy contest for seats. Starrett saw Markley enter behind Susanna. Markley seated Susanna on an aisle, whispered a word to her, and came through the gate to the witnesses' area. He moved confidently, a tall broad-shouldered man with a horseman's lack of hips and an insolent grace of body.

Judge Waggoner struck his desk with a gavel. "Bailiff, what's the first matter for our attention?"

"You want the Garth business, Your Honor, or the Markley versus Starrett, *et al.*?"

"Markley versus Starrett."

The bailiff, a stout, waddling man with a round head and silver-rimmed glasses, commenced reading. " 'Comes now Zachariah Markley, who deposes and says that a tract of land belonging in part to him and known as the Mission Creek section of Spade Ranch is being unlawfully occupied by one Ruel Starrett, and who asks a restraining order against said Starrett until such time as the matter may be settled in a court of law.' Is Mister Markley present?"

Markley rose.

"Take the stand."

Markley came forward.

Waggoner rustled some papers. "By what authority do you claim this land?"

"Will Dalhart promised to leave me a half interest in it."

"But evidently he never made out such a will."

"No, sir, but when I was in Fort Worth one time, I asked a lawyer to look up that point for me. He said that a promise to make a will isn't the same as a will, but if it can be substantiated, any court will recognize it. So I never pressed him on it."

Waggoner said ironically: "This court's read a little law, too, Mister Markley. But what you say is correct. So it seems to be up to you to establish the fact that Dalhart promised you an interest in this piece of land. Can you do that?"

"I'd like to call a witness. Lisandro Garza!" Markley said loudly.

The courtroom was silent.

"Lisandro!" Markley repeated. Boots shuffled; men turned to glance about. The bailiff plodded to the door and called the Mexican's name. He turned back.

"Ain't here yit, Your Honor."

"Any other evidence?" Waggoner inquired.

Markley appeared disturbed. "Yes, sir. A grant deed that Dalhart wrote out last year.

It was to take effect on his death. I . . . I don't know whether that's legal, but it's proof of what he meant me to have." He glanced at Clyde Tilford. "Did you bring the paper, Clyde?"

Tilford looked white and nervous. Suddenly, in an instant, Starrett knew what he was going to say, and a core of fury began to twist in him.

Tilford rose. "I'd like to make a statement, Your Honor."

"Go ahead."

The banker placed himself beside Markley, facing the spectators. "The paper's been stolen, Your Honor. The bank was robbed last night."

The remark fell into utter quiet. But a murmur of voices began, and Tilford shook his head. "No money was taken . . . you don't have to worry. It's as sound as ever. That's what I say to you, before the rumors start. At a time like this, rumors could be catastrophic for all of us."

Markley slowly came to his feet. He swung his glance to Starrett. "That paper of mine was taken?"

"The envelope you deposited with me and asked me to bring this morning. I suppose that was the deed you mention."

Suddenly Markley broke from the stand

and walked toward Starrett. Starrett lurched up, but the bailiff rushed at Markley and pinned his arms to his sides, and Starrett halted while Clyde Tilford got in front of Markley and talked low and earnestly.

Markley was shouting. "What chance does a man have against a wolf like this! He robbed the Indians! He slaughtered my cattle and killed my foreman. And now, damn him, he steals evidence against him from a bank!"

Judge Waggoner pounded his desk, coughed, and at length had Markley seated in his own chair. Starrett sat gripping the arms of his chair, sick with rage. Abruptly he rose.

"I'd like to take the stand," he declared.

Judge Waggoner said dryly: "We'll hear from Miss Dalhart first. Sit down."

Susanna came to the stand, smoothed her skirts, folded her hands, and faced the court with composure.

"I'll put to you the same question I asked when your father's estate was closed," the judge said. "Do you know of any claims outstanding against Spade Ranch?"

"Yes, sir."

There was a general shifting. Susanna looked at her hands. Judge Waggoner reddened.

"In that case, young woman, you perjured yourself the last time you were in this court-room."

"Yes, Your Honor. But only . . . only slightly."

"How slightly?"

"I mean, the claim against the ranch is small. It's true, as Mister Markley says, that he was to have a piece of land. But it's only a small piece. We call it Barranca Roja . . . Red Cañon. And that's about all it is. My father took it over at a tax sale. It was appraised at three hundred dollars."

Zack Markley shook his head and glanced out a window. "Call Lisandro Garza again," the judge said.

The bailiff went into the yard. Rex glanced at his father. "Somebody's got to him," he whispered. "I told you there was something behind his going to church. He was either telling the truth all along or he'd confessed to the priest that he'd been lying."

"That's a lot of help to me, ain't it?"

The courtroom grew noisier. Finally the judge said: "In the absence of the corroborating witness, we'll proceed to the other matter on the calendar. Milt Howard. Thomas Goss. Come forward."

Howard and Goss stood by while the bailiff read the description of the action near

Comanche Spring. They gave their divergent views of what Markley had ordered Clay Garth to do with the herd. Markley took the stand and repeated what he had said to Marshal Bennett regarding the incident. Harold Tompkins, the coroner, reported his findings. Ruel Starrett gave his version of the affair. As Rex was called, Starrett gripped his arm.

"Don't tell them you did it," he whispered. "One of us has to stay in circulation. They'll have me in jail while they hunt Garza, the way it's going."

Rex had been prepared to tell the truth about the killing. But as he went forward, he realized that what his father said was true. After he was sworn in, he began to talk.

"We went out there to keep Markley from moving his cattle onto Spade. When Garth wouldn't turn the herd, we began to shoot the cattle. I was up on the hill, and I saw Garth draw a bead on my father." He hesitated. "Then my father ducked and Garth missed him. He got ready to fire again, and that was when my father shot him. It was self-defense."

"But you went out there to slaughter cattle, eh?"

"Sick cattle."

Waggoner leaned back. "Seems to me you Starretts are great ones for passing laws as you go along. What law gave you the right to kill those steers in the first place?"

"It seems to me," Rex countered, "there ought to be a law against keeping cattle like that around."

"Nobody's asking how it seems to you," the judge snapped. "Excused." As Rex stepped down, he said: "Ruel Starrett."

Starrett rose. He stood hipshot, pouring the venom of his eyes at the judge.

"You are without question," Waggoner drawled, "the damnedest fella I ever knew. You swindle a poor Comanche tribe. . . ."

"Who were robbing me blind."

"I'll talk! You butcher a man's cattle without reason. You kill his foreman . . . whether or not in self-defense will have to be established. You, or a cohort, break into a bank to destroy evidence against yourself. And now . . . now you tamper with the only witness against you for possession of Spade Ranch. How do you expect me to rule?"

"If it pleases the court," Starrett said sarcastically, "you're the damnedest jurist I ever saw, too. You've just convicted me of all the things you were supposed to set trial dates for."

"I'm not convicting you! I'm telling you

how your behavior looks!"

Waggoner began to write. At last he said: "Mister Markley has asked for a restraining order against your using the Mission Creek section, pending his suit to possess himself of this land. The order is hereby granted. You will remove your cattle and make no attempt to prevent use of this land by Mister Markley."

"I'd like to ask Your Honor a question," Starrett said.

"Go ahead."

"What's your cut of Spade going to be?"

Waggoner lurched up. "Bailiff, remove this man's gun! Ruel Starrett, you are hereby bound over without bail on suspicion of murder!"

Marshal Bennett bounced up as the room began to stir. "Your Honor, only a coroner's jury can. . . ."

Waggoner's gavel thudded. Conversation broke out. In this moment of confusion, Starrett turned to Rex. "Get out of this stinking town, Rex," he said quickly. "They wouldn't know justice if they saw it wrapped in ribbons. They'll be after you next."

"This is only a hearing, not a trial. You should have come with a lawyer."

"What good would a lawyer have done me? What I needed was time and cash. Now

I'm plumb out of both. Broke, like I've been all my life." He rubbed his palms on his thighs. "I'm taking off. I'll get Lisandro and fry him over a fire. And you get out, too, while they're hunting me."

"Dad!"

With Waggoner banging his gavel and Bennett protesting, Starrett walked quickly past the bailiff. The judge turned hastily as he saw Starrett coming up behind him. But Starrett caught him in the crook of his elbow and dragged him up out of his chair. He rammed his Colt into his back.

"Only one way to keep me from pulling the trigger, Judge. Get in front of me and shield me to the back door."

Waggoner stammered an incoherent protest. Markley was standing a stride ahead of his chair, holding a revolver. The judge blurted desperately: "No! Let him go!"

Dragging the judge with him, Starrett backed to the door. The mass of spectators reminded him of a picture, full of fear and movement, but without any real movement at all. But as he reached back to turn the knob of the door, he saw Susanna smile faintly, and he could imagine her saying: *Good luck.*

Starrett released the judge as he stepped out, slammed the door, and ran down the side of the building to his horse. He ripped the reins from the tie rail and rode to the rear of the building. Someone stood in the doorway now, and he fired into the wall beside him, and the man ducked back. Starrett headed for the hackberry woods east of the courthouse.

Later, when he turned the horse north, he could hear the sounds of pursuit. His mind was well ahead of where he stood. Cross the river — what else to do now? No one in this town had any authority in the Nations. And later, when it was dark or he saw his chance, double back and try to break the riddle that was Lisandro Garza, for he was the only worthwhile card left in this played-out deck.

Starrett crossed the sandy ribbons of water to the north bluff of the Red, put his pony up a steep trail, and topped out in a thicket of Chickasaw plum. The last of the river fog was clearing. He glanced back. A few men had collected on the far bank. They would come no farther, knowing they would be under fire if they started across the river. He was impatient to be back on Spade, tracking Lisandro. But he must wait until dark. Even then, crossing would be chancy.

He looked about, remembering the country from the days when he leased range from the Comanches. Then he saw the smokes of a nearby village. He started. Chief Jack. *If that old wolf learns I'm here. . . .* It was hard to settle in his mind whether he would find more mercy among the chief's braves or with Markley and his dehorned gunman, Billy Titus. Starrett hid his pony in the brush and settled down to wait.

XVII

Rex rode down to the river after the posse had swarmed after his father. He kept out of the way. One Starrett might serve a frustrated lynch mob as well as another. He saw that Markley was running the show, although Charlie Bennett had gone along. Rex could hear him posting guards along the low chocolate bluffs.

"Couple of you stay here. Couple more drop down about a mile. Signal will be three shots if you see him crossing. The rest of you come along."

Markley rode west along the river with the dozen men remaining. Rex saw Charlie Bennett angrily rein away from the group. He came back up the slope toward the village. When he was near, Rex called: "Charlie!"

Bennett spotted him in the pecan grove. "Reckoned you wouldn't be far off," he

287

said. "Now, listen. Take your bedroll from my office and light out for Trinity. They'd as lief hang you as Ruel, and hanging's what they're talking about."

"I'm not going anywhere until I find out what happened to Lisandro Garza. He may be the key to the whole thing."

"I don't have time to argue. I've got to get back and at least make a show of trying to capture Ruel. Just let me tell you this. There's lots of rope and plenty of trees in this country, and your name is Starrett. Your dad . . . there ain't much I can do for him now. But he's got the good sense to lie low. Maybe he'll slope down to Trinity to hire a lawyer. That's what I'd do."

"By that time the whole thing would be salted down. If Lisandro's taken off, he'd be out of range by then. If he's dead, he'd be buried twenty feet deep."

Somewhere a shot was fired, and glancing north Rex saw dust puff from a cliff. Starrett did not return the shot. He tried to think along the lines his father would think.

"Dad will be back as soon as the pressure lets up. The last thing he said was . . . 'I'm going to get Lisandro.' Another thing, he doesn't dare stay there long because of the Indians. Charlie," he exclaimed, "I've got to help him get back!"

"I don't know how. Even if we could toll them off for a few minutes, how could we get word to him? Anybody that crosses either way is going to be stopped."

"Anybody but an Indian," Rex said. Then they gazed at each other.

Bennett grunted. "Too bad Ruel ain't in with Chief Jack. We could send word by him. He's still around town somewhere, beggin' *wohaw.*"

"I could put it to him this way. If he did this for my father, Dad would kick in with what he owes the tribe."

Another shot echoed along the river bluffs. "Tell you what," Bennett said. "If you can talk the chief into it, I reckon I can pull the boys back for a while. There's a lot of old shacks up at the slaughterhouse that are a crime. I've been after McClintock to tear them down for years. Now, half the boys in the posse are volunteer firemen, and the rest . . . hell, no man worthy of the name can resist a fire."

"Give me a while to work on him. Start things rolling after you see him cross."

XVIII

Chief Jack always camped behind Stockdale's livery stable. Rex found him loading

289

odds and ends into the limber-legged wagon he drove. Rex offered tobacco, which the chief accepted without thanks. Rex glanced over the things he was taking back to the Indian village with him — a few hanks of tobacco, a bolt of red calico, a small sack of sugar.

"Slim pickin's, Chief," he said. He stacked two gold eagles on the tailgate of the wagon. "That'd buy some grub."

The clear jet of the chief's eyes searched Rex's face. "What for, eagle money?"

"It's a sight less than we owe you."

The Indian suspiciously examined the money. Then he pulled a dirty envelope from his pocket. "Thinkin' Long Knives go crazy."

Rex read the message Ruel had scrawled. He looked up with a curious expression. "Did my father give you this?"

"He say make peace. I don't make peace for fifty cows. I don't trust to go for cattle, neither."

It sank deeply into Rex's mind. A week ago Ruel Starrett had spoken bitterly against Chief Jack. But last night he had given him fifty cattle. Why? He was not afraid of the Indians. But sometime during the last few days he had changed his thinking about the chief.

"Ever make a mistake, Chief?" Rex asked thoughtfully.

"Trusted white feller once."

"And he trusted you. But you stole cattle and horses from him. Well, we expected some of that, but you overdid it. My father was pretty mad. But I think he's over it now. That's why he's started paying you back."

The Comanche smoothed the envelope on the tailgate of the wagon. He frowned. "This good, hey?"

"As good as the gold I gave you."

The Comanche glanced toward the river. "Big feller got heap trouble now."

"I'm not trying to buy your friendship because of that. He gave you this paper before he knew he'd need your help. He was sorry he'd put you in bad with the tribe. That's how I explain it. He always liked you before. Remember the gun he gave you?"

The faintest smile softened the Indian's mouth. "Shoot like hell!"

"I've been sore at the big feller, too. But this paper he gave you . . . maybe hard times are good for a man, eh?"

"Hungry belly not good."

"You'll have beef all winter, if you help me. I want to get a message to him. If you take it, you'll get the rest of what you've got coming . . . count on that."

The Indian clinked the coins together. "Hokay. Long Knife trick me again, I take warpath."

Rex told him where to find Ruel and what to say. "He's to cross where he crossed before. I'll meet him there. Here, take this and buy some things for me, too. Jerky, some Fifty-Six-Fifty shells, little sack of coffee. He may have to travel."

While the chief did his buying, Rex procured his bedroll from the marshal's office. There was a brisk traffic up and down the street — men hurrying to the river to try to get a look at Starrett, men running back with this or that rumor. Rex crossed near the church with his horses. Then he trailed down the alley to wait for the chief behind Stockdale's. The Comanche was long in coming. *What a setup for revenge,* Rex thought. *To pocket the money and beef, and let the tribe have its fun with Starrett.* But in about an hour the Comanche was back with two sacks of provisions. Rex shoved the coffee, cartridges, and jerked beef into his bedroll. The chief drove down the alley.

Rex was about to ride into the trees when he heard a horse enter the alley a short distance above him. He pulled back. The rider had come from the hotel stable. He saw that it was a young woman riding a

292

side-saddle; she wore a blue cape over her shoulders. She glanced nervously down the alley without noticing him in the shadows of the livery barn. Then she turned to ride quickly toward the county road running south from the village. It was Susanna. Rex watched her until she was hidden by a curve in the alley.

She would go back to the ranch and wait until it was over. She would make her peace with whoever returned. But she would stay at a decent distance from the violence. She was young; she was pretty; she could be charming. Susanna could not lose. The only risk she ran was of coming to attach too much importance to a love she had given up.

It was midday now. Rex rode quickly toward the river, but had to swing off the road as some riders came toward him. He was deep in the brush when they passed, but he saw them clearly and he turned his head to watch them ride into Spanish Ford. They were Zack Markley, Billy Titus, and Milt Howard. He lingered, curious. Had the bloodhounds given up the scent? Or was Markley planning a new approach to the problem — perhaps to cross the river in force?

Troubled, Rex rode on. He posted himself

on a timbered bench near the river. Two hundred yards north, two men rode slowly along the bluff. Across the river, the sweeping vacancy of the Nations was broken by a thick curl of smoke. Suddenly one of the posse men pointed with his rifle. A wagon came into view among the snags of old cottonwoods in the river bottom.

Rex watched Chief Jack drive his old wagon across the shallow ford and take the bluff road to the top. He waited tensely while the wagon struggled up and finally disappeared in the plum thickets. The guards began to laugh. Rex was puzzled, until he saw it with their eyes. It must seem that the chief was hurrying home to set the Comanche village on his old enemy, Ruel Starrett. It was about twenty minutes later when the fire bell began to ring.

For some time the guards remained at their posts, staring at the village. But when the black smoke of creosoted timbers began to cover the town, they took off. The bell was still clanging.

After another ten minutes, Rex rode down to the bluff and began to signal with a handkerchief tied to his carbine. Immediately a horseman broke from the frost-killed thickets and lunged down the trail to the river. Hitting the bottom, he came at a dead run across the muddy ribbons of water, a dark target against the water. Starrett reached the foot of the bluff. He appeared on the crest a moment later, raised his gloved hand, and they cut south into the hills.

After a half hour, they stopped. Rex unlashed his bedroll.

"There's a little food here and everything else you'll need. Bennett says you'd better head for Trinity and hire a lawyer."

"Bennett ought to know I wouldn't leave," Starrett said. Then his face softened. "That old Comanche! When I saw him coming, I figured the game was over. I still didn't believe him until I saw the smoke. How'd you talk him into it?"

"I couldn't have, if you hadn't already tried to make peace with him."

Starrett appeared half ashamed of his softness. "Well, I saw him shuffling along last night and he looked like a plucked eagle. First time I'd ever thought of how things must be between him and the tribe. Kind of like they are with me and the town. But it wasn't the chief's fault his bucks hit our herds any more than it was the village's. Well, I . . . fifty steers won't kill us," he said.

Rex smiled.

They passed through the community

pasture to the edge of Spade. A half mile farther was the ranch road. For some time Starrett gazed out across the hills.

"If you were an old Mexican," he speculated, "and figured you'd better lay low, where would you go?"

"Trinity," Rex said.

"More likely you'd hole up somewhere and wait to see which way the wind was going to blow."

Rex recalled the first meeting with Lisandro. "Remember when Markley called on him to back him up?" he said. "Lisandro stammered like a schoolboy. He was lying. Now, I suppose he got remorseful and told Markley he was backing out. Markley might have killed him. That's another possibility."

Starrett said: "That's the angle I'm going to follow up. We'll check at the ranch first to see if he talked to anybody there. But if I find him alive, I'll know how to handle him this time."

"If you find him dead," Rex said, "what then?"

"If he's dead, not even a Fort Worth lawyer can help me. There'd be just one place for me, then."

"Where's that?"

"The Nations," Starrett said. Then, gloomily, he sighed. "Maybe I was a fool to leave

296

it, Rex."

"After all these years," Rex said, astonished, "you'd have the heart to start over?"

Starrett shrugged. "Some ways, the Nations weren't so bad. I never had a year like the one we spent on Little Sabinas Creek. Remember? Man, that was fine country. And you were just getting big enough to make a hand. We even made a little money. I thought about it this morning while I sat in the plum thickets grinding on the fix I was in." The dark, lined face grew wistful. "When a man's ambition gets to dragging him around like a calf at the end of a rope, he'd better quit. That's what I decided."

"You've been a long time finding that out. But you'll never fit an ambition the size of yours into Little Sabinas Creek again."

"Won't I? I had things then I don't have now. Friends, for instance. We'd come to town and it'd be two days before I got through having drinks with everybody that wanted to set me up. But it was after that good year, when I had a couple of thousand dollars cash, that I started shoving. I hewed so close to the line that people like Clyde Tilford and Horse Ledbetter began to figure they had a grievance. Maybe they did. I don't know. But when I started looking around for friends . . . why, they were all gone."

"Well, if you have to go," Rex said, "I'll ride along. You'll need a rider or two till you get set."

His father gazed at him; he started to say something, but closed his mouth and turned his face to the road. He punched Rex's shoulder. "What did I ever do to deserve a son like you?" he said.

They rode over the winter-killed range, passing groups of Starrett's humpbacked Brahma cattle. Starrett's eyes bragged as he looked at them. The dream began to shimmer before him again. Little Sabinas seemed far away. *Lisandro, you old sinner,* he thought. *I'll have the truth out of you before a judge and jury, if you've got a breath left in your body.* Working southeast toward the ranch road, they crossed a familiar trail. With a jolt, Starrett remembered the sprawl of yellow grass running out toward a bois-d'arc thicket that flanked the road, climbing to a steep ridge at the right. He remembered with what care he selected this spot, for the clear shot it gave at the road and the nearness of trees to duck into. He saw again the blood-bay horse moving up it and remembered lying among the rocks while he trailed it under his sights.

"Hey!" Rex was staring toward the road. "That's where they dropped my horse the other day." He began to glance about. "The sniper must've been right about here when he bushwhacked me."

He dismounted and walked into a nest of boulders beside the trail. Abruptly he picked up two shining cartridges. "Fifty-Six-Fifties," he said. Immediately his eyes snapped to the rifle on his father's saddle.

Starrett, who had also dismounted, put out a hand toward his son, stunned. "Now, wait! I would've told you, sooner or later. It wasn't a bit harder on you than it was me! But I had to keep you here."

Rex dropped the shells, staring at his father. He strode to his pony. Starrett seized his arm, but Rex struck his hand away.

"I swear," Starrett groaned, "that I wouldn't do it now! I was plumb loco! But surely you can see. . . ."

"I can see that you risked killing me to get your way," Rex snapped.

He swung his horse through the brush to the road. He jogged along at a rack. *If he'd take that chance with me,* he thought, *what would have kept him from killing Lisandro? The danged old hypocrite.*

In his fury, he did not notice for some time that he was following a set of fresh horse tracks on the road. He stopped finally, gazing down at them. His father came up. Starrett's face was creased with anxiety.

"Rex. I told you I'd learned some things since we were over this road last."

Rex ignored his plea. "There's two horses been over this road," he said. "One was last night. The tracks are crusted a little from the mist. The other isn't an hour old. One of them must have been Lisandro." He glanced at his father.

Starrett retorted angrily: "By Joe, the other wasn't me. I don't have to prove that, do I?"

They followed the tracks down through a wash and up a steep ridge. The road entered a deep tangle of brush. It broke free on a sharp turn. A few rods beyond, a high tower of rocks overlooked the road. As he sat there, Rex realized it was a perfect ambuscade, and involuntarily he turned his pony aside. But there was no evidence of ambush, and he started on. Just ahead, he saw where the road had been torn by hoof marks. A horse had broken back here, swerved, and run into the brush. He saw dark drops in the dust, and dried blood on the leathery leaves of a shrub.

Starrett came up and studied the signs grimly. "If he ain't dead, he's ridin' a wounded horse. They've done for him, Rex. That means he was lying, and Markley followed him out here after he backed out of their deal. Look here!" He spurred to the base of the pile of boulders overlooking the road. "He shot him from up there. But it was dark, and he bungled it. D'you see where he came out of the brush later and tried to follow him? There's three sets of tracks, there . . . Lisandro's, Markley's, and the fresh ones."

He sprang down. Rex watched him candidly. Starrett knelt among the hoof marks, his excitement growing.

"By George, I'll wager the fresh tracks are Markley's, too. And here's boot marks. He came out after the hearing this morning to try to cover his tracks. He'd lost something in the dark, maybe . . . something that would mark him. Here we are!" He snatched something from the blackened weeds.

Rex went forward, still dubious after discovering the secret of the earlier ambush. But when he halted by his father, Starrett rose to face him with a strange expression.

"Nothing," he grunted. "Snuff-box lid. Wouldn't prove a thing." He pointed back up the road. "You can see how it went. He trailed him last night, but couldn't find him. This morning he came out again, weaseled around for whatever he'd lost, and then took off after the Mexican once more." He tried to fasten his own enthusiasm onto Rex.

"Let's see the snuff-box lid," Rex said.

"I threw it away. Don't you get it? Markley. . . ."

Rex caught his wrist. "Let's see it." A waxy grin came to Starrett's face as he opened his hand. Smiling but stricken, he let Rex take the cartridge from him and turn it base up to read the calibration.

"Fifty-Six-Fifty," Rex said. He felt tired, tricked. The hypocritical yarn about the old days on Little Sabinas. . . . "Damn you," he said.

Starrett struck the shell from his hand. He shook him by the arms. "What's it mean, anyway? Half the guns in this county are Fifty-Six-Fifties! Markley's got a lever-action rifle. Same caliber, I think."

Rex peered into his father's eyes. They were dark, tormented, but he was so full of histrionics that he might not know for sure, himself, where the truth became a lie.

"What do you want me to think? You admit one bushwhacking, but you won't admit another a half mile away. You try to hide something you pick up, and it turns out to be a shell that would fit your rifle. How do you know what caliber carbine

302

Markley carries?"

"I saw it yesterday in Bennett's office. Rex, at a time like this . . . look! I raise my hand to heaven!"

Rex moved into the weeds and found four more shells. Starrett drifted after him. "One thing's dang' sure," he grumbled. "If I'd been doing the firing, I wouldn't have needed more than one bullet."

Rex stopped, frowning at a boot print in the road. It was small and pointed and there was no indication of a spur chain. It had been pressed there by a woman's boot. Sudden fear congealed in him as his father knelt by the prints.

"Now, those boots I wasn't wearing, and neither was Markley. Those are a woman's."

"Susanna's," Rex said numbly. "I saw her leave the hotel this morning. And Markley . . . Markley left town with Titus and Milt Howard a few minutes later."

Starrett started. "If Markley's out here, too, he's tracking Lisandro. He knows he's got to find him and finish him. It wouldn't pay," he said, "for Susanna to get in the way of him."

Across the range came a soft thud of hoof beats, rising from the wash beyond the ridge where Lisandro had been shot. The horses were coming at a lope. They could not have traveled at that gait all the way from Spanish Ford, Rex knew. Markley had discovered their sign coming in from the river. He glanced at his father, but Starrett was ahead of him, appraising swiftly the odds of meeting Markley here.

"How many men with him when he left?"

"Titus and Howard."

"We could shoot it out with them, but a couple of them might corner us while the other went after the girl. Stay with me," he said abruptly. He spurred his horse into the thorny tangle of Osage orange beside the road. Rex breasted the spined branches close behind him. They hit a shade-starved clearing beneath a hackberry, crossed it, and swerved onto the deer trail Lisandro and Susanna had taken. Rex glanced back and saw a flash of horsehide as a rider loped past toward the rocks. After that, it was a scramble to stay within earshot of his father.

Starrett rode as if he knew the trail. Once he pulled up sharply and leaned over the side, studying something. Rex made out the large brown blotch on the earth. A man had lain here a moment in agony, but the hoof prints went on, and Rex could see the thin-shouldered form of the Mexican swaying in the saddle as he rode.

The terrain was level, but two miles south

the plateau was broken by a wide but shallow fault with gaunt rimrock walls, as though the earth had settled here. The graze grew abundantly on the floor of the basin. Along a creek stood cottonwoods with aprons of gold at their feet. It was a small cow horn of a valley such as a homesteader's wife might have picked, and, perceiving the spot such settlers might have chosen for their home place, Rex found a haze of trees and the ruins of a dwelling. Here the walls of the basin slanted in like the sides of a branding chute. The cabin commanded the entire basin, its back to the west wall, lying there like a stopper at the mouth of a narrow cañon.

Starrett saw the cabin and said briefly: "Smoke. They're yonder." He spurred down the narrow trail.

Rex heard horses ripping through brush behind them. He saw the dust before he saw the riders. He saw where they would emerge into the open, and, laying his cheek against the stock of his carbine, he waited. When the horses broke into view, he fired at the flinty trail. The bullet exploded in a puff of red dust. It wailed through the closely packed riders and they turned off into the brush. Rex used the gun barrel to quirt his pony.

Near the base of the trail, Starrett halted to gaze back, but, when he saw Rex, he loped on. He jumped the horse into the sandy wash of the creek, and Rex pelted after him. About a quarter mile downstream they came upon the body of a horse, still saddled. Starrett jumped it and loped on. Into Rex came an old, forgotten thrill — the cold wind stinging and disaster on a fast horse behind them, relic of their Indian days. They rode hard for several minutes. At last, over the low banks of the wash, they could see the cracked walls of the basin veering in toward them.

They scrambled from the creek to the edge of a little meadow. Not far off was a stone corral and a ruined adobe cabin. Roofless, it was the sort of shelter cowboys used on roundup. The old sheds were mounds of clay. From the branch of a cottonwood decked with mistletoe hung branding irons and scraps of harness. The smoke they had seen came from within the ruined cabin.

The echoes of distant shots poured down the basin; a spent bullet fell in the creek. Starrett, followed by Rex, started for the cabin, but at that moment Susanna appeared in the doorway. Her black hair lay on her shoulders; her eyes shone darkly.

"You can bring your horses in from the back . . . most of that wall is down. Will you fetch some water quickly? Lisandro . . . there's a bucket." She pointed. She started back.

"Is the old sinner alive?" Starrett snapped.

But Susanna had vanished. He swung his horse to the tree and procured the sprung cedar bucket. Rex rode to the rear. The wall was at full height, with the smudges of burned timbers at the top; it sloped to the ground at the far side. He rode in and saw Susanna's horse in a corner. The old man lay against the wall near the door. A small fire burned near him. Susanna had covered him with her cape. As Rex came up, she turned away and covered her face. Rex held her in his arms.

"He's dying, Rex! It's my fault . . . all of it is my fault! Oh, Rex!"

Rex stroked her hair. He could feel her heart pounding, like the heartbeat of a bird. "No, it wasn't any of your fault. But that's Markley coming. So if you aren't sure which team you're on, this is the last chance you'll have to decide. You can still ride down the cañon from here and cut to the ranch."

Her pale, frightened face turned up. "Do you really think I would?"

Rex gazed at her. Then he pulled her

307

against him.

Starrett rode in with the leaking bucket. He dismounted and strode to the wounded man, rifle in one hand, bucket in the other. Rex stood by Lisandro as the rancher knelt.

"How is it, grandfather?" Starrett's voice was rough but kind.

Lisandro smiled. "It didn't hurt at first, you know, but. . . ."

Starrett scooped water with the brim of his hat.

Lisandro drank desperately. He fell back. "Now it goes better. You know for what I am glad? That I go to confession yesterday. I do not sin since the priest gives me absolution, unless it was being a fool last night."

"How's that?"

Standing at the door, Rex saw the riders take to the creekbed. Two minutes — three minutes.

"Because I tell Meester Zack I would not lie again for him. And then I start for the ranch. Well, what do you expect? He follows. God does not forgive such foolishness easily."

Susanna was gently opening the old man's shirt, but he stayed her hand. "No, thank you." He smiled. She gave it up.

"Why did you do it, Lisandro?"

"Because I think it helps you. If I had not

held up the cattle drive, Spade Ranch would not have been in trouble. And I think you marry Meester Zack. So if I say the old *patrón* left him the good land, then I help hold it for you when you marry him. And I think," he said, with a glance at Ruel Starrett, "I think this fellow is very bad. But I learn different. He is not bad at all. Only . . . very loud."

Peering out the door, Rex said: "Dad."

"In a minute." Starrett offered Lisandro another drink. "Can you write, Lisandro?"

"No, but. . . ." Lisandro's hand traced words in the air. "Lisandro Garza. . . ."

"If I write down what you said, will you sign it?"

Lisandro closed his eyes. "Write it, *patrón* . . . but quickly."

Starrett found a splinter of a pencil in his jacket, but no paper. He yanked out his shirt tail and ripped a piece from it, spread it over his thigh, and wrote the confession painfully. He propped Lisandro up while the old man signed it. Lisandro sank back, staring up into the thin blue sky and smiling to himself.

A ringing volley of shots ripped through the broken doorway. Pebbly adobe was blasted from the lintel by a slug; another smashed the wall near the horses, and Susanna's pony snorted and tried to pitch. Rex saw the smut of black powder in some rocks on the bank of the wash. He fired back, and then ran to a window and crouched by it. He raised his head to fire, but a bullet tore through the frame and he ducked back. He could hear a man running. Then his father's Springfield roared and Starrett swore while the echoes still throbbed in the room.

"Markley! He made it to the corral. If another of them crawls downstream, they've got us in a sack."

Susanna hurried to one of the east windows overlooking the barranca. She had a small rifle in her hands.

Starrett scowled. "What in thunder is that thing?"

"My buggy rifle," Susanna said. "I brought it this morning, in case. I'll watch the gully here. It might occur to them to try to get up on the cliff from downstream."

"It might. Can you shoot?"

"I've killed rabbits when they weren't running. I don't know whether . . . whether I can shoot a. . . ."

Starrett gazed grimly at Rex. Susanna stood close to the window.

Starrett kept his vigil by the door, hatless and stolid, his iron-gray hair rumpled. *I suppose they think this is just another ruckus for me,* he thought. But his heart was sick with fear for his son and the girl his son loved. He knew Susanna was on the point of breaking. But if he showed her any kindness, it would only hasten her collapse. It seemed to him that all his life he had been in this position. He had had to be arrogant to keep the others going; he had had to be tough to show the hardcases he was not afraid, even when he was. So it had become a way of life, and the arrogance he acted out went into him, and he had been on the point of forgetting how weaker men felt when Markley came along to humble him.

A bullet passed through the doorway with a crack. It struck the wall with ringing force close to Susanna. Starrett heard her cry out. The horses, which had been moving restlessly, suddenly wheeled away. They cut through the broken wall and ran toward the trees. Susanna whirled to face the direction from which the shot had come, dropping her gun. Starrett walked four strides, caught her arm, and pulled her out of line. Then he scooped up her gun and thrust it at her.

"That was your father's good foreman," he said. "He wasn't trying to kill you . . . just letting you know he's got that window covered. We're under crossfire, you see. So you'll have to use this window here, which is just as good. But if anybody crawls up the cliff, I don't know where any of us is going to hide."

He peered back into the yard. The cabin was at the apex of a triangle — a gun in the corral, two guns in the wash to the right of the corral. His eye was caught by movement in the gully — a slow parting of the weeds on its bank. Then he saw the bronze glint of a rifle barrel. He snapped his shot with the quick, bone-bred instinct of the Indian fighter. The rifle set him back and smoke rolled across the bare ground. The weeds stirred. For an instant the rifle barrel canted to the sky. Then it clattered on the rocks in the gully.

He glanced at Rex, who grinned. "First blood! I owe you a new hat."

A man was running down the barranca, his spurs clinking. Susanna leaned into the window, holding her gun to her shoulder. She dropped her cheek to the tubular stock, trailing the running target, and Starrett waited for the shot. Then the sounds faded. The man had reached the mouth of the cañon.

Susanna faced Starrett, white as chalk. "It was Billy Titus! I could have shot him, but. . . ." She set the rifle against the wall.

Starrett shoved the gun forcibly into her

hands. "He'd shoot you, believe you me! Now, you just flax down to makin' a hand here!"

Susanna's eyes filled. Starrett struck her cheek and turned her to the window. "Now, suppose you watch that cliff, missy! If Titus holes up in those rocks, a pry bar couldn't move him."

He turned back, breathing heavily. He looked across the doorway at Rex, his eyes bitter as smoke. "I wish," he said, "Bennett weren't such an old woman."

Markley was wedged into the rock corral like a badger. There were small chinks here and there among the stones through which he fired steadily. But after each shot he would roll away. Starrett even glimpsed him, but his fire continued, steady and vicious. Starrett knelt and deposited a handful of cartridges on the floor. As he was reloading, he noticed a spur lying near him. It looked new enough to have been worn recently.

Susanna glanced around. "The spur? I found it where Lisandro was shot."

"It's Markley's!" Starrett exclaimed.

"Yes. I can tell by the broken tines. The rowels were cutting his horse, and he broke off every other tine."

Starrett began to chuckle. He threw the spur into the yard. "Here she is!" he shouted. "Come and get it! You came this far for it! Pick it up!"

Markley fired at the door, and at once Starrett pressed to the door frame and fired at the burst of smoke. There was a small, spiteful sound from a new gun. Susanna had fired her buggy gun upward at the cliff.

Starrett heard the thin whine of the smashed slug, and laughed. "You don't need to worry about killing him with that. If you hit him, he'd probably die laughing."

"Is that so? I can see him! He's on that ledge halfway to the top! Now he's . . . pshaw!" The gun had jammed.

Starrett spoke quickly to Rex. From Rex's position halfway across the room he could see the upper portion of the cliff. "What do you see?"

Rex peered across the top of the roofless wall. "I don't see much of. . . . Wait a minute!" He raised his gun, but lowered it. "I saw him for a minute, but he's back of the rocks. The ledge goes up like a regular stairway."

Markley's fire broke out again. As Rex turned toward the corral, Susanna cried: "Rex, he's going to fire!"

Rex pivoted to face the cliff. A bullet struck the wall and blinded him with grit. He went to his knees; there was blood on his fingers as he wiped his eyes. Starrett started to run toward him, but caught himself. He heard Susanna scream; he caught her as she ran toward Rex. He forced her back to the wall and said — "Now, stay there!" — and glanced through the window.

High up on the cliff he could discern a rag of smoke tearing in the breeze. He threw a shot at it, but Titus was entrenched behind the rocks. He turned back to Rex.

"Can you see anything?"

Rex raised his face to the cliff. "Not . . . not very well."

"Now, listen. I'm going to draw Markley's fire. The minute he fires, cross over here. Titus will be taking aim right now."

Starrett stepped into the doorway. Then he swerved back into the corner. Markley's shot came. The bullet ripped past and slammed into the far wall. Rex ran across the floor. Starrett caught him and wiped blood from his face with his sleeve. He grunted in relief.

"The cut's on your eyelid. It's just the grit that's blinding you. You'd better take Susanna's place as soon as you can."

He stared out again into the bare sunlit yard. From now on, the room would grow smaller. Markley would find a new vantage point from which he could drive them out of the corner. But if they moved, Titus could drop them. *Bennett, Bennett,* he thought desperately. *Deliver me from one-armed marshals.*

Then Rex raised his face from his bandanna. "Listen."

Starrett held his breath. The whole basin was silent, seeming to listen. Starrett heard the hoof beats grow louder, and he grinned at his son. "You don't reckon old Bennett's going to surprise us, do you?"

A gun crashed far up the basin. Markley's shot came an instant later, but it was not directed at the cabin. A man shouted in anger. Rex smiled at his father. "That's Charlie, all right! Maybe you're surprised. I'm not."

Now they could hear Bennett shout: "What goes on here? Starrett, where are you?"

Rex pressed close to the door. "Charlie, listen to me! We're in the cabin! Markley's in the corral and Titus is up on the cliff! Watch out for him! Work down the trees behind the corral and we've got them both!"

After a moment, Bennett called: "Got you!"

Rex took Susanna's place at the window. Starrett risked an aimed shot at the corral, but Markley was still staying down. He heard Rex fire at the cliff.

A moment later Billy Titus's voice drifted down: "Zack! It's no good! I can't git a shot at Bennett in them trees! Make a deal with them!"

Starrett heard Markley's savage reply: "The only deal we'll make is with a carbine! Now, pour it to them, you hear me?"

Titus resumed firing. The thunder of Bennett's fire came closer. Rex waited for Titus to rest. Then he whipped the rocks again. There was a long silence.

Titus shouted again: "It's no good, Zack! Marshal, will you make a deal?"

"What is it?" Bennett replied.

"I've killed nobody, Marshal! I've done nothing but steal a paper from the bank! If I throw down my guns, will you let me climb this cliff to the top and take off?"

Bennett was silent. "Any objections, Starrett?" he called. Starrett kept his gaze on the corral. "So long, Billy!" he shouted.

Titus's guns clanged on the rocks as they fell. And now all the weight of hopelessness was on the small rock corral. Starrett watched it in fascination. A moment later, Markley vaulted the wall and charged for the cabin.

Starrett held his fire as the ramrod came on. Markley could have been an infantryman in gray charging a blockhouse. He held his carbine before him and his face was greasy with perspiration and wild with a wildness that burned in his eyes. He was coming straight to the door. Susanna screamed; a tight grin stretched Markley's lips.

Starrett took a half step to the left. Markley's gun blasted. The bullet struck the lobe of Starrett's ear and jolted him. Blood splashed his cheek. Rex ducked aside to get a shot at the ramrod as Markley rocked the loading lever. But his father fired first. Markley staggered. He recovered, still trying to cock the gun, stumbling forward and never taking his eyes from Starrett's face. Starrett could see the blood on his shoulder. He could hear him sobbing, swearing, as he pulled on the loading lever.

Starrett raised his rifle to his shoulder and sighted down the barrel. He fired at the middle of Markley's breast. Markley faltered. He stumbled, caught himself, and drove on. Starrett threw his rifle down and drew his Colt. He fired a third shot into the ramrod's body, and Markley dropped his carbine. He came hard against the edge of the doorway, clutched it, and sprawled inside. He lay with his face pressed against the earth.

Marshal Bennett came from the trees. "Starrett! You all right?"

Starrett stepped out, holding a handkerchief to his ear. "I was never better." He smiled.

Sometime during the fighting Lisandro Garza had died. Bennett read his confession, appropriated it and Markley's spur. "There's no use lugging him back to town," he said. "He'll sleep as well in this earth as any other. But I'll send a wagon out for Markley and Howard, just to make it official. Reckon there ought to be a spade around somewhere."

Rex had taken Susanna outside. He could hear the marshal talking, and, looking at Susanna, he knew she had had all of the violence and the talk of violence that she could endure.

He entered the cabin and told his father: "Susanna and I will track down the horses."

"Go ahead," Starrett said. "And tell her I'm sorry about slapping her, will you?"

When he lowered the bandanna from his torn ear, Rex could see the notch in it. "They'll call you Gotch-Ear as sure as anything." He chuckled. "But they'll smile."

"I've been called worse than that, and they didn't smile."

The horse tracks led downstream. Rex put

his arm around Susanna. "Well," he said, "the Dalharts finally showed them."

Susanna tilted her head onto his shoulder. "All I ever want to show them, Rex, is you beside me. There won't be any Dalharts left before long, will there?"

Rex said — "Not if I can help it." — and kissed her, and with a sigh she came against him. She pressed her face against his cheek, and he could feel her tears. But they were warm and soft, and as happy as laughter.

ABOUT THE AUTHOR

Frank Bonham in a career that spanned five decades achieved excellence as a noted author of young adult fiction and detective and mystery fiction, as well as making significant contributions to Western fiction. By 1941 his fiction was already headlining Street and Smith's *Western Story* and by the end of the decade his Western novels were being serialized in *The Saturday Evening Post.* His first Western, *Lost Stage Valley* (1948), was purchased as the basis for the motion picture, *Stage to Tucson* (Columbia, 1951) with Rod Cameron as Grif Holbrook and Sally Eilers as Annie Benson. "I have tried to avoid," Bonham once confessed, "the conventional cowboy story, but I think it was probably a mistake. That is like trying to avoid crime in writing a mystery book. I just happened to be more interested in stagecoaching, mining, railroading. . . ." Yet, notwithstanding, it is precisely the interesting — and by comparison with the majority of Western novels — exotic backgrounds of Bonham's novels that give them an added dimension. He was highly knowledgeable in the technical aspects of transportation and communication in the 19th-Century American West. In introducing these backgrounds into his narratives, especially when combined with his firm grasp of idiomatic Spanish spoken by many of his Mexican characters, his stories and novels are elevated to a higher plane in which the historical sense of the period is always very much in the forefront. This historical aspect of his Western fiction early drew accolades from reviewers so that on one occasion the *Long Beach Press Telegram* predicted that "when the time comes to find an author who can best fill the gap in Western fiction left by Ernest Haycox, it may be that Frank Bonham will serve well." Among his best Western novels are *Snaketrack* (1952), *Night Raid* (1954), and *Last Stage West* (1959).

ABOUT THE EDITOR

Bill Pronzini was born in Petaluma, California. His earliest Western fiction was published under his own name and a variety of pseudonyms in *Zane Grey Western Magazine.* Among his most notable Western novels are *The Last Days of Horse-Shy Halloran* (1987) and *Firewind* (1989). He is also the editor of numerous Western story collections, including *Under the Burning Sun: Western Stories* (1997) by H.A. DeRosso, *Renegade River: Western Stories* (1998) by Giff Cheshire, and *Tracks in the Sand* by H. A. DeRosso (2001). His own Western story collection, *All the Long Years* (2001), was followed by *Burgade's Crossing* (2003), *Quincannon's Game* (2005), and *Coyote and Quarter-Moon* (2006). His Western collection is *Crucifixion River* with Marcia Muller. Its original title novella won a Spur Award from the Western Writers of America for the best short fiction of 2007.

The employees of Thorndike Press hope you have enjoyed this Large Print book. All our Thorndike, Wheeler, and Kennebec Large Print titles are designed for easy reading, and all our books are made to last. Other Thorndike Press Large Print books are available at your library, through selected bookstores, or directly from us.

For information about titles, please call:
  (800) 223-1244

or visit our Web site at:
  http://gale.cengage.com/thorndike

To share your comments, please write:
Publisher
Thorndike Press
10 Water St., Suite 310
Waterville, ME 04901